THE
BIRDS OF
PARADISE

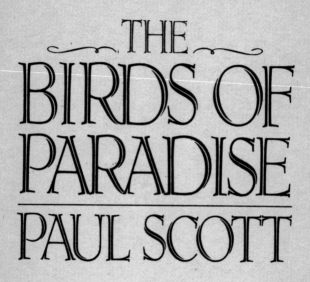

THE BIRDS OF PARADISE

PAUL SCOTT

Carroll & Graf Publishers, inc.
New York

First Carroll & Graf edition 1986

Carroll & Graf Publishers, Inc.
260 Fifth Avenue
New York, NY 10001

ISBN: 0-88184-232-X

Manufactured in the United States of America

To
Wilmorrow,
with gratitude and thanks
for my own sabbatical year

Author's Note and Acknowledgments

The Birds of Paradise is a work of fiction and the characters are all imaginary. Places like Tradura, Jundapur, the camp called Pig Eye, the island of Manoba,—these, the backgrounds to events, are imaginary too. I know of no trading company in the Far East called SIAT, no European Foundation with a medical research station in a place called Muzzafirabad. Ranjit Raosingh is, I believe, a common enough name, but Pandirakkar Dingit Rao and Krishnaramarao have been chosen more with an ear for sound than an eye for accuracy in the business of naming imaginary Rajput princes. If coincidence has been at work then, in all cases, particularly in Daintree's and Grayson-Hume's, I apologize for any annoyance caused to real persons whose friends think they recognize them and believe them, quite unfairly, to have provided a living basis for characters who live if they live at all, only in the following pages. Melba is real; although that is not her name, so far as I know.

I acknowledge, with grateful thanks, the help given to me by Mrs. Joyce Pope of the British Museum (Natural History) and by officials of the Commonwealth Relations Office who patiently answered questions about birds of paradise and the Indian Civil Service respectively. I am also indebted to Mr. V. P. Menon's book, *The Integration of the Indian States,* which I found invaluable as a political guide to some of the facts behind the fiction.

P.S.

Contents

"They are styled Birds of Paradise because when first discovered various and most extravagant fables were reported concerning them; amongst which, it was long generally believed, that whence they came, or whither they went was unknown; that they lived on celestial dew; that they were perpetually on the wing, taking no rest but in the air; were never taken alive, and consequently could only be obtained when they fell dead upon the earth; so that the vulgar imagining them to drop out of Heaven or Paradise, and being struck with the beauty of their shape and plumage, bestowed on them the singular name by which they are still distinguished."

(*The Flowering Moment*
by C. WREY GARDINER)

BOOK ONE

The Wheeling Horsemen

1

IF Melba interrupts her South American love song and squawks, "Wurrah Yadoor-a!" I take no notice, simply carry on with whatever I happen to be doing, but if the squawk is followed by the tinny sound she makes with her beak and claws when she tangles with the wire netting of her cage I leave the hut and go into the clearing to calm her down by tickling her stomach and ruffling the top of her head. It is always sunny on these occasions because Melba never sings when it is raining or when rain threatens. At night I bring her indoors and put her into the same small steel cage she was in when I first saw her and which she had to travel in when I brought her with me to Manoba. I cover the cage with a cloth because the light from the pressure lamp distracts her. The cloth is an expensive square of green silk decorated with pictures of monkeys and tigers—a scarf, in fact. I say good night to her and she says good night to me, but she says good night only to lull me into a false sense of security. When she thinks the silence has gone on long enough she shrieks at the top of her voice: "William Conway! William Conway!" I've nearly upset many a glass of whisky hearing my name called like that. She catches me a few seconds after my alertness has gone. Perhaps she has X-ray eyes and can see through the scarf.

I say, "Shut up, Melba. Go to sleep," and upon the degree of annoyance in my voice depends the length and tenderness

3

of the song she then sings to me, a song of the Paraguayan hills, punctuated by little rollings and trillings of the tongue. Gradually she hypnotizes herself into a state of such enchantment that sleep falls on her as gently and swiftly as the night falls here on the tropical ocean.

The cage in the clearing is a curious affair and got built in this particular form more by accident than design, although the design was in my mind right enough and obviously imposed itself upon the process of construction right from the beginning until at the one-third finished stage I recognized its ramshackle kinship to the stout iron cage that stands on the lake isle in the grounds of the Jundapur palace back in India, which, a month or so ago, I found unchanged after thirty years. It was then just a question of consciously finishing what I had subconsciously begun.

Two lads from the beach settlement helped me to make it in return for a full quarter-pound tin of Kwikkaffy. They cut the bamboo for the uprights and thatched the roof in the shape of an onion dome, as I instructed, with fronds that were green but are already going brown. The wire netting which is tacked to the uprights, and which Melba sharpens her beak on and clings to with her claws, pressing her pale green breast and stomach against it so that she looks as if she's holding on for dear life but, with that wild light in her parakeet eye, daring you to touch her, was given to me by Griffin.

Griffin is an Australian. He lives down on the beach and runs the trading post for the Straits, Islands and Archipelago Trading Company which is known from Singapore to Cooktown as SIAT. He had the wire netting tucked away at the back of his store's go-down which stands at the beach end of the jetty and smells like all such places do, of dust and tin and nutty fibres. I disliked keeping Melba confined in the small steel cage so I asked Griffin whether he had anything I could use to build something larger. There was a moment in which he looked as if he would say no. He was suspicious that the bigger cage for Melba was proof of my intention to stay in Manoba longer than I told him I was going to. Before I came, he and Dr. Daintree were the only two white men on the island.

The island of Manoba is volcanic in origin. No one has ever measured its rainfall, so far as I know, but it is probably in the region of one hundred inches a year. The island rises above five thousand feet, not high enough to produce the moss forest that can be found on the mainland of New Guinea which, on a clear day, I can see from my veranda. Apart from the boats that sail long distances and anchor beyond the reef to off-load stuff from and into Griffin's lighter, a mainland launch arrives fairly regularly to remind us, as Griffin puts it, that you can't get away from Them even on an island like this; although I expect he would fret if They stopped coming because there would then be almost nothing for him to complain of.

I'm told that the people of the interior live isolated from each other in tribal valleys and grow sweet potatoes, green vegetables, bananas, sugar cane. SIAT supplies them with what Griffin calls cargo, civilized amenities like tins of Kwikkaffy, clothing, ornaments, tobacco, novelties, and takes from them amongst other things native craftwork which ends up in the shops of Port Darwin and Melbourne, and a dye that comes from the root of a plant and is much sought after by the Chinese and the Malayans. In the old days there was trade in the plumes of the species of Great Bird of Paradise which is found in the higher reaches of the hills.

The people of the shore are fishermen and there is a small plantation of coconut palms which Griffin oversees and which adds to the sum total of all the copra in the world. When I first saw the island from the rails of a boat anchored off the reef it looked to be nothing but bunched up hills rising sheer out of an oily yellow sea, hills whose formations merged one into the other and were entirely covered with what the travel books call virgin jungle; but at eye level, riding the lighter into the lagoon, I saw how the hills might hide interior valleys. The beach is a narrow strip of silver sand, silver because the volcanic foundations have been overlaid with coral. A fringe of palm trees leans inland, blown into that position by the prevailing wind. Behind the palms are the huts of the settlement and these are built up on stilts as a protection from high tides when storms set in. I can just see the beach from the veranda of the hut I live in, where Daintree's last assistant used to live. Daintree has lived and worked alone now for over a year.

When I arrived, having climbed from the lighter onto the jetty and introduced myself to Griffin who was standing there like a port official on the lookout for undesirable aliens, shading his eyes from the glare, splashed with rippling lozenges of light reflected up from the sun-struck water, and walked at his direction towards his bungalow along the hot, hollow-ringing boards of the jetty, followed by the two men who had come out to the boat in the lighter and touted my three suitcases, myself carrying Melba who was shrieking and swearing in her cage, outraged it seemed by the very smell of Manoba, I had to march past a row of male Manobaons who stood on one side of the jetty (as they always do when a boat comes in, a lingering instinct from the days when strangers weren't welcome), brown, flat-nosed men in trousers, others in loin cloths, some with spikes stuck in their nostrils which I think are porcupine quills. One of them (the local clown, I've discovered since) wore only the phallic horn. I had seen photographs of this and in real life found it less untoward than I would have expected, but wondered nevertheless what it felt like to go around all the time with an encased decorated and artificial erection.

These men, and the view of the island, the situation in general, made me feel like an actor of contemporary drama who found himself miscast; in this case as a Victorian explorer; but not for long. Griffin has a sending and receiving set. He uses it to communicate with the mainland and between whiles lets it play music. The sound of jazz and rock-and-roll comes drifting up from the beach; and the beach, the settlement, even the paths in the forest, are littered with old Kwikkaffy tins which the Manobaons, after they've drunk the contents, fill with pebbles and shake, to make a kind of mambo-mambo.

Griffin is not much impressed with the tale that it is only to see the birds of paradise that I came to Manoba, particularly as I came armed with a letter of introduction to Daintree from a man called Cranston. I met Jim Cranston over eighteen years ago as a fellow prisoner-of-war in a camp in the north of Malaya that was called Pig Eye. Cranston has been to Manoba several times in the past few years but his only connection with the island is Dr. Daintree. Cranston is ten years younger than Daintree but he is Daintree's boss. Griffin knows this and suspects that my interest in Manoba is also Daintree, that I'm here to do something Cranston isn't prepared to do. This isn't quite true, but I don't blame Griffin for thinking it might be. He has never heard the expression Sabbatical Year and I'm neither his idea of a bird watcher nor his idea of a man in business in London taking time off, which is what I happen to be.

Whenever I go down the hill to the beach settlement to pass the time of day with him he looks my white, drip-dry suit up and down and says, "How's Doc Daintree today?" and only half believes me when I tell him that I don't know. Once he offered me a pair of field glasses which he said he had found in the go-down. I told him I already had a pair to watch the *Paradisaeidae* at close quarters if I was lucky enough to see them at all. He nodded and said, "Good on you," and then glanced up at the western arm of the hill where Daintree's dispensary is, which Griffin knows can be seen from my own hut. He was wondering how often I spied on Daintree.

When he talks sneeringly of Them, meaning mainland authority, authority of any kind, he does so with the look of a man testing you by verbal ordeal. He thinks I'm an investigator from the European Foundation that finances the Manobaon health service and which therefore employs not only Daintree but Cranston as well.

Griffin is a tall, broad-boned man, with sandy hair. We eye each other levelly but he is the heavier. His stomach bulges his shirt out above the waistband of his washed-out blue trousers. I judge him to be about forty-five, a few years older than myself. He married a Chinese girl in Singapore just after the war. She died about four years ago and was buried in the Timor Sea. He has three children, two boys and a girl who go around stark naked and have faces that perhaps remind him too much of their mother whom he loved very much. He says that it was only in places like Manoba that they could live together without being reminded every day of civilization's faint disgust, and when she died he found that such places had become a habit. He has been here three years, a year longer than Daintree. He talks of taking the children to Sydney when the eldest boy is ten.

The first "a" in Manoba is short, the second long; the "o" is hardly pronounced at all. You begin to pronounce it and then swallow it. The whole, spoken quickly, sounds like Man'Bah, but with this little break, this whisper of sound dividing the syllables. Before the war the Manobaons of the interior lived in almost total isolation. They were contemptuous of the people of the coast who have their living mostly from the sea. The missionaries tried to get at them once or twice but in those days there was no permanent trading post, no established or accepted white man through whom the missionaries could claim any kind of authority or on whom they could rely for protection, and their attempts at salvation were pretty much hit-and-run affairs. It is to a different kind of religion the Manobaons have now succumbed: the religion of goods, what are called consumer goods, what is sometimes called cargo—a cult rather than a religion; the cult of the happiness that must follow in the wake of the tins of Kwik-kaffy which have already made the white man rich and power-ful and lie on the sands, the paths and the tracks, like shiny manna fallen from heaven, gone rusty, but no less potent for that.

My sabbatical year began several months ago, in the April of 1960, six months after the final decree in the divorce suit brought by my wife Anne, to whom I was married for just over ten years and who is the mother of my son Stephen, now getting on for eleven. He and Anne live on with Anne's new husband in the house in Surrey called Four Birches which used to belong to my Uncle Walter and Aunt Ethel.

The idea of taking a sabbatical year only occurred to me last January but I had no real plans until my partners in London said, "Where will you go?" Before I quite knew what I was saying I said I'd go somewhere warm, perhaps to India where I was born. It was a mistake to mention any-where. In business there is hardly a square mile of land where there isn't some man, firm, body or institution you should look in on if you happen to be passing. There is al-ways some tentative proposal to explore even on holiday, some suggestion to make and leave simmering, some idea to be picked up; and there is always this man: Our Man at the Source of the Amazon.

My sabbatical year was planned for me from the mo-ment I opened my mouth; at least its opening stages were planned. Telephones rang, cables were sent, seats reserved on jet aircraft which flew God knew how many thousand feet above the oceans I'd rather hoped to chug across slowly in a banana boat—not, I imagine, that I should actually have gone in a banana boat if left to myself. A man of forty-one is not much given to the stench of oil and ripening fruit if circumstances haven't made him get used to them. When I go down to the beach to see Griffin and I smell the stink of the petrol he keeps to run his generator, the odour of things going bad at the water's edge, and climb the steps of his wooden bungalow with its notice board hanging from the roof: Straits, Islands Archipel. Trg.Co, Manoba Division, Lew Griffin; grin at his naked children, Tony, Len and Lucille (who, when first I arrived, covered their private parts with grubby hands as if this were a form of salutation), when I push through the bead curtain that suggests an old-fashioned South Seas interior but actually gives on to a living room furnished with a plastic-topped table, steel and canvas beach chairs, a studio couch and a flight of china ducks fixed to the wooden walls, I settle for the fact that here in Manoba is as much the likeness of my banana boat as I should care to have. I gratefully accept a glass of beer cold from Griffin's refrigerator, a meal of packet minestrone and tinned breast of chicken with asparagus heads (both heated up on an electric hot-plate) followed by strawberries and cream; and acknowledge my thankfulness that all is not as I might once have wished it to be, long, long ago.

The hut I live in is primitive enough, although that—because it is practically empty—is tidy and borrows its atmosphere less from the jungle on one side and the view of the sea on the other than it does from my white suits, tropical mesh shirts, wild silk ties, gold cufflinks, Schaeffer fountain pen, sharkskin swimming shorts and my hide suitcases which one of the lads from the beach polishes every day with Wren's to keep green mould at bay.

I swim every morning and brown my body before the sun rises too high for comfort, return to the hut to do my exercises, for I take the sight of Griff's sagging stomach and flabby chest muscles not as stirring proof that a man can still look derelict, still look in the latter half of it like an early twentieth-century remittance man from the fiction of my boyhood, but as a terrible warning of what can happen to him after forty if he lets himself go. Afterwards, I go out to the makeshift shower, pull the string and wash away salt and sand and dirt, dry myself on a fluffy white towel which I have to forgive for never really being dry, and deodorize with a preparation called Clipper Tang. There is a boy in the settlement who cuts hair European style and I have him up to trim mine once a week. One acquires habits of comfort.

Griffin gives me meals, a service I pay for both in money and in time spent coaching the eldest boy in the technique of keeping a straight bat. He has a spirited square cut but a tendency otherwise to scoop everything off his legs. We play on a length of matting in the flattened compound behind their bungalow and for this period the boy consents to compromise his sense of proper manhood by wearing a pair of shorts.

From Griffin's bungalow I can see whatever men, women and children climb the hill to Daintree's dispensary for treatment and I can judge circumstances by the time that passes before they come down again and by the manner in which they come—in ones and twos or as a group. If they come down in ones and twos I count them and when they've all returned sometimes go up the hill myself, past my own hut and on up the steep winding track which rises through forest to the cleared plateau where Daintree lives and which, when I went there on the day of my arrival just as the sun was setting, seemed in its air and on its ground to glow with a tangible pinkness, as if flocks of invisible flamingos had just flown over shedding minuscule particles of their pigmentation. But if the people come down as a group I carry on bowling to Tony until it is time for another swim, another shower, and lunch, and the drowsy pleasure of rest and sleep and desultory reading.

I have not been into the hills yet to see the birds of paradise and since that first occasion have only seen Daintree twice to talk to. On some evenings I play chess with Griffin, but it is the evenings when time hangs heaviest, evenings when my sabbatical year begins to be irksome, for I've always been active. But I'm determined to see it out, to go on making use of it, and Daintree's presence on the shoulder of the hill, the cage outside my hut which reminds me of the cage at Jundapur, prevent me from leaving and spending the last few months in top expense account places. And while I've no real hope of being able to do the small thing I should like to do for Daintree before I go, I feel I mustn't leave Manoba a day before it becomes absolutely essential to get on a boat and begin the long journey home, in case, just in case I do get that opportunity.

Daintree must be nearly sixty-five now. He was barely fifty when Cranston used to wake me up in Pig Eye with his nightmares, calling, "Dane, watch it, Dane." I asked him who Dane was, told him that he had called out to someone whose name sounded like Dane, telling him to watch it. He said that Dane was what he called a man called Daintree, that he was dreaming the Japanese had got Daintree too. Now, Daintree's hair is silvery white. It was nearly that colour, Cranston told me recently, when Daintree, who had indeed been captured by the Japanese, got out of prison camp in Java. On the two occasions in Manoba when I've been able to talk to Daintree since the evening of our first and unsuccessful introduction, he's looked at me from eyes that are very black and piercing (as I always imagined them to be although I don't think Cranston ever described him to me in much detail) but as if he's never seen me before and is a bit troubled by a memory of a letter which told him who I was. On the last of these occasions he interrupted me in the middle of what I was telling him about the problems of modern industrial finance, pointed at me and said, "I know. You're the chap who wants to see the birds of paradise. Cran told me about you."

I depend on him to see me in to the hills because the people from the beach settlement never go. I'm almost convinced that they don't even know the way, small as the island is. The hill people come down to trade with Griffin but I depend on Daintree really to take me in and bring me back, and I must wait. Perhaps he will never take me.

When I came to Manoba I had no intention of putting things down on paper. It is the way time hangs on my hands that has started me on it. There has also been something compelling in the way Melba sings of the hills, valleys and forests of her youth (for it is said she is very old), sings as though she sees them through her wrinkled lidded eyes, which she half closes. There is contentment in her singing, happiness in recollection and a mature acceptance that so much of her youth was maya, so much of it illusion; and then when she breaks off and pokes her head forward (I have watched her at it without her knowing) and suddenly arches out her wings with that abrupt and belligerent movement that just as abruptly fades off into a graceful slow-motion folding back of them, begins to bounce from side to side and squawks my name: William Conway! and, Wurrah Yadoor-a! I feel that it is my youth she has been singing and not her own and at times like this I go up to her cage and we stare at each other and try to break down the terrible barrier that exists between man and beast.

2

THERE are no tiger in Manoba, but if I were to go out into the forest now I could take a tiger with me. He is here,

picked at random from the recollections I have brought to
the island with me like invisible luggage, in the dark corner
of the hut where the lamplight doesn't reach, his head in
profile like a gigantic Egyptian cat, flat-topped and jutting
along the line of his broad, wedge-shaped nose. He comes
complete with his own Indian background of thorn-sharp
fronds, emerges from it into a sunlit clearing and I can see
under the loosely worn but close-packed hairy hide the eruptions of his arrested muscle. He stands stock-still, red gold,
with black, tapering, disruptive whiplash stripes, his white
wiry whiskers curving out from his mask. Now the muscle
shifts, articulating the bones, moving over the soft corruga-
tions of rib, and the hot tiger smell reaches me where I
perch, an awe-struck boy, alone with Dora Salford, a little
girl dressed as I am in a white shirt, jodhpurs and topee, in
the makan that has been built in a previous year around the
forked branches of a tree. I am armed with a gun but have
lost faith in its powers. It is my first and last experience of
Indian shikar.

I came into the world to the whizz of rockets and the
whirl of Catherine wheels as if I were heir to great and
noble opportunity. I was born in India at the Residency in
Gopalakand in 1919, when my father was acting as assistant
to the Resident. The fireworks were ordered by the ruler of
Gopalakand, The Maharajah, Sir Pandirakkar Dingit Rao.
He was known to the English as Dingy Row. It never occurred to me to ask why there should have been fireworks to
mark the birth of a son to a then junior civil servant, but I
suppose Sir Pandirakkar was in a pro-English mood and
thought the fireworks as much a proof of his own good
nature as a compliment to my arrival.

I remember nothing of my life at the Residency. When I
was two we moved to a place called Pankot. The only things
I remember of my mother are the pretty features of a photograph, her timeless isolation in a darkened room, a bed, and

my father's head resting in his hands as a signal of her death.
She died in Pankot when I was four.

Mrs. Canterbury was the first woman in my life. I called
her Canterbury Bell, or Canters, or—if piqued—Old Mutton. She was my nurse first and then my governess. She had
flaky lips which she softened and tinted with what she called
lip salve. Her nose was long. It was the outward sign of her
authority. Her shapeless bolster bosom was the outward sign
of her sex and the hard bone buttons that ran down it a suffi-
cient reminder that her motherliness was paid for. They were
uncomfortable to the cheek and provided an effective barrier against behaviour unseemly in a boy, which is as she
would have wished.

I don't think she was at Gopalakand but she was certainly
at Pankot. There was an Indian woman too, an ayah. Did I
call her Amy? I think so. And I think Amy was at Gopalakand. It may have been Amy who told me about the fireworks. Perhaps she returned to Gopalakand from Pankot
when we left for Tradura where nearly all the major boyhood recollections belong. It must be a failing in me not to
remember things more clearly. Other people seem able to.
I'm sure that Melba does. But the fact is that beyond the
knowledge that an ayah existed and the remaining sense of
her as "Amy" she is quite gone. My father probably distrusted the influence of a native woman and got rid of her
early on. When I was eight he sent Old Mutton packing too,
to Jundapur, and brought in a man called Grayson-Hume to
be my tutor until the time came for me to go home to school
in England and stay during the holidays with my Uncle
Walter.

Except on our annual retreat to a hill station, I had few
connections with children of my own age between five and
ten, the years coinciding with my father's appointment as
Political Agent to what was called the Tradura Agency. We
lived in Indian India which was as different from British

India as chalk from cheese. Indian India was made up of
the princely states which one way and another accounted
between them for something like a third or more of the
whole land mass, which I have found surprises people who
always thought of India as just India with the British ruling
the lot from Whitehall and putting a Viceroy in to make it
look good. The states had treaties with the British Crown
and were left to govern themselves for good or ill, except in
matters of external affairs, defense and communications; but
the British Crown represented the paramount power and so
they had to govern themselves under the eyes of British
residents and agents.

Apart from Tradura there were five neighbouring principalities in the Agency: Jundapur, Shakura, Premkar,
Trassura and Durhat. None of them held any British in-
stallations. In consequence there were no cantonments, no
English officials except those employed by the rulers, no
English clubs, no Anglo-Indian life. In Jundapur there was
an English doctor called Henderson. He came to see us
quite often and sometimes stayed the week end with his
wife and daughter. He had dry, chalky hands, polished
magenta lips, and called me Little Man. The daughter was
three or four years older than myself. The chief of police
in Shakura was a Scotsman who had resigned his commission in the Indian Army. He commanded, for a salary
paid out of the ruler's treasury, a small force of native
policemen, had a Eurasian wife and light-skinned children
with mauve shadows under their brown eyes. We seldom
came in contact. I remember them chiefly for the air of
untouchability attaching to them. The ruler of Premkar had
an English dewan (prime minister) but the dewan was a
bachelor and I gathered that Father thought poorly of him.
I think I met him three times. My father used to travel the
agency territories in a Residential progress, but I never
received the summons to accompany him.

My father was a tall, thin man with narrow chest and shoulders. He married in 1917 when he was thirty-five. He had entered the Indian Civil Service more than twelve years before but the exodus from the political department of seconded army officers during the Great War enabled him to transfer permanently to the States branch of the service, the branch in which his father, my grandfather, had served before him. My great-grandfather was a soldier. The Conways had been in India for a long time.

When my mother died my Aunt Sarah, Father's spinster sister, came out from England. She too was tall, thin and narrow. They looked very much alike. Her arrival, and a moment that must have preceded it by several weeks, are the most vivid memories I have of that time. I was climbing the steps to the veranda of the Pankot bungalow. The bungalow was red brick and the veranda was constructed of creosoted wood which smelt pleasant when the sun got onto it. These places were called bungalows but they had upper storeys. There were gables at Pankot. There were what I remember as willow trees and a kind of wistaria. It was very English. I was climbing the steps ahead of Mrs. Canterbury who at that time still wore an Edwardian straw hat perched on piled-up hair. My father was on the veranda reading a letter. It would have been at the end of 1923, December probably. Pankot was the most northerly station we were ever in and the winter climate would have been like an English spring, but hotter during the day.

"Is it news of your sister, sir?"

That is what Canters said. I was puzzled. News from your sistersir. What was a sistersir? I understood that it was female and that I would see it soon, probably because my father said something like, "Yes, she's agreed to come and stay." I also understood that it was a kind of sister, but a special kind peculiar to men in Father's position; and if I'm any judge of my own small boy's character I did not try to puzzle it out too long for myself but went at what I thought was a suitable moment to the sole but often reluctant source of casual information, Canters, and said, "What is a sistersir?" And I expect she said, "What on earth are you talking about, William? Go and get Amy to wash your hands and knees." I wasn't very good at judging suitable moments. A certain un-Conway-like impetuosity of temperament showed up very early on.

By the time Aunt Sarah reached Pankot I must have worked out that Mrs. Canterbury had only run two quite ordinary words together, otherwise I should certainly have said to Sarah, "Are you a sistersir?" whereas I said something else. At some time just before or after the clicking into place of sistersir's real meaning my father told me that my Aunt Sarah was coming out from England to help look after the household and to sit at the other end of the table from him when there were guests at the Agency Bungalow. Aunt Sarah arrived in a dress of brown silk that was blown against her stick-thin legs by one of those hot Indian winds that can stir up the most placid day. I stared at her and said, "You've come a jolly long way just to sit at the other end of the table."

She may have hoped to find a husband ("even at her age," a phrase that sticks in my mind and has the ring of Mrs. Canterbury talking privately to herself in my presence), she may have accepted Father's invitation to join us mainly for that reason. Later, when Grayson-Hume replaced Canters and Sarah was the only woman in the house I used to describe her to myself as "looking soppy about the Old Gray Hum." Dora, when grown up herself, said she remembered Aunt Sarah as what she called a nice grown-up to kiss. Aunt Sarah was always kind to me but there was this feeling of suitcases and restlessness wherever she went. She read time tables, booked tickets, wrote letters and cards for table places, made out lists—even lists of lists that would be needed presently. Nearly all her actions were ones of preparation. Perhaps the only things she ever finished in her life were the railway journeys which took us up to the hills in the hot weather, but even those involved preparations for disembarking and seeing that we weren't cheated by the station coolies. Her great asset, apparently, was distinction at the dinner table. I gathered she sat at the other end of it very well, always making ready to cover up an awkward lull in the conversation, planning the right moment to catch the eyes of the ladies so that her signal to rise should not be missed.

3

As a boy I used to think that if you disregarded the King-Emperor, George the Fifth, Father was the second most important man in India, the Viceroy being the first. This evaluation of his public as distinct from his private splendoor began when I left Pankot and childhood behind me and entered boyhood and the Tradura Agency. There was an element of household excitement at the move which communicated itself to me in the form of mystery. Father had been promoted. This was in 1924. I was five. The old ayah either stayed in Pankot or returned to Gopalakand. Canters was in charge of me and Aunt Sarah would have been in charge of the packing. This major upheaval made me ask questions. "Why are we leaving here? Why are we going to Tradura? Yes, but what does Father do?"

"Your father," Mrs. Canterbury said, "tells all these princes what to do."

I remember her saying that. I have the image of her kneeling on the bare boards of the nursery floor at Pankot

gathering up lead soldiers and putting them higgledy-
piggledy into their box when they were supposed to go
neatly into their rightful cardboard sockets.

Mrs. Canterbury's remark coloured my whole attitude to
the things and people of Tradura right from the moment we drove up to the entrance of the squat, white, porticoed building that was our new home. Here there were
peepul and chinar trees; a mass of green which hid the
house until you were right on top of it. Unlike Pankot it
was very Indian; Anglo-Indian, rather; grandeur in miniature, Whitehall scaled down to dominate with proper dis-
cretion a Moghul landscape. The house—still called a bungalow—was actually in the grounds of the Maharajah's palace
but separated from the palace garden by an interior wall of
mellowed brick. Beyond our own formal garden at the
back of the bungalow there was a wilderness of rhododen-
dron-like bushes growing in the shadows of taller trees
and a pathway leading through it to a wooden gate set in
the wall. This was our private entrance to the palace garden.
It was seldom used because relations between palace and
bungalow (I discovered much later) were not as cordial
as they could have been, so that visits tended to be official
rather than social. I came to look upon the private gate as
my own.

At the front of the bungalow a gravel drive curved from
the porticoed entrance through trees and bushes down to
wrought-iron gates. Day and night the gates were guarded
by sentries, men from the Maharajah's private army. They
wore orange turbans and orange sashes but otherwise their
uniforms were regulation khaki drill. Just within the gates
there was a wooden hut which served them as a guardroom.

From the wrought-iron gates the prospect was rural.
You could turn left or right along the unmetalled road. In
the rains I have seen the road running like a yellow river.
In the dry weather the bullock carts, the bicycles, and the

one-decked Indian bus which occasionally went down it left clouds of smoke-signal dust behind them. If you turned left the road led you past cultivated fields and then through hills and secondary jungle to the Maharajah's hunting lodge, and onward to the neighbouring state of Jundapur. If you turned right you went past flat, sunken fields on one side and on the other the high, white stucco wall which enclosed the palace grounds. From outside the grounds you could see nothing of the palace itself. The wall was sharp with radial spikes. Behind it banks of trees gave the impression of a walled forest. The wall continued for half a mile before it brought you to the fine set of main gates. Here again there were sentries, but the palace guardroom was a much grander affair than ours, of red brick with yellow facings. At least, I thought it grand but it must have been a bit of an eyesore.

If you didn't go in through the palace gates but continued along the road you came to a wide, open stretch of flat parkland, like a playing field, grassed and treeless. This was the maidan* which separated us from the town. I was allowed onto the maidan alone provided I was on horseback and to the other distant side of it if accompanied by Paluji, our head syce. In no circumstances was I allowed into the town. The entrance to it was dominated by the yellow mutti-walled prison, the police and army barracks and the parade ground. Behind these you could see the beginnings of the narrow dusty streets.

In Tradura "all these princes" meant simply the rulers of the cluster of six independent, self-governing and auto-cratic states for whom the paramountcy of the British Crown was represented by Father's person. Of these Tradura was the largest and most important. The maharajah was entitled to a salute of eleven guns when entering Delhi and therefore to a seat in the Chamber of Princes which had

* phonetically: My-dahn.

been inaugurated as a reward to the states for the way they had come to the aid of the British in the war of 1914-18. But even Tradura had not much more than eight or nine hundred square miles of territory to call its own. Jundapur was much smaller than that. Shakura, Premkar, Trassura and Durhat lay a bit to the east of Jundapur and were separated from it by a few miles of British India. These were smaller even than Jundapur, but estates would have been a better name for all these other five principalities in the agency.

"All these princes," Canters said. Six of them. In India there were nearly six hundred but I didn't know that at the time. Six was a powerful number of princes to tell what to do and because he was always the tallest man at any gathering, represented the King-Emperor and the Viceroy, and was my father, I stood in an awe of him that was loving, possessive and proud.

But apart from height, relationship and investiture there was what existed inside the man himself: the sharp, blue-green ice of his personality which I did not question until early manhood when I saw it only as a puzzle. As a small boy I must have seen it subconsciously, interpreted it sub-consciously, as the natural aura of a man who was one of the keepers of the sacred trust laid upon a certain kind of Briton to guide, punish and reward those whose mother's milk lacked the vital element that would make real men of them—fair-skinned rotters, for instance, or dark-skinned heathen.

There were days when I did not see him at all. Instruc-tions to me when I was eight or nine not to worry him because he was busy and had vital work to do were not, I'm sure, new instructions, but I remember the exclusion more clearly in regard to the time when I was old enough to feel excluded; not in any frustrated sense, though. There was always this inner knowledge that as I grew older I should grow into his consideration, that he would turn to look at me—as if to say, Well, let's see what these people I've employed have made of you. It was as though there existed a future initiation of body and soul, something that would kindle the flame I used to feel burning inside me into a kind of immense conflagration of arrival. Arrival at what I did not know exactly but, to be sure, I should arrive.

From Mrs. Canterbury I had at first the most romantic conception of his duties. That Tradura was not in the grip of excesses that would make Suraj-ud-Daula and the Black Hole of Calcutta look like a vicarage fête was, she implied, entirely due to him. A lot was owed, she admitted, to his predecessors, to the Political Department in general, past and present, but—"in India you never knew," and everything finally devolved upon the "man on the spot." My father was the man on the spot, alone, unarmed but ready like Gordon at Khartoum to quell an angry mob with a look. At any moment the good fellows in the guardroom at our gate might turn against us as the sepoys of British India had turned against their British officers in the mutiny of 1857.

To Mrs. Canterbury the mutiny was of absorbing interest. There was a time when I thought she had actually been involved in it, then that her mother had been, then her grandmother. She had a special compulsion for the well at Cawnpore. From the stories she told me I built up a childhood picture of it crammed with bodies, so crammed that the limbs of those on the top layer stuck up stiffly at odd angles over the edges. She spoke of a pink satin slipper, a relic of the bodies in the well, that could be seen in a museum in London. I used to imagine that the slipper had belonged to someone in her family. I had nightmares about the well and would wake in the dark, bite my hand to stop myself crying out; but in the daytime I dug deep, narrow holes in the garden and stuffed them full of lead soldiers with relish.

"What are you doing, William?" my Aunt Sarah said, finding me at this task on the way to one of her own. I told her that the hole was the well at Cawnpore and the soldiers were dead bodies.

"What a grisly old game," she said and smiled abstractedly, continued on her errand, notebook in hand.

As I grew older I suppose Mrs. Canterbury adjusted her sights higher in order to cope with my inability to equate the greys of life with the blacks and whites of the stories she told. The soldiers in the guardroom, for instance, were my good friends. I used to sneak away and pester them when they were off duty, sitting on their hunkers smoking bidis. They showed me how to throw a rifle about—not that I could do it because the rifles were as big as I was— and encouraged me with cries of *Shabash!* in my muscle-trembling attempts to hold one in the firing position with the right hand only as they could. I couldn't imagine one of them throwing us down a well, nor could I bring myself to think of them tied up and blown from the cannon's mouth as a fitting punishment for having done so. Mrs. Canterbury's mutiny was quelled by its own growing perspective but, as a child does, I put down any past impressions that we still lived with the threat of it or its like to "the kind of mistakes you make when you're a kid."

By the time I was seven—and in my own eyes no longer a kid—I knew that the mutiny was a thing of the past. Mrs. Canterbury even scolded me once for talking about it as though it still hung over us. Indeed, it was she who first explained that the Indian princes had been on the side of the British "to a man," that they had always been the loyalest element in British Indian life, as had been proved in the Great War when they gave money and men to the allied cause. But this, now, was offered as proof not of their virtue so much as of the virtue of "men like your father," which was one of her favourite expressions. "Men like your father have put down all the old feudal injustices." "Men like your father have given them standards." "By leaving them with the crowns and palaces they had when we first conquered India, men like your father have shown them that the English understand true values."

And—"One day, William, when you're a man like your father, it will be your job to go on helping these people to live better lives."

When I was eight and Old Mutton told me that she was leaving and I asked her why, she said that there were important things a boy could only be taught by a man, particularly a boy like myself who would one day bear great responsibility, and that my father, who always knew what was right and would want me to be a credit to him, had found and engaged a tutor who, it was said, would lick me into proper shape.

"Aren't I a proper shape already?" I asked.

She laughed and said that I was a proper shape for my age but that I was growing older and must learn things no woman could teach me.

I wasn't reluctant to lose her, simply fascinated by this sudden revelation of her ignorance. I asked her what sort of things she couldn't teach me. I don't remember exactly what she said, although boxing was mentioned, what she called the "manly arts." It made perfect sense to me. When she went she patted my cheek. She wasn't going far, only to Jundapur, to be governess to the son of the ruler, a boy whom Dora and I knew later as Krishi. I asked Canters how old this young prince was. She said he was about my age, so I asked her whether he ought not to have a man teacher too.

"It's different," she said. "He's an Indian, you see."

I shook hands with her when she left and shook hands with my tutor Grayson-Hume when he arrived. Between the two events I had begun to look upon him as an innovation not at all to my liking because in a terse interview my father had made it clear to me that Grayson-Hume would have full authority to inflict corporal punishment. I wasn't sure what corporal punishment was, so I asked. My father said, "Flogging," and dismissed me.

To me, flogging was something that only happened in books to sailors, usually to the hero who might faint but never uttered a cry. To be flogged in a book was therefore heroic. To be flogged by the old Gray Hum upstairs in the schoolroom sounded distinctly unpleasant by comparison. When I entered Father's study to meet him I half expected to find him armed with a cat-o'-nine-tails. I know I partly understood that the full severity of nautical punishment wasn't likely, and yet there was that uncompromising, leathery word. Flogging. So when, some weeks later, having been lulled into a sense of security by Grayson-Hume's good nature and friendly grin, and in consequence having strayed into a natural misdemeanour, he said he was going to cane me, I said, "Oh, is that all?"

Afterwards he made us shake hands, which struck me as very forthright and proper, very fitting to the occasion. Grayson-Hume was nothing like as tall as Father, but he was broad and very strong. I admired him deeply. He had dry yellow hair and blue eyes and a lot of hair on his chest. I thought him tremendously handsome and hoped that one day I should be like him. Years later he got into trouble for interfering with young boys in a wood in Berkshire. He never interfered with me but once lectured me long and earnestly because he caught me interfering with myself. He instructed me pretty fully in the facts of life when I was nine, and made it clear that he had my father's permission to do so. He called it a "thing." The man's thing, he said, goes into the woman. I asked, genuinely puzzled, "Who puts it there?" I expect he told me but for some time after that I visualized the act of begetting children not only as the sole reason for putting it there but as an act almost wholly disembodied and only gradually realized that the juxtaposition of things also involved the close proximity of boy and girl from head to toe.

I had learned the three R's from Canters. Grayson-Hume taught me mathematics, Latin, French, science, biology. From Canters I had got to know some colourful geography and some inaccurate English History. Grayson-Hume extended the geography dully with isobars, prevailing winds, deciduous, coniferous and tundra regions, and Mercator's projection. History became a business of Plantagenets, Tudors, plots, massacres, thumbscrews, racks, Thomas à Becket and Mary, Queen of Scots. It was a formidable program for a boy who at school in England was only described as "lively, active, of average intelligence, and good at games."

My favourite subject of all, though, was the history of the British in India. It was a subject in which Grayson-Hume excelled. Now I see his excellence as motivated by an ambition to do well as the tutor of a political agent's son. I suspect that he read it up before he came to Tradura. But at the time there was always a feeling of mutual excitement whenever he closed a book and said, "Right, Bill. Let's go for a walk and talk about your father's job and how it all began." The inference was that my father's job had an immediacy and reality better appreciated away from the schoolroom, that like that of an heir to a throne my training was to be dedicated and specialized, at one remove from the ordinary business of book learning because I had to be, in the future, at one remove from an ordinary run-of-the-mill man.

In the grounds of the bungalow, moving from sun to

shade, breathing fresh air, surrounded by the whole of my natural world, the liberal aspect of my education began. "We haven't always been kind," Grayson-Hume said, "and of course we haven't always been wise." I asked whether there would be another mutiny, hoping a bit for that kind of physical excitement. He talked about Indian leaders like Gandhi who would rather starve than fight. You had to fight a bully, but the kind of fighting we were talking about proved nothing, except that one chap was stronger than the other or used less strength with more skill. I asked what starving proved. I think he said it didn't prove anything either but drew attention, like civil disobedience and non-violence, to social and political injustice in a way that fighting couldn't because in the heat of battles there wasn't room for anything but anger. Sometimes, though, civil disobedience got out of hand and then you had to treat the leaders like rebels, you had to put them in prison, they had to pay for the hot-headedness of their followers. On one of these walks I said, "What does Gandhi want, what's swaraj?" He said, "Independence for British India. Freedom. What we all want, old man." "Will he get it?" I asked. Grayson-Hume said perhaps, but there was a long way to go. There was so much we had to teach the Indians before they could rule themselves. That was what Father's job was about, although the princes were a different problem. We had two jobs in India. The princes knew how to rule but we had to teach them democracy. The Indians of British India knew about democracy but had to be taught how to rule. "It's quite a job, isn't it?" he said, and punched me lightly in the ribs. "You'll have to give it everything you've got. Your life won't be any bed of roses." I frowned and said, "We're like the Romans, aren't we, sir? Like the Romans in Britain." It was a serious but exciting thought. I thought the Romans were fine fellows.

In "term" the program was rigid. We rode every morning

before breakfast, meeting at the stables which lay behind trees to one side of the bungalow. Sometimes we rode onto the maidan and galloped to the far side to watch a parade of the Maharajah's army which consisted of cavalry and foot soldiers and a battery of two cannon (which I don't think worked). At other times we took sticks and ball to practice polo shots, or rode down the Jundapur road and watched the villagers at their early morning work in the fields, breathed in the sharp enticement of dung fires. Sometimes I scattered pice to the scrabbling, naked, pot-bellied children.

We breakfasted alone in the dining room, wonderfully cool so early in the morning, and comfortable with its old carved black oak furniture and Jacobean chairs, and Father's silver reflected on the table top. I liked opening the cupboards in the sideboard because they had an old, closed-up smell of salt, pepper and sweet resin. The furniture was not ours but this fact somehow increased my sense of Father's consular power. It wasn't ours but we used it as we liked. The silver on the table was the symbol of his reign.

After breakfast I had half-an-hour to myself to go to the lavatory, wash my hands, and go upstairs to prepare the schoolroom for the morning stint. This was a tall, narrow, spartan room lighted by two small windows high up in the wall which could be opened and shut by long double lengths of cord that gave a bit, like elastic, when you pulled them. There was a cupboard for books, a table at which the two of us sat—Grayson-Hume on an upholstered chair, I on a plain wooden one.

At half-past ten we went downstairs to the dining room where the servants had left a tray of biscuits and tea for him, biscuits and nimbopani for me. Between eleven and twelve we worked upstairs again and then I was free until tiffin at one, at which meal I would see Father and Aunt Sarah for the first time that day—unless Father was out, which he

often was, or there were important guests. If there were
guests I might or might not be told to present myself in
the anteroom while sherry was drunk, might or might not
be told to take my place at table. Quite often the old Gray
Hum and I had our lunch in what was called the chota
dining room which was separated from the main dining
room by closed mahogany doors. Over the fireplace there
was a picture of the battle of Plassey, with Clive brandishing
a sword and flags fluttering in the breeze although the rest
of the picture looked very hot and still. After lunch I was
free until five o'clock when we met in the garden on the
lower lawn. Here there was a tennis court, a space for two-
man cricket. If we were boxing, we met at the stables so
that no woman guest strolling in the grounds would see our
bare chests. Stable and house staff joined in our sports—as
ball-boys at tennis, fielders at cricket, cheerers-on at boxing.
At six we bathed and changed and then I was alone to do an
hour's prep, to eat a solitary supper in the chota dining
room with a book—usually a Henty—propped in front of
me, and then to knock at the drawing-room door, enter and
say good night to my father, Aunt Sarah, Grayson-Hume
and any guests there might be. Sometimes I sneaked over
to the stables afterwards to talk to Paluji or waylay Bapu, the
old servant who looked after me.

Always I took Digby for a walk, admonishing him in
whispers not to bark or he'd give me away and I'd be for it.
Digby was only an imaginary dog. Apart from the horses,
which were a means of locomotion, Father did not permit
animals. With Digby snuffling around my ankles I would
watch the luminous sky, identify what stars I could, breathe
in the heady smell of India which, in those days, I took for
granted as the natural smell of night.

4

On each of my birthdays I had tea with His Highness, the Maharajah of Tradura, Ranjit Raosingh, Lord of the Sun, Giver of Grain. At four o'clock in the afternoon an open carriage arrived at the bungalow. The coachman was dressed in a brocade uniform of turquoise blue with silver facings, below which he wore the white native jodhpurs. On his head there was a blue and silver pugree and around his waist a blue and silver sash. There were blue and silver bows of ribbon on his long whip. It was always the same man, very fierce and handsome, I thought. It was the first thing I looked for when the carriage appeared around the bend in the drive: this unsmiling, familiar face that I saw on no other occasion. The footman who hung on behind was dressed similarly but without the silver facings and in a cloth duller and rougher than the shining brocade. As the carriage rolled to a halt the footman jumped down, salaamed and opened the carriage door for me.

For a reason which was never explained but which I never questioned because it seemed perfectly natural, part and parcel of my training, I had to be alone in the porch, enter the carriage aided only by the footman, go alone to the palace, be alone with the Maharajah, and then return alone. I did not mind in the least, in fact I enjoyed it all hugely. To begin with I liked the feeling that I was my own master and the way the well-sprung carriage dipped when I put my weight on the footplate. I liked the gleaming black coachwork, the blue velvet upholstery studded with blue velvet buttons, the blue carpet on the floor and the white mat above which for the first three or four years my feet used to dangle. On my ninth birthday I found that my feet rested fair and square on the mat if I sat forward a bit.

The carriage was drawn by two black horses. I counted it a sign of good luck if one of them broke wind before we reached the road. I used to wait eagerly for the arching out of their tails, the quivering reverberations, the fine stable smell.

At our gates the soldiers on sentry-go presented arms, but whether to myself or to the Maharajah's carriage I was not sure. They presented arms to my father but never to me except on these occasions. It must have been the combination of palace carriage, political agent's son and occasion which brought them excitingly slap to attention, palms ringing on wooden butts. Ordinarily, whenever I passed through the gates they grinned or winked at me, but on the birthday passage our faces were stern, our backs very straight. I acknowledged their presentation of arms by removing my topee as I had been taught, and holding it with the brim flat against my chest so that it should not appear to have been removed languidly or condescendingly. Taking my topee off like that always made my heart come up into my throat. I compressed my lips and stopped breathing until the hat was safely on my head again, its wide brim restricting my vision and making me a bit cross-eyed.

The performance of presented arms and removed topee was repeated at the main gates of the palace. From here the drive took you by sunken lawns and fountains (which were never working) towards another gateway set in a high, very thick wall of red brick similar to the wall which separated the palace garden from the agency bungalow grounds. As soon as you had passed through this second gate you saw the ground floor of the palace between the boles of many trees whose branches, interlacing, cut off your view of the rest of it, and by the time you had got beyond the trees and there was no further obstruction you were so close, coming into a paved courtyard at such an oblique angle to it, that I suppose I never had the opportunity of fixing the front of the palace properly in my mind.

There were pillars and moghul arches which formed a deeply shadowed arcade whose floor was raised some five feet above ground level. I think there were narrow stairways every few yards which enabled anyone who walked in the arcade to come down to the courtyard without going to the main entrance, which was a shallow-stepped affair of marble.

From the back, under a moon, the palace was of icing-sugar beauty. Under the sun and close to, crumbling stone and flaking stucco gave it more an air of romantic decay. "Romantic decay" is not an expression that would have come to me as a boy. I don't think I would have made any conscious assessment of it, but I must have noticed crumbling stone and flaking stucco for them to have come with me over more than thirty years. I can't have imagined crumbling stone, but just what stone it was that had crumbled I don't know for certain. There were stone elephants guarding the marble steps. It may have been those. Perhaps the decay is something I noticed when I was nine or ten and romantic has simply attached itself to the word because it now seems to describe properly everything to do with the external appearance of an Indian palace that was part of my boyhood.

When the carriage had stopped and the footman had helped me to get out I went alone up the marble steps and always paused to look right and left at the black and white tiled arcade which went off in fascinating perspective to either side of me. There were pigeons. Their droppings spoiled the symmetry of the black and white squares. One year there was a naked holy man occupying a pitch about halfway down the arcade to the right of the main entrance. He glared at me. His body was daubed with grey ash and even from that distance I thought his eyes glowed red; but this may have been fancy. The eyes of sadhus are generally supposed to glow like hot coals although none of the holy men I saw later had eyes that did. The redness is supposed to be caused by bhang, the eating of which inflames the passions.

I was met by a servant who helped me to take off my shoes and put on embroidered slippers with Aladdin toe-caps. So shod I followed him into the palace. The entrance hall was very dark. This was because, facing the doorway, there was a curious wooden contraption like a gigantic tapestry frame. On it there hung a gloomy, musty-smelling curtain. By peeping I discovered behind the curtain an immense glass door which gave a view of an inner courtyard. The palace was hollow in the middle. Within the hollow there were a formal garden of clipped shrubs, flowers, fountains and summerhouse. I was told that on certain occasions the giant frame was wheeled to one side and the window opened so that from the top of the marble steps you would appear to be entering directly through an archway into the inner courtyard, and that at times like this the courtyard was floodlit and the fountains turned on.

We first turned left along a corridor parallel to the arcade, then right. The corridor continued. There were mahogany doors with brass knobs at intervals leading into rooms on our right, but were there really aspidistras in brass bowls, set along the tiled floor between them? Yes, I think there really were, and drooping maidenhair fern in tall mahogany stands, and brown varnished lincrusta like that in the agency bungalow to the height of my shoulder. Above the lincrusta, thick as postage stamps in an album, hung uncountable highly coloured prints in rosewood frames. These at least were Indian and not Victorian. Most of them depicted scenes from Hindu mythology but amongst them, like sheep from another flock, were pictures of Indian boys and girls throwing balls or playing blind-man's buff.

We came presently to a set of double doors which sealed the corridor off. Behind them was an anteroom: lincrusta, black and white tiles, aspidistras and a large leather sofa with a gold-framed reproduction in colour on the wall above it of George the Fifth and Queen Mary, crowned and robed in Delhi. In this room I was always left alone for a few minutes. The servant left by the door through which we had come. On the other side of the room, in the centre of the wall, there was another double door. I think that on the first occasion it must have been explained to me that I should sit down and wait for this other door to be opened.

Perhaps in time I became a bit blasé about the whole thing, but what I feel now as I think and write about it is the leap of the heart when the doors were opened slowly by two servants who were invisible to me and I found myself with one foot on the long, wide strip of Persian carpet which formed a red and blue pathway across the great Durbar Hall of rosy pillars and fretted stone to the cloth-of-gold backed dais on which was set the enamelled and jewelled throne of Tradura, illuminated by arc lamps concealed in the recesses where pillars met the carved and painted ceiling.

And seeing a small figure already seated there I bowed deeply from the waist and then set out on the long walk to say hello to old Ranjit Raosingh.

He would have been about sixty. To me he looked immensely old. When I reached the last central medallion in the design of the carpet I had to halt, bow again and then stand still and upright, looking him in the eye until he beckoned me to climb onto the dais.

On these occasions he wore an achkan (the highnecked long-skirted coat) of gold thread, a white turban, white jodhpurs and tiny gold slippers. He was a small-boned old man. He can't have been much more than five-and-a-half feet tall. He was thin, but his hands were sinewy. On one of them he wore an emerald ring. His skin was a luminous yellowy brown, not so yellow when I saw him away from the light of the arc lamps. What fascinated me most were his eyes. Below each of them the skin had fallen away so that the pink, lower lids were turned out and down. The upper lids were hooded by a fall of flesh between eye and eyebrow. The eyeballs were yellowing and red-veined, the irises brown. A white moustache covered his lip but his chin was clean shaven. He looked wise and venerable but the truth was that he was stubborn and tortured by restless energy. I discovered later that there were long periods when he would have nothing to do with Father except through his dewan and that this was mainly due to a difference of opinion over his right to appoint his successor.

The first thing that happened after I joined him on the dais was the one part I hated. He picked up a silver shaker and sprinkled me with attar of roses. It made me feel damp and silly and I used to complain to them at home that I always came back from the palace stinking like a girl. After the sprinkling he gave me a sticky Indian sweetmeat. I wiped my fingers surreptitiously on the seat of my trousers thinking that I couldn't very well lick them so near to a throne. I sat half-facing him on a footstool which placed me at quite a disadvantage in the business of meeting his eye with frankness as I knew I must.

We had tea just where we were. After ten minutes or so of formal conversation he pressed a button on the under part of the right-hand arm of the throne (which, close to, had the disappointingly dull, encrusted look of something lain long in a junk shop) and then palace servants brought in cakestands and dishes loaded with European-style confectionery. There were bottles of ginger pop and straws to drink through. Ranjit Raosingh had nothing but a glass of milk but he encouraged me to eat and drink everything in sight. While I did so he talked.

My *Yes, sirs* and *No, sirs* spurted from my swollen mouth with little jets of cake and biscuit crumbs. I fancy there was a high old mess on the floor, but he didn't seem to mind either the mess or the uncontrollable burping brought on by the pop. I sat there, spasmodically galvanized into a position of hunched shoulders, with tightened chest and compressed lips, and with the air puffing out my cheeks and fizzing down my nostrils, and presently wanting very badly to pee, a sensation which when long enough frustrated induced in my face an expression I could feel was idiotic.

From the other end of the hall we must have looked an odd pair. The first tea party would have taken place when I was six. Mrs. Canterbury thought I was pulling her leg when I told her the king (as I used to call him) had entertained me from his throne. It was a natural enough background to me but to her it seemed as unlikely as the King of England wearing his crown at breakfast. On my seventh birthday she told me I shouldn't expect to have the experience repeated because no doubt he had received me that once in the Durbar Hall "so as not to disappoint a little boy." Now I was seven. Sterner stuff was to be expected. Returning to the bungalow I was asked where tea had been served this time, and I quite clearly remember saying, "In the Durbar Hall, of course. He's a *proper* king."

And this, I think, was the whole idea. There may have been plenty of avuncular kindness in his choice of tearoom; he would have known that it would be the greatest disappointment to a small boy to be invited to the palace and not to see him on his throne; but there was a distinct element of artificiality in it which was naturally lost on me at the time, lost on me for what it was but not for what it did. To me he was a great and powerful ruler. The throne, the great Durbar Hall, the long carpet, the button he pressed which rang a bell and conjured a prince's tea, the blue velvet upholstered carriage, the coachman's glittering uniform, all proved it. And then, as well as being a great and powerful ruler, he was a kind old man who, having been bowed to properly, unbent and threw attar of roses at me as a sign of honourable welcome, and filled me up with ginger pop. He was giving me a lesson in benevolent autocracy. What he would not have known was that this projection of himself as great and powerful only served to increase my loving awe of Father, who told him what to do.

Ranjit Raosingh never spoke to me against Father. I know that in the later years when a more practical interpretation of Father's duties had put me on the defensive, I was on the alert for any remark or drift of conversation that could have been taken as slighting or mischievous. After each occasion Father questioned me; but that was a moment of glory, not of inquisition. I felt like a trusted emissary and left his study glowing with a sense of duty done. I knew that when I was alone with the Maharajah I was Father's representative.

It is difficult to separate what I guessed of Father's work in Tradura then from what I knew of it later. I find myself very uncertain what Ranjit Raosingh talked to me about. What I can say I know about the State of Tradura between 1924 and 1929, I know from such a variety of sources (from which my own imaginative deductions aren't excluded) that it's impossible to remember accurately who told me what or when or why. To that extent my Tradura is and was, perhaps, illusory.

The illusory Tradura was not by any means a model state. There was feudal poverty, inefficiency and corruption amongst officials. When I say "there was" I mean that my illusory picture did not exclude those probabilities. On the other hand it did not admit dire poverty or inefficiency and corruption on any grand scale and the fact that it did not was due to the faith I had in Father's ability to curb tendencies in that direction with his sound advice and shining example, and the power he subtly wielded as the representative of the British Crown which could, if it had a mind to, depose a ruler or refuse to acknowledge the claims of his legitimate heir, but which would not otherwise much meddle in a state's internal affairs.

Ranjit Raosingh's succession was assured. He had sons, five I think it was. The eldest by his first wife, the Maharani, was a man of middle-age. There were grandsons and daughters. There was a second official wife and there were two concubines, one of them a Goanese half-caste who had been beautiful. I saw a woman once who must have been the Goanese, and thought her fat and blowzy. The eldest grandson, the son of the heir, would have been about fifteen when we left Tradura, ten when we arrived there, but he was at school in Switzerland most of the time. Father's predecessor had had trouble over this grandson's education. The education of young heirs was something of very special concern to the Political Department. Father's predecessor had advised English tutorage followed by a few years at an English public school. Ranjit Rao had sent his son to Switzerland in the face of stiff opposition and was credited with the remark, "My grandson must learn the value of time," a reference to the Swiss national industry which the then political agent was said to have taken a year to understand.

During Father's term of office Ranjit Raosingh was preoccupied with the belief that his eldest son intended to enforce his abdication on the grounds of age and health. This was the excuse, anyway, that he put forward to Father to justify his wish to nominate as heir his son by the Goanese half-caste. There was once a poison scare. The Goanese was seized with violent abdominal pains after a meal. "Indigestion," was, I believe, Father's explanation, but Ranjit Rao told him he suspected the Maharani of trying to get rid of the concubine because she believed it was the concubine who was turning him against his true son. He used what he called the problem of the succession as a delaying tactic in the business of forming some kind of elected or nominated government, a gentle form of democ-

racy such as men like Father were always urging on the
princes as a protection for the princes' own futures. Ranjit
Rao, I believe, took the line that there was no point in
reforming the constitution if the succession to the throne
wasn't in the hands of a man who would foster and further
it. He tried to persuade Father that his eldest son would
simply destroy any such constitution. And Father refused to
see any connection between the one matter and the other.

All this explains the long sulks into which Ranjit Rao
obviously retreated. I can visualize the way Father would
stand, looking at the old Maharajah, and the way the old
man would look back at him from those pulled down eyes
of his, accusing his own family, testing the edges of
Father's sympathy and credulity, trying to get him to say
in advance what the Political Department's attitude would be
to the son by the Goanese succeeding to the gaddi; and then
dismissing him, refusing to see or talk to him for months,
but sending messages through his prime minister; not,
I'm sure, because of anything Father said but because Father
said nothing and simply got brighter and brighter, frostier
and frostier, until the old man had to freeze to his throne
and wait for the comfortable murk of ordinary human
fallibility to fall around him again.

The plots and the poison also explain why the palace
always struck me as strangely silent, deserted. It must have
been filled with the old man's displeasure and suspicion
and the dying flickers of his passion for the Goanese whore,
as she was called by some. He kept his women in palace
purdah. Grayson-Hume, discussing Hindu customs, told me
that on the few occasions Father met the Maharani she and
her women talked to him from behind a screen. At the time
I accepted it as a custom, but it was policy. Both sides,
palace staff and agency bungalow staff, lived in conditions
of armed truce.

Father always seemed to me to be the busiest man in the

world. He had an Indian secretary called Moti Lal who smelt of tombs and taught me Hindustani on Tuesday and Thursday evenings. I also remember a clerk and a chaprassi. I was not allowed to have much to do with them, nor with the palace children. Not having much to do with the staff was part of the rule of not pestering or interfering with Father and his work. Not having much to do with the palace children, none of whom I cared for much (the girls were sullen and the boys, I thought, crybabies) was almost certainly due to the climate of palace versus bungalow which I grew up in and did not think odd. My only real Indian friend, apart from Paluji, the head syce, and the son of one of the palace gardeners, was young Krishi of Jundapur and even that friendship did not ripen until the spring of 1929, my last year of Indian boyhood.

Nineteen hundred twenty-nine was the year of the great hunting party, the year of the Kinwar tiger, the year I met Dora, the year of the birds of paradise in the cage on the lake isle at Jundapur.

5

EACH year, at the beginning of March, what was called the hot weather began. By the middle of April the lawns were turning brown and Aunt Sarah was arranging the luggage for our retreat into the hills. But in March the lawns were still clipped, watered, and as green as emeralds, and in the palace garden there were these white peafowl, a cock and two hens, moving across them with arched necks, smoothly bulging breasts and trailing tail plumes. When they rested on the grass with their legs tucked away they looked like Viking ships at anchor. The cockbird curled up the tips of his folded fan as if he didn't like it to be in contact with the ground and he looked more like a Viking ship than the hens did.

I used to tease the peafowl, particularly the cockbird. This was my first consciously erotic experience. I was allowed into the palace grounds through the gate in the red brick wall, on our side of which was my wilderness of rhododendrons, and to go across the lawns as far as the giant cedar of Lebanon. I believe this cedar was unique, either the only cedar or one of the very few successfully planted in India. If any of the palace children were playing I could go further than the cedar and play with them. I preferred to play with the son of one of the malis whose job was to water the flower beds for his father. He was a bit older than I, a ragamuffin with holes in the khaki shorts that had been handed down to him by the son of the previous agent. Playing with the gardener's son was always interesting because he would get his ears boxed if his father caught him slacking.

He taught me rude words in Hindustani and I reciprocated to the limited extent of my knowledge with rude words in English. He was the first boy with whom I compared, but that was curiosity, ordinary boy business, not eroticism. He said that I was a Muslim dog because I had been cut, so I hit out and landed a lucky punch on his nose which I think surprised me as much as it did him. I was interested to see that his blood came out the same colour as mine. I already knew that his water did. I was proud because I could pee further than he could. He was better at spitting, though. I let him beat me at spitting after I'd hit him on the nose, so that he would feel better about it. We smoked bidis and sometimes I stole cigarettes from the box in our dining room that had a filter on the lid to keep the contents dry. He was allowed to smoke, but English cigarettes were a great luxury to him. In exchange he gave me betel nut which I liked because it made you look as if you had a bloody mouth.

Sometimes he must have been working in the grounds at

the front of the palace, and I suppose there was a time when he wasn't working there at all, being too young. I don't remember how or when we first met. It was probably when I was seven or eight. He was part of my secret life, like the soldiers in the guardroom. I have forgotten his name.

What I liked best was to sneak out of my room during the heat of the afternoon when all the others were having an after-lunch nap (what we called So Jao), tucked away in their separate places, embalmed in the lowered temperature of the tatti-becalmed bungalow like bodies awaiting the last trump, and to go soft-footed over the flinty gravel path that struck fire-hot and sharp through thin plimsoll soles, until I reached the dappled area of sweating rhododendrons and the high, red brick wall that at this time of day cast almost no shadow and hummed faintly when you put your ear close to it. Then, having made ritual water amongst the nettles, a small havoc of heavy splash jostling frail, fuzzy leaves, I would follow the wall to the gateway and enter the palace garden.

Beyond the framing darkness of trees there was the green lake of grass and beyond it the white palace—arches, and shuttered windows and lattice-work in the stone, mysteriously deserted, behind taut, transparent veils of heat. Advancing as far as the great cedar, to stand in its saw-mill smelling shade, on the bare earth that radiated soft and prickly from its trunk, I searched out the peafowl.

And yes, I took Digby with me and used to whisper to him, "Fetch 'em, boy, sic 'em, pup," a fascinating and at the time fairly incomprehensible saying I had got from P. C. Wren's novel, *Beau Geste*. How did you sic a thing? I asked Grayson-Hume once, "What's sic 'em?" He said it was on the borders of Tibet and Nepal. The dog was called Digby after one of the Geste brothers. Perhaps it was the Geste brothers' game of making paper boats for Viking funerals

which first made me think of the peafowl as Viking ships,
but whether or not that was so, there being no Digby except
in my mind I had to sic 'em myself, and this usually involved moving cautiously beyond the cedar into no man's
land, the desert beyond Fort Zinderneuf, from one oasis of
shade to another, until I found them: white, elegant,
strangely inflammable of my passions. I was sorry for them,
covered as they were from head to tail with white feathers,
because this branded them cowards and they naturally had
to be baited to see whether they were. I set Digby onto
them, encouraged him by snapping my fingers and saying
pssst and waving my arms. The hens usually jerked away
into the undergrowth as if they had remembered all of a
sudden to go gathering nuts, but the cockbird swung around
to face me, and this is what I wanted him to do.

I did not always find them in the same place but the
place in my mind now was a miniature area of sunlit grass
with the trees very big and black all around it and shadowing
the hen birds to a midnight pallor as they thrust up in-
quisitive necks from positions of safety, watching the cock
who stood in the open so close to me that I could see the
waxy gleam of his long quills in repose.

And then, without warning, the bird began to swell and
the great fan came up, stiff and icily tumescent, its gossamer
tips trembling in the disturbed air.

"You beauty," I said, "you fine, brave, white beauty," and
felt the blood gather in that curious well of sensation that
lay hidden in the tassel of flesh.

There was music: *Tales from the Vienna Woods,* alternating with *The Blue Danube.* The palace orchestra—all
bulged-out brown bearded faces and gleaming convoluted
brass—was playing under an awning. The palace garden
was full of people. I saw her moving slowly along the
fringe of the lawn, this girl called Dora, a white girl of

roughly my own age, in a white organdy frock tied around her waist with a shiny white ribbon.

"You followed me," Dora said, years later. I asked her how she knew unless she kept turning around.

"I don't think I turned round," she said, "but I knew you were following me. I believe I wanted you to, but when you got me under the cedar you were horrid to me."

I asked her what she meant, "got her under the cedar." She said that the impression she had was of being got there, of being driven there so that she would find herself alone under the cedar with me, but I think it was just a case of catching her up to stop her sneaking through my private wall in the garden to my private rhododendrons. She told me that eventually I agreed to let her go to the rhododendrons. She had been looking for a place. Afterwards I had to take her to the bungalow where she did it again properly. The first time hadn't been a success. I was standing guard and she thought I was sneaking a look. In the tatti-darkened drawing room of the agency bungalow she played the piano, announced each number in an assured little voice: "Queen Mab, from *Forest Fantasies,* by Walter Carroll."

"You said I was showing off," she accused me when we met again as man and woman.

Did I? She played well. I could swear that I told her so, swear that I was impressed, even a bit startled that she could play what I called grown-up sounding music right there in my own home.

But remembering what we said isn't important. What is important is the picture of her in her white organdy dress. Close to, she smelled faintly of eau-de-cologne. Her mother made her put it on her temples to counteract a tendency to giddiness in the heat. I remember kissing her. I don't think the kiss was in the bungalow but I can't be sure. The kiss, like the texture and whiteness of her dress, the dark bronze colour of her hair, is isolated; all extraneous details have been rubbed out long since. There were beads of perspiration on her face. Our mingled breath was a small, hot pressure on my own. She did not turn her cheek but lent her whole head solemnly to the occasion in perfect stillness. Her eyes were grey-green. To describe their later, grown-up expression, I would use words like frank, searching, and because in her woman's face I could see faint traces of the child I had known those qualities of frankness and curiosity were probably in her eyes that afternoon, thirty years ago, after I had kissed her and we stood wherever it was, on the porch of the bungalow, by the gate in the red brick wall, or in the shade of the cedar of Lebanon, cast up on a little island of experience from the blinding seas of innocence.

We did not speak of the kiss afterwards, not even when we met again as man and woman. But I don't think Dora forgot it either. That we never spoke of it seems to be proof that for each of us it was a moment of private revelation. To me was revealed something of the way the flesh will suddenly feel imperfect, insufficient, as if it has become detached from what it properly belongs to, and the kiss did nothing to satisfy this sense of deprivation, only increased it and induced, like the erupting peacock fan, an immature erection which at the time I don't think I connected in any conscious way with what Grayson-Hume had told me about the act of procreation—although the subsequent recollection of the strange disorganization of flesh and spirit was almost certainly the main bridge I threw across the gap separating what Grayson-Hume had told me from what he had left to my imagination.

But even when the bridge had been thrown across and I realized that a man would actually hold a woman close in his arms and somehow manipulate a physical possession, it was my curiosity in grown-up people that was aroused, not my curiosity about Dora and myself. I remember watching the behaviour of men and women as they stood in groups, or walked together, apart, or arm in arm, talking, silent, laughing, serious; clothed, and infinitely removed from whatever cold consideration it was that turned them towards each other in a way I could not picture the exactness of. And yes, cold is the right word to use with the word consideration, for the real heat had not yet come up behind my eyes or the bitter-sweet juices into my loins, and there was nothing in the way these men and women looked at each other, touched hands, absent-mindedly kissed, which seemed to have anything to do with the way I had felt compelled to lean towards Dora, and kiss her.

Dora remembered the garden party, our first meeting, as a debit item in the balance sheet of my behaviour to her, or said she did, whereas I have forgotten things like behaviour, the gestures and actions of child and child; but if Dora said I was horrid I must have been. She had it quite clearly. The way, she said, I stood with my fists stuck in my pockets, legs astride, topee pushed to the back of my curly black head, and smelling of peppermint. She said I had a grim look, was very conscious of male superiority and of being the son of the Political Agent; that I got a lemonade for her but was sullen about it as if I knew it looked to her like currying favour. We had been introduced before the rhododendron business. It was the lemonade and being too shy to ask where a lavatory was that led to our meeting under the cedar. After I had given her the lemonade she said I left her to it and talked to a girl with a fat bottom and blonde ringlets called Brenda Boscombe. I remember no family called Boscombe and no girl with a fat bottom called Brenda, but Dora remembered her, even that she wore a "terrible pink dress" that was too tight for her. I teased Dora about this recently, told her that she must have had her eye on me, otherwise she wouldn't have remembered her set-backs so clearly, and that if I had been so taken up with

Brenda Boscombe how did I come to be following Dora Salford and getting her under the cedar?

She said, "Because you laid claim to me by getting the lemonade and I shouldn't have gone away without permission, even though you weren't taking any more notice of me."

Her father was an officer in an Indian Infantry Regiment, a major at that time. The Salfords were stationed in Marpur which lay to the north of Trassura outside the agency territories. Dora said that the fact that her father was a soldier was what made me get her a lemonade. Apparently I said, "What's *your* father?" as if she must know already what mine was, which she did. She pointed him out to me and almost at once I offered to get her a lemonade. When I came back I let slip I knew he was a major and gave away what she had seen for herself, my long detour to the refreshment marquee to get a close look at him.

I don't recall any of this, but I'm sure she was right. I was fascinated by army officers. In a cantonment of British India they were two a penny but in Tradura they were a rare enough sight in uniform and in the hills they all seemed to wear tweeds and grey trousers and look like any other man. The only parades I saw were those held on the maidan for the soldiers of Ranjit Raosingh and none of his officers was British. According to Dora her father wore dress uniform that afternoon, which is likely because in spite of the heat all the men were dressed to kill and the women wilting beside them like chiffon ghosts protecting their pallor with sunshades.

The Salfords were at the garden party as guests on what was called the Trassura List. There were six lists in all: the Trassura List, the Shakura List, the Tradura List, the Jundapur, Premkar and Durhat Lists. It would have been in February that the lists first began to be mentioned. They were connected with the business of the Kinwar tiger.

Kinwar was a speck on the map of Tradura which hung on the wall of my father's study; on the ground, a huddle of crumbling mud huts and thatch roofs in a small cultivated valley enclosed by hills of secondary jungle.

I went there with Grayson-Hume and an official from the palace some time in January 1929. At the end of April I was due to sail from Bombay, school-ward bound, and to live between terms with my Uncle Walter and Aunt Ethel in their house in Surrey. I think it was entirely due to Grayson-Hume that I was allowed to go to Kinwar.

The story of the tiger begins with a feeling of "The boy ought to see for himself"; not of Father saying these words but of Grayson-Hume saying them. If I think of the probability of my having overheard Grayson-Hume say this thing to my father I can at once conjure a picture of an open door, interior gloom, exterior sunlight, the smell of leather gone musty, the smell that always came from Father's study and was more noticeable just outside the door than inside the room.

"The boy ought to see for himself, sir."

If I add the "sir" to it, it is definitely Grayson-Hume talking to Father, but with the "sir" or without it the trip to Kinwar is indivisible from this memory of my understanding that I ought to see for myself. I know that when I rode to Kinwar I was conscious of being about to do so; which shows the inaccuracies a boy collects around himself because if there were truly anything Grayson-Hume had said I ought to see for myself it wouldn't have been Kinwar but what Kinwar was a prelude to: the hunting and killing of a tiger.

The Kinwar tigers had appeared first in 1923 and again in 1924. An interval of three years elapsed and then the male returned in 1928. The villagers swore that it was the same tiger and that it had come back to a familiar, easy haunt because it was getting old. At night it could be heard snuffling close to the huts. The people were convinced that it had turned man-eater. It made a daylight attempt on a young calf but was observed by some of the men who frightened it off by banging drums and brandishing staves. When the rains came it left the district, for water was plentiful abroad, but in January 1929 it returned, bolder than ever, being observed on two successive days standing only partly concealed by scrub-jungle on the edge of cultivation, watching the villagers at work, swishing its tail. Kinwar had had enough. A petition for shikar was sent to the palace.

Standing in those same fields a week or so later with Grayson-Hume and the palace official, and what seemed to be the entire male population of Kinwar, my fancy was caught by the image of the swishing tail and the gathering odds against the lone, aging hunter. I remember saying to the old Gray Hum, "Why don't they kill it themselves?" There were enough of them and several of them looked lusty.

Grayson-Hume said that while it was in Tradura state the tiger belonged personally to the Maharajah, and couldn't be killed without his permission. He picked up a clod of earth and crumbled it. "This," he said, "and everything in it and on it belongs to the old man."

Writing, here in Manoba, of that distant afternoon at Kinwar I can still see the whole gang of us trudging back across the fields, the brown-skinned old men with ugly, stretched muscles, and the younger ones who smelled of sweat and cotton cloth, salaaming and calling us Huzoor, meaning Great Ones. In this picture the Great One from the palace seems to have assured them that the shikar petition already has the ear of His Highness, the Giver of Grain. The dust kicked up by our feet is the dust of achievement and satisfaction, and the boy, riding-breeched, white-shirted, tapping his leg with his crop, moves through the

dust with his head up and his shoulders back to bear the
weight of privilege and authority which automatically
presses upon him because of his white skin. Before leaving
the fields the boy turns and looks back at the several places
where the tiger has been seen lurking. Does his heart miss
a beat? Is it sadness for the old tiger that comes up into
his throat and is swallowed again? I think it does, I think
it is, but who can swear that this was so? It was so retrospectively, it is so now, it is so out there in the darkness of
this island just beyond the veranda, that black screen onto
which this picture of the fields at Kinwar has been pro-
jected.

Here is another picture. We are leaving Kinwar in the
fine smell, the fine creak and jingle of our horses. The
official leads off, Grayson-Hume behind him, myself bringing up the rear. The village children run to keep up with
us for a while and I scatter them with a small flung handful
of annas. Presently Grayson-Hume twists his broad back
around, grins, winks and puts his thumb up, the gesture
he and I call "Roman for Good Show," I give him Roman
for Good Show in return, spur to join him, not sure what
show he means is good but accepting it in regard to the
day's work done, the hardish ride ahead and the addition-
ally friendly warmth that has entered tutor and boy relationship now that the end of it is sadly in sight. He nods in
the direction of the official and says, "We'll get our shikar,
old chap," which surprises me because I went to Kinwar
believing it to be the first step towards a shikar that was
a foregone conclusion.

"The boy ought to see for himself, sir," the grin, the
wink, Roman for Good Show and, "we'll get our shikar,
old chap,"—these are clues, part of a total evidence that
it was not Kinwar I ought to see for myself but whether
I liked hunting. Like dogs, guns were not part of our
household at Tradura. Every so often, particularly after our

retreats into the hills where I mixed with boys who had guns and went out with their fathers, I had asked when I should be taught to shoot. "Not yet," they used to say, or, "When you're a bit older. It's up to your father to decide." I think Grayson-Hume forced the issue. He may have done so for the simple straightforward reason that I was old enough and ought not to leave India without experiencing this particular Indian sport, or for more complex reasons that had to do with something he detected in my father's attitude.

It is not really extraordinary that a man like my father with no taste for the shikar should have risen virtually to the top of his profession in India. There is always a wide gap between popular supposition and actuality and the Indian Empire was not built and maintained only by red-necked men with guns in one hand and chota pegs in the other. Neither is it extraordinary that he never said to me, "My boy, I do not believe in the hunting and killing of game." It would only have been extraordinary if he had. He was never a man to tell you what he believed or why. His pleasures and displeasures were communicated to the world through a series of indistinguishable silences.

The shikar was fixed for the beginning of March and old Ranjit Raosingh decided to conduct it with all the pomp and display at his command. Why did he decide that? It may have been that for years the old man punished Father by refusing all permission for official shikar, thinking that like so many of his countrymen Father enjoyed nothing better than stalking about the countryside shooting everything in sight. Once he had got this wrong idea into his head his stubbornness may have been such that no whispered confidence that Father didn't like shikar anyway could shake his resolution. If that is the truth then the shikar arrangements coinciding with my departure from India and the termination of Father's term of office in Tradura were meant to reflect Ranjit Rao's final generosity. To me this does not ring true.

I think Ranjit Rao knew from the beginning, even before our arrival in Tradura, that the new agent's tastes did not run to blood sports, even guessed that he had an odd, deep-rooted objection to them. Perhaps he thought that by refusing all permission for royal shikar on the pretext that the state treasury couldn't afford it he was cunningly high-lighting a quirk in my father's nature which could, in certain lights, be seen as a cowardice which he, the ruler, was too well-mannered and sensitive to bring to public notice by arranging entertainments Father would not attend.

In that case the shikar for the Kinwar tiger was Ranjit Rao's final and subtle insult. It was presented as an occasion of honourable farewell. In this way, perhaps, hoping to see Father made to look cranky, foolish and ungrateful, he avenged himself for Father's obstruction of all his efforts to nominate an heir other than his eldest legitimate son. But if an insult was intended it was hardly successful. Father, so far as I can recollect, held himself physically aloof from the junkettings, only being present when protocol demanded it.

Several miles down the road from Tradura, turning left from the Agency Bungalow gates, was the hunting lodge, a large and imposing building constructed almost entirely of wood and looking rather like an immense Swiss chalet with verandas encircling each of its three floors. There was room in the lodge for something like a hundred guests. People were invited not only from the other states in the agency but from neighbouring provinces of British India. It was at the lodge that Major and Mrs. Salford and their daughter Dora stayed during what was called Shikar Week.

The lodge was in its own grounds of sorts, but these were really no different from the light jungle which darkened

the hills thereabouts and there was an exciting air of camp-
ing out. What lawn there was was used for the big dining
marquees. Wherever you went within a radius of several
hundred yards from the lodge you came upon tents—servants'
tents, soldiers' tents, beaters' tents, cookhouse tents, tents for
bachelor guests whose civil or military status didn't qualify
them for one of the rooms in the lodge.

The most distinguished guests were housed in the palace
at Tradura and the palace at Jundapur. Even our agency
bungalow was crammed with people, very carefully selected,
elderly and dull, and I had to camp out in the agency
garden in a brown canvas bell-tent during the first two
days of the celebrations. After that I camped out in the
grounds of the hunting lodge with Krishi.

The celebrations began with the garden party at which I
met Dora and on the following day there was a banquet at
the palace which none of the children attended and which I
remember chiefly as a scene of grand evening departure
from the bungalow, with Aunt Sarah in *grande toilette,* almost unrecognizable, shining and glittering, and with something odd having happened to her eyes and the way she
held her head.

In the dark I crept from my tent and went into the palace
grounds to stand beneath the cedar. The palace was floodlit
and I cared for it less like that than when it lay under
moonlight like something long drowned. People were moving on the terraces and there was music: waltzes and synco-
pation—*Yes, sir, she's my baby,* and *Paddlin' Madeline
Home;* and I experienced what I called the cold fountain
effect up my backbone, breaking, cascading across my shoulder blades, an effect produced by excitement and the sadness of wanting to hold a moment from slipping away.

And when, after a long eye-aching time, I turned away
into the warm night I muttered, "Come on, Digby. Come
home, boy."

6

I was to ride an elephant in the Maharajah's procession. Such an invitation had to be interpreted as a command.

"Is there room on it only for me?" I asked, and on being told I might choose a companion I chose Dora Salford. The garden party and the kiss had made their marks, turned me romantically towards the idea of having a girl.

I wrote a note beginning *Dear Dora* which Aunt Sarah made me write again beginning *Dear Miss Salford*. The note was delivered by bicycle to the hunting lodge and the chaprassi came back with a note of acceptance addressed to Master W. Conway, beginning *Dear William* and signed *Dora Salford*. This correspondence must have taken place on the day after the garden party, the day of the grown-up banquet. I'm sure it was only after the garden party I heard about the procession and that anticipation of it contributed to my restlessness on the night of the banquet, heightened the magic of watching the floodlit palace from a place of hiding.

The Maharajah's procession marked the real beginning of the royal shikar, the central event of which was to be the beating-out of the Kinwar tiger. The shikar was laid on with an almost military precision. Kinwar lay some three miles to the south of the hunting lodge. Experts had been at work in that area for two weeks and a plan for flushing the tiger and driving it on to an open stretch of ground and onto the guns had been worked out to the last detail; or so I gathered from Major Salford who explained it to me by making marks on the ground with the toes of his highly polished boots.

In the old days when the ruler of Tradura went out to the hunting lodge the procession had gone from palace door to lodge door; but in my time it formed up at a makeshift overnight camp about two miles from the lodge and when it was ready the principal actors, who had driven there by car and bus and lorry, took their places and moved off to the sound of music. The overnight camp was needed for the elephants and soldiers and the host of servants who caparisoned them.

My father was not in the procession. He had the job of greeting the Maharajah, on the latter's arrival at the lodge, on behalf of the British guests. The Maharajah's invitation to me to ride Ranka was like the annual invitation to tea— kind, thoughtful, but full of subtleties only my father and some of the officials may have perceived. Riding on one of the royal elephants in the shikar procession was an honour, but it was an honour you took up at His Highness's rear, as subservient a position as that taken up at his feet in the throne room when he sat you on a low stool and stuffed you with fine boy-size grub. I remember no discussion with Father about the procession invitation. I think it was all done through Aunt Sarah, because he was unwilling to discuss the shikar with me at all.

And Grayson-Hume had gone unexpectedly to Bombay, which was described by myself as a terrific swizz, a business of thumbs down, Roman for Bad Show; but apparently unavoidable because it was said to involve our sailing arrangements for the end of April.

My plan with Dora for the elephant ride was that I should go to the hunting lodge where she was staying and then be brought back with her to the starting point of the procession in her father's car. I rode to the lodge accompanied by Paluji, who helped me to find the tent I had been allotted. My kit either followed me or had gone before. All that is hazy to me, as is my first meeting with Dora's parents, but I remember the car, a Buick, half-convertible with the driver sealed off by glass panels. It was dark blue

with bits of yellow here and there. Mrs. Salford was dressed in
colourful georgette and struck me as bossy. She dabbed eau-
de-cologne on Dora's temples before we started out and the
smell of the cologne filled the back of the car and seemed
to bring me out in a kind of rash, although it must have
been only a tingling flush of sustained embarrassment. Dora
said that we sat as far apart as the seat allowed but that
when we drew near the forming-up area I became excited
and overbearing, and on reaching it got out of the car
without turning to help her until too late, when I contented
myself with slamming the door, pushing my topee away
from my eyes and jamming my hands in my pockets and
trying to look as if she were with me because of some
unavoidable mistake. She said she remembered feeling that
she could put up with this typically masculine behaviour
because in the car she had suddenly appreciated to the full
her victory over Brenda Boscombe (whoever Brenda
Boscombe was). She had hooked what Brenda had let
wriggle away and what she had hooked was "nice looking,
particularly when it scowled." She was quite content to act
the weak girl rôle.

But this is not in the remotest degree the way I remember
Dora on the day of the procession. I'm sure that I was scared
stiff of her most of the time. What she called getting excited and overbearing as we drew near our destination was
probably a case of saying whatever came into my head out
of sheer funk, and bad manners in getting out of the car
the result of all but shattered reflexes, because I was usually
good at what the old Gray Hum called "manners" or at any
rate tried to be if only to please him whose whole bearing
I admired, whose very gestures I consciously and unconsciously copied.

And I was scared stiff of her because she was beautiful
and remote in a clean white dress, and because two days
earlier I had had the colossal cheek to kiss her. Was the

elephant ride secretly a black-hearted device, an attempt at
bribery to keep her silent on the matter of the kiss? It was
partly bribery, I think, and also partly continued curiosity
and the built-in determination of my sex to stick its neck
out to see what might come of things.

Overnight the elephants have been painted. Patterns of
lozenges, stripes and circles, in white, vermilion, green and
orange, decorate the swinging trunks and the big humped
heads on which, between the eyes, also rest bright medal-
lions. Huge thimbles of silver filigree encase the stubby, sawn-
off tusks. The largest and oldest of these animals bears on
his back a glittering silver howdah with a tasselled shade of
turquoise blue silk. Our own howdah is of polished mahogany
with brass fittings and the shade is green and casts blue-
green shadows into the folds of our white clothes. The
howdah bucks and sways, sideslips like a boat caught beam-
end on by a wave. My horseman's muscles stiffen and so for
a moment I lose equilibrium for I do not sit astride my
pony but upon a turbulent barrel of air; and in the end I
hang on to the rail of the howdah as Dora is doing, and push
my topee away from the bridge of my nose.

Ranka's mahout is a boy of fifteen or sixteen, a South
Indian with a blue-black skin and well-developed body
naked to the waist. He gleams at us, sweats and smells of
musky elephant odours and coconut oil, squatting below us
behind the hump of Ranka's head, coaxing the animal,
crooning quarter-tone melodies which have no end and no
beginning but which are sometimes interrupted by his
shouting hoarsely and flinging both arms out and leaning
far forward as if in supplication to some horizon only he
and Ranka can see, a performance which strikes me as
hotly magical, revelational of a mystical partnership between boy and elephant.

We are the last elephant, far back in the procession, but

when the yellow dust road twists we catch a glimpse of the
silver howdah in which old Ranjit Rao sits, wearing cloth-of-
gold. Ahead of him are horsemen, courtiers and ministers
in scarlets and whites and peacock blues; musicians whose
music we only dimly hear because between Ranka and the
next elephant ahead there marches a detachment of the
military band. They play English patriotic songs and on
Ranka we are a moving island distinguished by our special
tunes; *Goodbye Dolly Gray; Men of Harlech* and *D'Ye Ken
John Peel?* The elephant fifty yards in front of us is the
purdah elephant and the curtained howdah concealing the
Maharani and one of her women looks like a covered relic
in a religious procession. Between the purdah elephant and
the Maharajah's comes the elephant bearing the son of the
Goanese concubine. Behind Ranka there are more horsemen and foot soldiers.

Presently everything becomes obscured by the churned-up
dust which hangs in the air like a threat of thunder. The
hard hot sunlight which, when we started, lay upon the
road and scrub-jungle clean and bright is now diffused,
translated by the floating particles into dirty grey-yellow
smoke and when the road turns and gives us a glimpse of
the leading elephant the silver howdah gleams like the
minaret of a mosque seen through a sandstorm.

We pass through a village and the sandstorm somewhat
abates because the inhabitants have watered the road to keep
the dust down. They prostrate themselves as the Giver of
Grain goes by but are on their feet by the time we reach
them, calling out something I don't catch, the men salaaming in a cheerful way, the women keeping their faces covered
which pleases me because it makes me a man by implication.
I want to take my topee off and hold it to my chest but
make no move because Aunt Sarah has told me that only
the Maharajah and his family may acknowledge demon-
strations. So I smile at any whose eyes I catch and try not

to catch too many, but keep the smile going so that the impression we leave shan't be one of sullen superiority.

And when the village is behind us I feel that all the magnificence has drained away.

According to Dora, when she and I talked about the procession recently, I was concerned about "that old woman in rags." Dora still had a clear picture of her, the way she knelt by the roadside holding out her palm. I remember no old woman in rags, but I remember the feeling of the splendour suddenly gone. I think what happened was that both Dora and I saw the old woman, even discussed her, but that afterwards I retained a general impression while she retained the particular one. What I have never forgotten is how the procession suddenly looked unreal and tawdry. The way I would describe it now is to say that in the midst of the magnificence I saw the face of damnation.

I shared a tent with Krishi, the son of the Rajah of Jundapur. He looked a weakling as a boy, with thin arms and thin, knobby-kneed legs, but in later life he has put on flesh, is handsome, a rare whoremonger, and no credit to Mrs. Canterbury who tutored him until he was fourteen. He succeeded to the throne, or gaddi, of Jundapur in 1946, just in time to relinquish its powers to the new Indian government and retire to live on a pension and brood through his periods of impotence in the decaying palace which stands on the shores of the lake I have yet to tell of.

Until the shikar I had had almost nothing to do with him. It was due to Old Mutton's influence that we found ourselves sharing a tent. She had often tried to bring us together, and efforts, however determined, to bring children together are usually forlorn hopes. It interested me that he was a prince and would one day be a rajah, but looked at simply as a boy he struck me as a dead loss. His hands made my flesh creep because they were narrow, long-fingered, cold and damp, like stick insects brought in out of the rain. His skin was olive-brown and he had eyes which Dora thinks of as like those of a gazelle now that he is grown up. His hair was much too oily for my liking when he was a boy, and the tent, I remember, smelt of jasmine and sandalwood. I suspected him of bed-wetting because there was also a powerful stink of urine every morning and his bearers changed his sheets every day.

The only thing I envied Krishi was his gun. I asked him whether I could clean and oil it for him but he said the cleaning and oiling was done by a servant. He let me hold it though and showed me how to break it, load and fire. It was the gun which brought us together. I asked him whether he would use the gun to have a bang at the tiger. He said that he would probably only be allowed to go along for the ride when it came to that, which made me feel better because that would make two of us. Krishi had been at the lodge from the opening of the shikar. He knew where everything was. He took me to a tent marked "Shikar HQ" and introduced me to an imposing Sikh with fierce moustaches who was in charge of the general administration. There were some twenty elephants in the lodge stables and elephant compound. There was a chart showing the names of the elephants and the names of people who would ride them on the tiger hunt. There were first-line elephants and second-line elephants. I was on second line and riding with nobody whose name I knew, and my own name was not distinguished by the word "gun" after it in brackets.

In the grounds of the lodge there was a .22 rifle range and a practice area for clay-pigeon shooting where people went to get their eye in. Parties were got up every day to go off in trucks and cars on small shikars for duck and game. With Krishi I spent one glorious afternoon on the rifle range. I started from scratch. At the end of it a man said, "That lad's a natural shot." He had a sandy, close-clipped moustache and wore a blue mazri shirt and he is engraved thus permanently on my memory in a blaze of sunshine and the smell of cordite.

Later, Krishi lent me his gun and I went with him to the clay-pigeon butts. A couple of Englishmen took an interest in us. The first hour was tricky but all I now properly recall is the burst of pride at getting the hang of it, and rubbing liniment into my shoulder before going to bed; and of making a fool of myself next day by hitting nothing and having to grit my teeth every time I tucked the stock into the fiery aching pit between arm and chest. And this was a very special disaster for me because I had invited Dora to come and watch, and she was there, in white, mute, accusing, witness of my shame and degradation.

It was called Shikar Week, but it would have been nearer two weeks in all. Dora said there was a rumour at one time that the tiger had been seen in another district entirely, that the experts reported the tiger gone from its haunt above Kinwar, that it was expected there would be no big-game bag in consequence.

She said that after the procession I ignored her for a day or two. She remembered watching me at the butts. It was then that she first met Krishi. She said that they ganged-up on me a bit, she to take me down a peg, he because he fell in love with her and saw me as a rival. I know we became a threesome, but it wasn't until some two or three weeks later, during the period when we both stayed with Krishi at the palace in Jundapur and used to row every day across the lake to the island that I see, retrospectively, Krishi as more than a thin boy with a gun and a habit of generosity.

It is not only that time hazed the memory of Shikar Week but also that the business of the tiger stood out in isolation for both of us—in such isolation, in fact, that what led up to it exactly is uncertain. Dora thought it was the result of a dare, hers, and that the dare had been caused by boasting, mine. She thought I was mistaken when I said it was simply an adventure of which I was the ringleader, and mistaken too in saying that Krishi had also been in it when it was first planned. But I know he was in it. He cried off at the last moment but let me take the gun. Afterwards there was a suspicion that I had taken the gun without his permission.

The grounds of the hunting lodge were enclosed by a wall. In it was a high, narrow gate, obviously not one of the main entrances to the lodge grounds, a gate not unlike that in the wall separating the palace garden from the agency bungalow garden. Beyond the gate there was jungle, and a pathway through it; scrub-jungle at first, but abruptly getting fairly dense. The ground rose and the track took you to a clearing where in the forked branches of a tree was the makan, built in some previous year but still serviceable.

It was one of the Englishmen who helped me at the butts who told us about the makan. I had never seen one and so he took the three of us to the clearing. We climbed up into it and he explained how it would have been used; how the clearing might have been baited with a live, tethered buck or calf; or how a tiger might have been driven into the clearing and so onto the guns of the shikaras who waited in their tree-fork observation post.

There was never any doubt about what we had to do, at least, not in my mind. We had to go alone, the three of us, with Krishi's gun, and wait for the Kinwar tiger. The clearing held for me a mysterious promise of excitement from the very first moment that I saw it and I always fancied that I had seen the tiger lurking there, watching us from the shadows. When I first stepped into the makan I was lost in a dream of adventure which only ended when the adventure itself ended.

Perhaps the rumour of the Kinwar tiger no longer being in the hills partly explains our foolhardy expedition. There may have been this unspoken understanding between us that no risk was really being run. That Dora should have remembered the rumour and I have forgotten it, in itself suggests that this was so. She would not like to think her dare had led us into unquestionable danger and I, as the boy, would not like to admit that the adventure was anything less than dangerous.

There were to be two attempts, the first late in the afternoon and the second very early in the morning. We decided that these were not only the best times to get away but likely times for the tiger to come to the clearing—before nightfall when it would be out "looking for a waterhole," and just after dawn when it would be "on its way home to lie up during the heat of the day," (remembered phrases which sound like young Conway laying down the law). The first attempt fell through. We were to meet just outside the gate in the wall, but Dora didn't turn up and Krishi was unwilling to go without her. It was the beginning of his defection. When it was too late in any case to set off for the clearing I went alone to find Dora. Her mother had wanted her for something. I accused her of crying off and warned her that she wouldn't get more than a few minutes grace for the morning sortie.

But it was I who was late the next day. I had wasted time trying to persuade Krishi to come. He thought Dora wouldn't be there, that the whole idea was silly, that once I found myself waiting alone I'd give it up. It was lucky that he stayed behind. He was able to tell people where they'd find us.

I had to run the gauntlet of tents and stirring servants, and Dora the gauntlet of corridors and stairways in the lodge. We met in silence and thin grey light and walked side by side up the track. She was wearing jodhpurs and a shirt.

I was more afraid than I had expected to be. The track

was narrow and as the scrub-jungle grew denser it seemed no longer to be morning but night.

But it was she who stopped and said, "Let's turn back, William."

Then she put her hand on my arm. I was holding the gun in both hands, carrying it in front of me in something approximating to the high port position and my muscles were tense. As boys will I was always doubling my arms, testing the biceps with my fingers to see how much nearer they were to bulging up like a grown man's, sometimes with genuine curiosity, sometimes absent-mindedly. I had compared them with the gardener's son's and had invited Grayson-Hume once or twice to pronounce judgment on them, but this had been like comparing your height or the shape of your hand. The sensation which tingled along my arm from the gentle weight of Dora's hand, a weight that made the muscle feel bigger and tougher, was like the sensation which had awoken me on the day I kissed her and it was as if she had touched me not on the arm but on the most intimate part of my body, so that I found myself wondering what it would be like if she really touched me there, there where no woman in my conscious memory had ever touched me except through the thickness of a bath towel when I was younger.

I said, "Come on. It's not much further."

It was light in the clearing. I helped her up into the makan. I had brought a water bottle and after we had wet our whistles she produced a bag of toffees and we sat there chewing and getting our breath back. Then we stood up. I gave her the job of "guarding the rear" while I watched the clearing. If either of us saw anything we were to touch the other on the hand. I got my eye in by drawing beads, then settled to wait. The sky brightened. Before long the sun was filtering light through the trees. The dew sparkled on the grass.

.   .   .

And there was this wave of panic, not in my own breast, but in the distant heart of the forest; a shrill piping of birds and shrieking of monkeys which went on for a long time and then died away until there was no sound at all, no breeze to stir the smallest leaf or cool my hot cheeks. I reached out behind me, signalling to Dora, caught and held her wrist until I sensed that she had seen the place on which my own eyes were rivetted: the continuation of the track we had come by, at the other end of the clearing, well to our left, visible to us only as a shadowy opening. There was a clump of bamboo growing there, and several of the sharp, slender blades had shifted, as if pressed aside by something heavy which still held them rigid.

Inch by inch I brought the gun up to my shoulder and when I had it there and was bringing the edge of the bamboo into its sights I found I was trembling, questioning for the first time the wisdom of what I had got us into. I had to shut my eyes for a moment, to clear them for aiming, to steady myself, to get a grip, and in the darkness there was the ruby light of the blood in my lids. I remember the words, "blood lust," coming into my mind, and then the stab of my own lust for the blood of the tiger like a pain low down in my throat.

I opened my eyes. My skin prickled. When I opened my lips to get air into my drowning lungs there was a taste of metal on my tongue and the smell of it in my nostrils. From the clump of bamboo there had emerged the black, white and orange mask of a gigantic cat, the head bigger and higher from the ground than seemed possible to me. The makan felt thin and ricketty, and there was this fluttering of the heart because the blood had grown too thick to pump. A pressure was building up, duller but heavier than the pressure in the throat which had come in anticipation of the taking of the tiger's life. It was a pressure involving the whole body, it produced a compulsive rigor of the limbs which only a decisive and physical act would dispel. I was being compressed like shot at the bottom of a gun barrel by a ramrod.

As in a dream I brought the bamboo patch back into the sights and sought a point of focus on the tiger's head, knowing now that I could not miss, and that it was all up with him. Abruptly he moved and my finger, moving to the trigger, froze to the guard. I heard Dora catch her breath but dared not alter my position for fear of attracting the animal's attention. I knew that tigers had little sense of smell, but the slightest movement in the makan could be dangerous. Holding my head still I followed him with my eyes, planning to whip around directly he caught on to our presence and turned his head towards the makan; and from this oblique, uncomfortable angle I saw him emerge from the shadow into the morning sunlight and stand arrested, staring at something that aroused his curiosity in such a way that mine was aroused too and almost unconsciously I turned my head and so saw not what the tiger saw, or fancied he saw, but Dora's profile: the small speckling of sweat on her upper lip, the partly open mouth and lowered jaw, her perfect stillness, the isolated pulsing movement of a vein in her neck—her appearance of being bewitched and totally unafraid.

At once the waves of her enchantment made themselves manifest in a faint vibration, a sawing of the air all about the makan; a compound of our breathing and the tiger's breathing. The tiger stood quite in the open now, but I made no move to bring the gun to bear on him. He made a perfect target. The phrase "perfect target" was in my mind but there was something wrong with it and presently, when quite unexpectedly he lost interest in whatever it was he had been looking at or listening to and moved to a patch of dappled sun and shade, lay down and began to lick his paws, I knew it was the word target that was wrong. There was no target in that place, just myself and Dora, the surrounding forest and the tiger washing himself.

And then it was not a question of being awestruck by the tiger's burning bigness or of seeing in it a kind of savage nobility. Big it was, and in the sunlight seemed to burn so that later Blake's poem came to me with an authority it would not otherwise have done. It was savage and, I suppose, noble in its way. It was a question of being awestruck by something quite other than these things: by the realization that it had a right to be where it was, as much right as I and Dora. Not *more* right, but as much right.

My lust for the animal's blood drained away. It left a sediment behind and I felt soiled by it. I wanted the tiger simply to go away, quickly, without having seen us. If it saw us it would attack and then I should have to fire at it, try to kill it; perhaps we should have to watch it die. At once the image of what the gun might do was obliterated by a sudden and terrifying lack of faith in the weapon I held. It was not powerful enough to kill a tiger. I was afraid and ashamed. I was ashamed to have brought any gun but more ashamed to have brought this particular gun; ashamed to be there in the makan with a gun in my hands that wouldn't protect Dora.

Inch by inch, hardly knowing what I was doing, I began to move the barrel across to realign the sights and at the instant Dora put up her hand to stop me the tiger saw us, was on its feet growling, twisting and leaping away with a bounding jump into the jungle. The gun jerked upwards. The explosion and the thrust against my shoulder were the only indication I had that I had actually pulled the trigger and then Dora and I were crouched on the floor of the makan with the gun behind us somewhere, listening to the noise that sounded like a boulder crashing down a wooded slope. There was a screaming of monkeys high up in the air. And then from someway off the tiger roared.

"It's coming back," I said, and groped for the gun.

"Please don't hurt it. Please."

She held onto my arm, trembling, and like this we knelt in the makan until the rescue party reached us twenty minutes later.

Of the tiger nothing more was seen or heard that day.

Two days later I saw it again when it hung, dead, from a contraption of ropes and poles, one immense paw swinging loose. The body, swollen by the pressure of the crisscrossed ropes, had a jellied look. The acid smell of sudden and violent death still issued from its half open mouth.

I had not been in at the kill. Dora had asked me to give up my place in the howdah to someone who wouldn't mind seeing the Kinwar tiger shot, and throughout the afternoon I had sat with her in the shade of the lodge veranda, a boy divided in himself, not sure that sitting with a girl while there was man's business afoot was really what I wanted, and when towards four o'clock the runners came to the lodge with news of success I left her and went down to the open space in front of the main marquee where the court photographers were preparing their cameras and tripods, and waited for the shikar to return.

I expected trumpets, music, the clashing of cymbals, something to make the killing heroic, but the hunters came back sweating and bored and too tired to talk much. They gathered around the body for the photographs and I waited for a long time, until they had all gone, before going close. The bearers lowered their burden to the ground. One of them placed his bare foot on the tiger's stomach and the stomach rolled flabbily as if it were filled with ruptured entrails. The men ribbed me about my exploit in the makan and I stood there grinning. They invited me to kneel down and touch the tiger and so I knelt and stroked its hairy neck. Its eyes were only half shut and the body was still warm.

I said, "Puss, puss," to make the bearers laugh. They copied me, "E-push, e-push."

When I got back to the veranda Dora had gone. I wandered about, kicking stones. A truck drew up near the marquee and the tiger was flung into the back to be taken away somewhere and be done something to—skinned, cut up. I wondered whether people ate tiger meat.

Back in my tent I found Krishi resting. He told me how the shikar had gone, how towards the end the Kinwar tiger had broken cover in an attempt to reach the safety of a ravine. He said I was a fool to have missed it. He said people would know the tiger had scared me two days before. He said he had heard two men talking about the resident's son having made a bit of a fool of himself. I could only think to say my father was agent, not resident. He said he had seen me being made a fool of by the bearers a few minutes ago. He had heard, "E-push, e-push." He said people were asking why neither the political agent nor his son had joined the shikar, that perhaps both of them were scared.

I went for him. He was stronger than I expected. Soon we were struggling on the floor, fighting like girls, going for each other's hair. In the end I had best and made him take back. When he had taken back I let him get up. He went out of the tent to sulk. Apart from the punch I had landed on the mali's son's nose it was my first fight. I had fought Krishi for calling my father a coward. I sat on the edge of the bed, sweating. The calves of my legs were trembling from the exertion and excitement of finding that life was just as they said it was in books. I kept saying to myself, I licked him. I jolly well licked him.

On the evening of the day of our adventure in the makan Father came out to the lodge to hear my explanation. I don't remember how it came about that he heard of the incident or whether his visit was a surprise to me. Neither do I recollect what questions he asked or how I answered them. "You'll be dealt with when the shikar is over," he said.

During the three days of waiting to be dealt with I wasn't treated as if I were in disgrace, neither were Dora and I kept apart. Her parents behaved as if the escapade, if not a joke exactly, was so nearly so as made no difference. It is too long ago now for me to remember whether this made me think it would all be forgotten and I can't bring back to mind the course of events back in Tradura which found me held by the shoulder and marched by Father through the hot sunlight to the black shade that smelled of horses. I remember my father taking my crop and giving it to Paluji, using that word again, flog, so that I held my hand out thinking that's all he meant. I remember my indignant and frightened protest when I discovered he really meant flog and that I was going to get the crop on my bare backside; my cry of, "But she was quite *safe*, Father!" which shows I thought I was to be whipped simply for taking Dora alone to hunt the tiger, or perhaps it shows I was pretending to think it was only for that and knew in my heart that there was more to it, more even than having offended once again against the equivocal rules and incomprehensible sensibilities of the adult world.

He had to tell me twice to take down my jodhpurs. He said, "I have had to tell you twice. You are no son of this house." He spoke very gently, gave each word its weight. To be thrashed is always a humiliation; it was a humiliation now, but a curious kind of dignity entered. By "no son of this house," I told myself, calmly, he meant that I was a bastard. I knew what a bastard was. Grayson-Hume had told me in the course of a history lesson. So this was the truth. I was a bastard. I had offended, but I had fought Krishi for calling my father a coward. The thought that I had beaten Krishi for saying that, was now to be beaten myself in a much more painful and degrading way, was a bastard, an outcast, set me to work with hot, sticky fingers at belt and buttons, strengthened me as much as the bunched and stuffed-into-the-mouth shirt-tail in my determination not to cry out. The crop drew blood. When he told the syce to stop I could not look at him and there were standing tears in my eyes. He told me to go to my room, wash myself and use iodine. The stable-yard was deserted, the house was silent— as though the scene had been set and people had made themselves scarce. I bathed the cuts but could not take the iodine. There was blood on my underpants, blood on the handkerchiefs I used as swabs. I was ashamed to put them in the dhobi basket. I did not want any of the women in the house to see this unspeakable evidence of guilt and punishment. I hoarded the handkerchiefs and the underpants in my room and, on the fourth day, took them out to bury them in my secret hiding place, the tangled area of rhododendrons.

But the hiding place wasn't secret. There, digging with a trowel, I was interrupted by Grayson-Hume who had just come back from Bombay. He knew nothing about the tiger, nothing about Dora, nothing about the punishment. He asked me what I was doing. I can hear him now: "What on earth are you doing, Bill? Digging for gold?"

I tried to hide the stained bundle but he took it, opened it up. I remember all this very clearly. He was wearing a blue shirt and grey trousers. The shirt was cotton and had a check design. He knelt by my side and put a hand on my shoulder. The hand on my shoulder was the kind of gesture I wasn't used to. I burst into tears and sought comfort against his huge expanse of chest; and there was this small shock, this shock of finding that a man's breast was warm even though it was hard. In the midst of the weeping I realized that my father had never held me in his arms, that I could remember. The thought made me cry out, "He said I was a bastard."

Poor Gray Hum. If the episode in a Berkshire wood was anything to go by, his temptation must have been sore. He patted my shoulder and then eased me away. I think he told me to be a man. It would have been in character. Now I was more ashamed of my tears than of the bundle. I expect it was a relief—even a secret pleasure—to tell him the whole story.

"Did you howl?" he asked.

"No!" I said fiercely, then added, "Not till now, anyway."

At that moment the suspicion that I might be a bastard evaporated entirely. But Grayson-Hume didn't leave it there. My father sent for me. The interview is locked in my mind as one of apology, although there was nothing really for him to apologize for. I remember desultory talk about the arrangements for sailing from Bombay, followed by a long pause. And then came words which still reach me clearly, in Father's level tone of voice.

"You are my son. Your mother was my wife before you were conceived. Do you understand?"

I said, "Yes, Father."

I felt like a young prince who had been lost and found. I know that I loved him. That same evening I went to the stables for the first time since the episode of the crop. The undersyce saddled my pony. Paluji busied himself elsewhere. He was still ashamed. It must have gone hard with him to beat a white boy. There were times, later, when I thought Father's getting Paluji to beat me had been his way of showing his contempt for us both; later still that perhaps only a man like Father would have allowed it, that it was his way of showing us that Paluji and I were both born equals into the world and that what we became later was up to each of us.

Mounted, I caught Paluji's eye. I wanted to smile at him but a smile wouldn't quite come. I said, rather too loudly, "Hello, Paluji," and then whacked the pony so that I set out too quickly but still seated and glowing with a sense of duty done—for it was, I knew, my duty as young master to speak first and show him I bore him no ill will for having done his. I was ten. He was middle-aged.

I rode down the curving gravel drive, through the iron gates and took the road to the maidan.

I imagine I am not alone in remembering my boyhood as a series of pictures, some vivid enough to carry with them the sound of voices and of words actually spoken, most of them dimmed by coat after coat of the varnish of time and forgetfulness. Nor do I think I am alone in finding that between these two extremes of picture lie others: mysterious, magical, tenacious and insubstantial as dreams. Such is my evening ride to the maidan.

I came to the maidan. The heat during the day had been intense. The wind that blew across the flat, wide plain of scorched grass was warm. The sky was pearly pink. Crows circled the branches of a lone, high, roadside tree. Their sore-throated croaking was the only sound in the world, and the world, the maidan, lay all about me, deserted, enticing. My pony was trembling. I put my hand on his neck. I loved the feel of the tough, smooth hide over the iron muscle, the dry tickle of the coarse mane. Presently we would gallop. In the distance I saw a dim host of riders, far on the other side of the maidan where I was not supposed to go unaccompanied. The lowering sun which glowed on the low, ochre walls of the houses in the town reddened the dust which all but hid the riders. Their horses seemed to be wheeling around and around as though in their midst there

was something that had been hurt or someone who had been
taken prisoner. I thought I saw a speck of white.

It's Dora, I yelled. They've got Dora.

Digging in my heels and lying low we sped across the
maidan into the wind, and I was a lancer, arm extended
forward and out, the hand holding the crop like a sword. I'm
coming, Dora! I'm coming to save you!

I never told her this, never once said to her: One evening
on the maidan at Tradura I thought I saw you surrounded
by wild horsemen and galloped to rescue you. I never told
her because I couldn't be sure that it ever happened even as
a game of pretend. And yet, "It's Dora, they've got Dora,"
and "I'm coming, Dora, I'm coming to save you," are words
I must have spoken for they ring more truly to my man's
ear in my boy's voice than any of the words I recall from
boyhood.

How did that splendid moment end? I don't remember.
That is why the rational side of me distrusts the memory.
Perhaps I daydreamed it so strongly as I sat still in the saddle,
listening to the crows, watching the empty maidan, that it
seemed even on that very day really to have happened. Perhaps there were riders in the distance, mounted soldiers
from the palace, at exercise. Perhaps I rode towards them.
But at some point, a point somewhere in the middle of the
maidan, the experience stops. At one moment, in the recollection, I feel the surge and thrust of the powerful little
pony and see through my narrowed eyes the cloud of dust
around the cluster of riders getting nearer and nearer—
and then it has ended and I have galloped bravely off the
edge of the world into silence and darkness.

7

I SPENT the last week of March and the first week of April
as Krishi's guest in the palace at Jundapur. Mrs. Canter-

bury was behind the invitation. On the afternoon I arrived
she said she did so want Krishi and me to be friends. With
all the bluntness of a ten-year-old I asked her why. "Because
you are my two boys," she said, and patted my cheek in a
way that made me thank God that Father had replaced her
years ago.

That fortnight, whenever she found Krishi and me together she said, "Ah! There are my two boys." If she found
me alone she said, "Where is my other boy?" I assumed
that when she came across Krishi playing by himself or with
Dora she said exactly the same about me. Where is my
other boy? She had become possessive. Perhaps she always
had been so but the years of living without her would have
weaned me from her clutches and caused me to be on guard
directly she seemed in this highly unsubtle way to be laying claim to me.

And it was not just a matter of "her two boys." When she
spoke of Krishi's father, His Highness (an elevation he was
not entitled to), she made it sound as if she really said, "My
Highness." Similarly, her references to the palace implied
a personal stake in it. Our Palace. So it was with the servants,
the staff, the lake, the cage, the boat, the terrace. When it
came to "My Room" she left you in no doubt at all about
her sole and exclusive ownership.

Of course, it was Dora, the girl of the party, who brought
this evidence of female possessiveness to Krishi's and my
conscious attention, and Dora who had the instinctive curiosity to ask where *Mr.* Canterbury had got to. Krishi said
he'd always assumed Old Mutton was a widow and added
that in the old days she would have committed suttee. "But
she's not a Hindu," Dora said. It was the first time I really
noticed how absurdly practical women are. It spoiled completely the fascinating picture of Canters flinging herself
onto her husband's funeral pyre. ("My Pyre.")

I had readily fallen in with the plan for a two week stay at

Jundapur because Krishi had said Dora would be there. I was sailing for England soon. I might never see her again. The party was to be made up simply of Krishi as host, myself and Dora as guests, and Mrs. Canterbury as chaperone. On arrival I discovered to my delight that there weren't even to be any parents. We had the palace virtually to ourselves. Krishi's mother and father and their other children, all girls, were in Bombay. The Rani's sister was married to an industrialist whose house there had greater attractions than the ancestral home in Jundapur which Krishi himself described as ramshackle.

Dora was at the palace some two or three days before me. She said this was because her mother had had to bring her in the car and could only manage to do so on a certain day. I pretended to accept this explanation but suspected Krishi of having invited her earlier so that he would have her alone for a bit. Whether or not this was so, I was, at first, something of an intruder. Forty-eight hours or more of each other's company had enabled them to evolve a code of private behaviour to which it would take me some time to find the key unless one of them gave it to me voluntarily. They had ways of talking, ways of silence, ways of standing which excluded me. I was part disdainful, part jealous.

But the taboos of childhood broke up this immature triangle. Old Mutton's "There are my two *boys*," may have helped as much as sneering remarks of mine such as, "Where did your two girls get to?" Boys' pride and solidarity were finally stronger than boyish jealousy. The triangle disintegrated and then reformed with poor Dora contained but isolated at its apex—an apex reversed, suspended in a position of inferiority below the male angles of the base line.

This was a state of affairs I think Mrs. Canterbury approved of. She was set on making a man of Krishi. But when the state of affairs had gone on long enough—a day, two days—she thought it time to remind us that there was an English concomitant for "man."

"You are neither of you," she said one afternoon, having found Dora alone and her two boys elsewhere dissecting a live worm, "behaving in what I should call a gentlemanly manner to the little girl."

And smiled down at the wriggling pieces before shaking her head and making that unspellable noise usually spelled *tch-tch*.

The palace at Jundapur had walls of grey, pitted stone and had been built, it was said, in the eighteenth century by an English nabob, which would certainly have accounted for its palladian style. It was nothing like as big as the palace at Tradura and even so some of the rooms upstairs were empty. The ruler of Jundapur, styled Rajah, was little more than a titled landlord.

The palace, standing upon a low hill in rolling parkland —grounds whose encircling wall was crumbling away and gave free access and egress to stray cattle so that the quiet of hot, trembling afternoons was constantly interrupted by the shouts of bereft herdsmen giving chase, the skyline broken by their waving sticks and thin, silhouetted bodies—looked woebegone.

The special picture I have of it from youth (disregarding as much as possible the recent picture of it) is one towards evening when the fading light seemed to darken the stone and dazzle upon the glass of whatever tall sash-window had been closed and left unshuttered, so that it looked like a shell with fire still at work inside. At the back of the palace, beyond the strip of formal garden with its geometrically laid out paths, was a lake. Krishi and I referred to it as the tank, but Dora hated the word, insisted it should be a lake. And so lake it was, a quarter of a mile long and two hundred yards across at its widest part. In the middle was the island, isle, lake isle, islet, as we variably called it, thickly wooded. The island could be reached by the boat that was tied alongside the slimy green steps built into the palace shore.

All around the area of the steps, but leaving a channel for the boat, water lilies grew in rubbery-leaved profusion. Beyond them the water was thickly speckled with fragments of green and cream stagnation and over it invisible creatures hopped and flew and marked their presence with tiny expanding ripples. Beyond the areas of stagnation the water reflected sky and island and was disturbed spasmodically by the curving eruptions, the flick and nibble of fish which accompanied their sport with muted noises, like corks pulled out of submerged bottles.

I first saw the island from the bedroom Old Mutton had got ready for me. The island was part of the total secret evolved by Dora and Krishi before my arrival. "Is there anything on it?" I asked them and they looked at each other before Krishi said something like, "Nothing much," so that I knew there was something, but shrugged my shoulders and made out I didn't care. It wasn't a part of the secret they could keep for long, however. Soon Mrs. Canterbury was saying, "Why don't you take William and show him the little island?" and my first trip across the lake found me still in my role of odd man out, sulking a bit and letting Krishi row, taunting him by telling him to "put a bit of beef into it, man."

Because of this the magic of the place was slow to work. I saw the island and what was on it with the eyes of a boy bent on finding no particular pleasure in anything, on holding himself aloof even from himself. Shallow stone steps marked the landing place and close by them was a stone lingam which made me blush because I knew something of its meaning, connected it in that childlike combination of knowledge and instinct with what Grayson-Hume had told me about men and women. The lingam was, to me, a peculiar and fascinating distortion of what made my body different from a girl's and I knew it had its place in the very odd assortment of idols and objects which Hindus got worked up about.

From the stone lingam a path led you through trees to a clearing in the middle of the island and in the middle of the clearing there was a hexagonal cage with an onion-shaped roof. The cage was tall enough and big enough to have held several fully grown giraffes and given them plenty of head-room. The slender iron bars of the walls were crisscrossed in latticework fashion which gave the whole structure an air of delicacy and also produced an optical illusion of movement within when you moved your head from side to side. The mosquelike roof was plated with copper that had rusted over and now looked like pale green velvet if you stared at it long enough.

Because it was so tall, light entered restricted only by the domed roof and from outside the impression was that the huge cage had simply been lowered over whatever vege-tation had been growing at the time, but inspection showed the interior growth to be more exotic than that of the cage's surroundings and Krishi said that all kinds of shrubs, trees and plants had been imported from New Guinea and that what we saw were the survivors.

You got into the cage through a section of the wall that slid to one side on wheels. When I first saw it this sliding section was partially rusted into the half-open position so that you had to go through the opening shoulder first. No-body seemed to have thought of scraping the rust from the rail and wheels and oiling them. This handyman job was the excuse I used to return to the island the following day, the first of the escapades with Krishi from which Dora was excluded. Overnight the cage and its contents had worked on my imagination and morning found me at the bedroom window looking at the island, trying to catch a glimpse of the rusted copper roof, creating fantasies whose magic needed sharing with someone before they could be really satisfactory.

In the cage there was nothing to see at first except the unfamiliar leaves of the imported flora. I think I turned to Krishi and said, "Well?" or, "What's it for?" and I think he told me to look up. I may have said nothing at all but looked above me automatically to see whether the onion-shaped dome was hollow or levelled off flat. But there is still this impression of my having been obtuse and of their catching me out, rather as though we played "hot and cold" or—as it was called at that time—"How green you are!" a game in which this phrase was chanted repeatedly, pianissimo, fortissimo, depending upon how close you were to discovering an object the others had hidden.

The roof was hollow but once you looked up you were not concerned with it but with the *Paradisaeidae* suspended there in simulated flight, swooping, hovering, and soaring, above the leaves and branches of their natural forest.

There were thirty-six of them. We counted them too many times both then and later for me to have forgotten the exact number. All but three were males. The females were insignificant, small, dun-coloured specimens of the species *Marquis de Raggi*, so insignificant that Krishi had to point them out to me. They were perched on a branch, beaks pointing upwards as if hypnotized by what was going on above them. Of the thirty-three males two were perched: the velvety, redly-black *Princess Stephanie*, with emerald green breast and tail plumes hanging down a full two to three feet, and the blue *Rudolphi* in a position that caused me to say, "That one's fallen over." I was looking for faults.

"It hangs upside down to attract the hens," Krishi ex-

plained. I made an ass of myself by saying, "Why's it interested in hens?" in such a way that they knew I meant the
farmyard type. I can't remember whether they laughed but
I do remember the flush of shame, the feeling of being a
balloon of pride blown up with ignorance but pricked now
and filling the cage with the faint hiss of all the things I
didn't know. Re-asserting myself I laughed at the birds,
said they looked moth-eaten—but at night I pictured them
living, flashing their wings, screaming, startling the whole
island so that it trembled and woke the fish from their wet
green slumber.

The birds had been collected by Krishi's grandfather in
the last years of his life and in his day their plumage had
been worth a fortune. Their wings and bodies were cunningly supported on wire cradles and braces and only the
rods connecting them to the domed roof were dimly visible from below. In a bower formed by the flora there was a
glass-topped cabinet with coloured drawings of the birds,
descriptions of them, accounts of their habits, legends of
them. Being under glass, the drawings were well preserved
and the colours, like those on packets of seed, more magnificent even than the reds, greens, blues and buffs and violets
of the stuffed specimens which had hung in the upper air for
something like twenty years.

Periodically a Muslim servant called Akbar Ali, using a
tall iron step ladder which could be unclamped from the
walls of the cage, climbed up and unscrewed the birds from
their rods one by one, and brought them down to inspect
the wire frames. In the leather bag he brought there were
coils of wire, pliers, a pot of vaseline jelly and little bottles
of fluid which he applied to the body feathers with a brush
and sprayed onto the delicate networks of tail plumes with
a contraption like a scent spray.

It was the fact that the birds were dead that gave them
their special power. Their deadness was more disturbing

than the restlessness of a cage full of living birds, so—as a man—I was able to analyze the feeling which had puzzled me as a boy. Dora said that when she was a child the cage gave her toothache and that we teased her so badly when she insisted it was the cage that did it that she ended up suffering in silence. I do vaguely recollect this, but like my desperate ride across the maidan a lot of my memories of the things we said and did and felt on the island when we were children fade off around the edges into deeper memories of things I'm no longer sure we did or felt, and Dora's toothache is like that.

Were we, for instance, ever alone on the island, Dora and myself? Was it that, the three of us being there, Krishi had set himself apart for a while and played a joke on us so that Dora and I awoke to find the sun already set and the boat not in its usual place and, thinking ourselves stranded, stood on the shore of the island and called? Did I dream that we were alone, that in the gathering darkness we saw the boat coming to the rescue and the lanterns of a search party in the palace garden? Recently I asked Dora what she remembered of this. She didn't remember it at all, neither did Krishi. But Dora having no recollection of being stranded on the island with me and Krishi no recollection of taking the boat and leaving us does not prove my own memory wrong. It isn't quite the same as the memory of the charge across the maidan which had no ending. It has an ending: the returning boat emerging from the massed shadows of the opposite bank. And after all, Krishi and Dora both had memories of the island which didn't coincide with each other's. Krishi could not remember locking Dora in the cage. Neither could I, but she swore he did and thought it was when they were playing a hiding game and the two of them were alone. She said she remembered the panic quite clearly, the dread of being left there forever with the dead birds. She said she lost her head and screamed and that he became afraid then and let her out. Krishi's unshared memory was of saving me from a snake (and yet there were no snakes, either on the island or in the lake). We were alone, Krishi said, sitting at the water's edge. He saw a snake coming and told me in a whisper to keep absolutely still. And it slid harmlessly into the undergrowth.

When, two grown men and a grown woman, we discussed these questionable memories we laughed and Krishi said, "The island was haunted in those days." It was Dora who noticed that none of us had a memory of the three of us together which the other two questioned, and that it was only when two were alone on the island that an event seemed to have taken place which might not have taken place at all.

Krishi dismissed it, saying, "It is all deeply Freudian, no doubt."

There was a legend about the island. Once, long ago, in the days of the old palace, before the palladian mansion was built on its site (something that was supposed to have happened while the rajah and his family were in exile or in prison and their estates taken from them temporarily by the East India Company) the king's daughter fell in love with the young boatman whose job it was to row the courtiers to and fro across the lake. She did not know that this handsome peasant was really the god Krishna in one of his many amatory disguises. After several days of watching him from a window and understanding his gestures of silent invitation she escaped one night from the vigilance of her women and ran to the shores of the lake where Krishna waited. The lovers fell into each other's arms but were seen by the prince, the girl's brother, who—himself in love—was wandering by night in the garden composing a poem. By the time he got to the lake shore his sister was disembarking at the island. He cried out but she heard only the cry of a heron because Krishna had the whole lake under his spell. The brother plunged into the water and swam to her rescue, an act of courage and foolhardiness with which the god had not reckoned, and surprised in the act of embracing the girl Krishna rose up and revealed himself in his true identity, whereupon the brother swooned and, on regaining consciousness found Krishna gone and his poor sister dead from fright.

There were variations. One was that the girl was only struck dumb, another that the brother and sister were both turned into herons whose lament might still be heard when the moon rose after midnight.

Poor Krishna. Poor Krishi. His real name is Krishnaramarao. Sometimes, in that childhood summer, I called him The Heron. We were always re-enacting the story of the king's daughter. Krishi was the god. We painted his face blue and he borrowed a flute from the store of musical instruments in the palace. I, naturally, was the princess's brave brother. We ransacked a chest for clothes to dress up in. I darkened my face with burnt cork, wore a curved dagger as a sword and a turban of tarnished silver which smelt like metal polish. For Dora, Krishi pinched some of his sisters' clothes. She coloured her cheeks and lips and darkened her eyes with Kohl, clipped one of Mrs. Canterbury's earrings to her left nostril and wore bangles on her arms and legs.

The game was electrified by the clash of our freed personalities. The conflict between Krishi and myself came closer to the surface. In the game we were enemies. Finding him with Dora, I had to let out what our unscripted scenario called a "blood-curdling yell" and wrestle with him until he said, "in a haughty voice," "I am the Lord Krishna." Sometimes he had to say it several times before I would let him go. "I'm the Lord Krishna. Krishna! Krishna, you ass!" When I fainted, which I hated having to do because only women fainted in such circumstances, I counted it a point of honour to fall hard and lie there with my head ringing, and nearly knocked myself out once in the process, which gave me the idea of pretending to have hurt myself; but this ruse only succeeded once.

There was an occasion when the wrestling bout between Krishna and the prince turned nasty. When we picked ourselves up, hot, dirty and out of breath, we found that Dora had left us to it, that we were alone in the clearing.

Krishi said, "You always spoil everything."

His eyes were watering. So were mine. His cheeks were a mess of streaky blue paint, the burnt cork from my hands and his own brown skin showing through. I said, "You're blubbing." My bruised lips felt as if I'd had an injection at the dentist. He smiled to prove he wasn't so I said again, "You're blubbing." I hated the dead feeling in my lips. "Blubbing," I said, "because I licked you again."

"You didn't," he said.

"Then I'll do it now."

I went close to him, fists clenched. Because of him I'd been humiliated beyond endurance in the hot, dark stables. Suspicion that I'd taken his gun without permission had, I felt, added a few strokes to the awful beating I got. The ones, I told myself, that drew blood. "I can lick you any time," I said, "because I'm British and you're only a wog."

As men we are friends, and I thought when we were together this year that he had not only forgiven but forgotten. Now I'm not so sure, and I think he forgave without forgetting, forgave not once but many times, as often as some gesture or mannerism of mine reminded him of the boy who had said this thing to him. For myself, I still go cold or burn with shame whenever I think of it. I am diminished by an intensity of feeling, wishing it had never been said, knowing it can never be unsaid.

At the time we were both stupefied by the enormity of it.

Presently he walked away, a prince in torn finery, and left me there by the cage against whose bars we had crashed several times. My shoulders ached. I went into the cage, looked up at the birds. Between Krishi and myself there was a dirty boy's joke about the birds shitting on you if you weren't careful. I glanced at the cocked and splayed plumes and thought, *Let 'em shit;* then slouched away in case they did, peed onto the glistening leaves of a eucalyptus and stood with my hands curled around the bars, looking at the clearing—a prisoner. I entered a fantasy in which I had been tortured but had revealed nothing. *Water, water,* I said. Dora would come and give me water through the bars. My lips were parched. There were weals on my wrists where I had been strung up. You'll get nothing out of me, I gritted (gritted because that's what heroes did in these circumstances). Because I'm British. I bent my head, closed my teeth on my shirt sleeve.

Looking up I *felt* imprisoned, locked up in a place where nobody ever came. Behind and above me I heard the birds beating their wings, trying to get out. Sometimes, I knew, a sparrow would get in through the lattice mesh of the bars and fly round and round, outraged or terrified (you can never tell which with birds), until it came to its senses and found the way out again. But the fluttering pandemonium I heard and dared not investigate was made by many birds, each much larger than a sparrow.

They began to fly closer to me. I could feel the air fanning my neck. Slowly, like a climber working his way on a rock face, I moved around the cage holding onto the iron bars, handhold by handhold, making for the exit, keeping my eyes on the clearing outside. Suddenly I knew I had been seen. Feathers flicked at my ears. I gripped the bars and closed my eyes, saw the whole cage and the swooping *Paradisaeidae* flashing like kingfishers in the split second before there was only the innocent darkness behind my own eye-lids, the sunlit clearing when I opened them, and stillness, silence.

Letting go of the bars I turned around, grasped the bars again, my hands behind me, my back pressed against them, staring at the stuffed birds, seeing for the first time what extraordinary and magnificent creatures they really were. Leaving the walls I walked into the middle of the cage and sat down on the ground. Presently I pretended that I was dead too, a squatting mummy. I composed my legs, feet and arms into a position that made me feel I looked like a kind of Buddha.

I don't remember how long I sat there, or what I thought of. I expect I got bored or lonely or suddenly felt a fool and pretended I had only been sitting down to rest. I don't think they came to look for me. I think I left the cage and wandered about until I found them.

I needed Krishi as an ally in the fight against female in-vasion of my boy's world. It was a world the right girl might enter if she stood long enough in admiration of it. Dora was the right girl. She was pretty, she smelt nice, she didn't cry, she didn't sneak to Old Mutton if I teased her or hurt her accidentally. She had tried to take equal blame for the escapade in the makan. I had kissed her. I had been beaten for her.

And I needed Krishi as a standard of comparison as well as an ally. I humiliated him physically not only for the pleasure of getting best or making him take back, but in order to ag-grandize myself in front of her. I was stronger, handsomer and braver than he, but he had to be on my side, there had to be a group of which I was the leader. Once he joined with Dora against me there would be no group left.

For a day or two after I had called him wog we scarcely spoke. Whenever we found ourselves alone my determination to apologize in what Grayson-Hume would have called a frank and manly way seemed to solidify in the place where it had its source, my heart—and I thought, My heart has turned to stone.

Another girl might have seized the opportunity of our quarrel to monopolize Krishi, but after pretending for as long as she could that there was nothing wrong, nothing spoiling her holiday, Dora lost her temper. She said she was fed up with us both because we were always fighting and when we weren't fighting we were sulking. She threatened to write to her mother and ask to be taken home.

I looked at Krishi, poor skinny little Krishi, I put out my hand, I said, "I'm ready to shake if you are." There was no end, really, to my histrionics. Krishi shook. Later on that day we became blood brothers, cutting our wrists, tying them together so that our blood should mingle. We made vows to stand forever in defense of one another and in defense of Dora.

"Dora must give us her rakhi," Krishi said. Rakhi was a bracelet a girl gave her brother at the festival of rakhi-bandan. In return he gave her something to wear. The exchange was a token of mutual loyalty and love. The boy need not be her real brother, but if he took her rakhi he accepted her as his sister, dharm-bahin, and she claimed his protection as her brother, dharm-bhai.

With one exception the bangles Dora wore belonged to Krishi's real sisters. The exception was a thin, silver hoop. She took it off, looked at our wrists, then slipped it over Krishi's narrow hand. She said my hand was too big and clumsy and that she'd have to find something for me later. Krishi said she could keep the sandals she was wearing.

"Won't you get into trouble?" she asked.

He said it didn't matter, that the real sister to whom they belonged would never notice they had gone. None of us believed this but it made his gift more exciting. I had nothing to give her. I said I would buy something in the bazaar. It was left that she and I would "do rakhi-bandan," later. She picked up the penknife which had been held to a flame in the little campfire in the clearing, snicked her wrist. Krishi's was still bleeding. Leaning over them to tie their wrists together with my handkerchief I saw her bitten lower lip. Pride hollowed me out. She said, "Your turn next."

The cut in my wrist was already closed. Eagerly I picked up the knife, but Krishi stopped me. He said we couldn't mingle our blood until she had given me her rakhi.

"Mingling blood isn't part of rakhi-bandan," I protested.

But my new blood brother insisted. I gave way.

We never did rakhi-bandan. She found no bangle, I bought no garment. Krishi was content with things as they were.

The childhood pictures are ending. But here, before they fade, is the lake and the boat drifting, Krishi asleep under his topee. We have a line out but the fish are sleeping too. There is a sunshade. Beneath it Dora is lying on cushions. The water reflections are jazzing on the undersurface of the shade and down from there all over her face and body so that through my half-closed eyes she seems to be float-ing amongst sun fish in a lake of air. We have been swim-ming from the boat beyond the areas of stagnation. Our bathing costumes are old-fashioned, black, mine like hers with shoulder straps but without the panel which in hers is meant to veil the curve between her legs but which has rid-den up and lies in little corrugated folds above the place where nothing bulges out. I turn away, close my eyes, want-ing to put my hand in under the warm wool, to feel what it is like, wondering whether she would let me if I asked her. Men, after all, did more than put their hands there. How? Did they ask first?

I lie there in an ache of erotic doubt and bewilderment.

And here are Dora and myself—where? On the steps down to the water? On the terrace overlooking the garden? There is an atmosphere of uncertainty, of time run out. She is in white again. She smells of eau-de-cologne.

"Bill," she says—I have stopped her calling me William long since—"we never did rakhi-bandan."

I catch the strap of my topee in my mouth and chew on it toughly. "We can't," I reply. "We can't be brother and sister in case I decide to marry you when we're old."

When I leave Jundapur, Dora has already gone home. Mrs. Canterbury kneels in the bedroom to adjust the belt of my jodhpurs, makes me kiss her. There comes a time when Krishi complains, "She was always ramming you down my throat as the perfect specimen, she worshipped the ground your rotten old feet trod on." I have a horrible suspicion she is going to cry. She says that I'm going to England, which of course I already know, know too well but face up to as a sad but necessary exile. She says we may never meet again. Neither do we. Nor does she cry. She blows her nose and I am glad to get away from her. For years she writes to me for my birthday and for Christmas. I think she waves to me from the palace steps, and then it may be I push the topee away from my forehead, scowl and walk, hands in pockets, kicking stones and smelling of peppermints, across the courtyard to some waiting conveyance to drive back to Tradura, and thence to Bombay, out of the prison of my Indian boyhood.

BOOK TWO

On the Banks of the Water

"One day I got under a tree where a number of the Great Paradise Birds were assembled, but they were high up in the thickest of the foliage, and flying and jumping about so continually that I could get no good view of them. At length I shot one, but it was a young specimen. . . . I still hoped therefore to get some. Their voice is most extraordinary. At early morn, before the sun has risen, we hear a loud cry of 'Wawk-wawk-wawk, wok-wok-wok,' which resounds through the forest, changing its direction continually. This is the Great Bird of Paradise going to seek his breakfast."

(*The Malay Archipelago:* the land of the orang-utan, and the bird of paradise. A narrative of Travel, with studies of Man and Nature; by ALFRED RUSSEL WALLACE. Vol. 2., Macmillan & Co., 1869)

1

THERE used to be engraved on a column of the Viceroy's house in New Delhi (and perhaps still are, although there being no Viceroy any longer the house isn't his) the words: "In thought, faith; in words, wisdom; in deed, courage; in life, service." These words were engraved elsewhere, on the invisible columns that marked the end of the narrow path along which I was prodded, blind and deaf to the truth. In my mind's eye, I was not being prodded but beckoned by those who had already passed beyond those columns into the stoic but exciting world which lay on the other side of them—Mrs. Canterbury, Grayson-Hume, Aunt Sarah. I would include Father were it not for the fact that I don't think he did any prodding and the fact that he seemed to me, when I was a child, to have gone so far beyond the columns that his beckoning was difficult to see unless, as I did, I continually made an effort, squinting into the distance from under the wide brim of my little topee. But it was prodding, not beckoning. They prodded me forward; also, in a sense, backward, into the kind of world they themselves had been taught as children to think existed and the idea of which they still clung to in the part of them they would think of as their better natures. I can't blame them for that. After the war, in England, I married Anne and we had a son we christened Stephen. Having Stephen taught me to see how impossible it was as his father not to join the conspiracy to keep his eyes shut to the ways of the world for as long as possible. He will be nearly eleven now, a year older than I was when I left India and sailed for home, accompanied by Grayson-Hume who was taking up a teaching post at a school in the Midlands.

I never loved Anne but cheated myself into thinking I did. I married her because I couldn't have her any other way. Her not letting me have her any other way was the result of her built-in determination to maintain social status by marrying for money, a determination stronger than her physical appetites which she saved up to indulge after marriage as another woman might save an appetite for bridge at half-a-crown a hundred. Fair-haired, she had that warmed milk English look that blooms in the open air and cold bedrooms. She wore soft tweeds, twin-sets and pearls. I should have known better.

I was left money by my Uncle Walter. Walter was Father's younger brother and it was he who, with his wife Ethel, brought me up in England from the age of ten. They neither prodded nor beckoned, perhaps because they saw I had already been prodded too far for their more realistic, down-to-earth tastes, for they were untouched by the mystique of Empire building. They had no children of their own.

Uncle Walter was a widower when Anne first knew me. She knew I would inherit everything. Uncle Walter's money and Father's knighthood were what made Anne want me as much, although in a different way, as I wanted her. There was nothing to choose between us. Whatever tender feelings I had for her can only have arisen as the result of compensation for the frustration of not being allowed to sleep with her. Her coldness and physical withdrawal simply aggravated the excitement that mounted the moment we came into contact. I mistook the coldness for shyness and she wasn't really to blame for either. Her family, like some of the Conways, were cold fish to a man; second generation middle-class living on capital, with any ordinary emotions they might have had buried deeply beneath layer after layer of simulated upper-class conduct. I can't hold her later promiscuity against her either. It was always implicit in the darkening of her eyes and the little raspberry-coloured flushes on her cheek when she pushed me away. After we were married we were for a time as happy as anyone in the world could be whose sex lives seemed to have achieved a perfect balance, and of course I was flattered by the idea that I had awoken her, tried to ignore the possibility that I had done no such thing, but, by marrying her, simply unbunged the barrel. After a year she began to complain that I neglected her, was moody. I knew it but would not admit it even to myself. I was doing my best not to acknowledge the cause of it: the satiation of my lust for Anne as a body and the stubborn refusal to emerge of tenderness towards Anne as a person. Her pregnancy saved our marriage in order that we should destroy it more spectacularly later on. When the child was born a boy I was absurdly, conventionally proud. His birth was like the pressing of a button that set the clock back thirty years. I set about arranging his life to the pattern of what in those days I still liked to think my own had been, as if this were an opportunity to live it again.

Anne and I lived, by then, in Surrey, in what had been Uncle Walter's house, the house of my English upbringing. It was called Four Birches. You can picture it—vaguely Tudor with gables, a half-timbered garage, six bedrooms, in several acres of ground which sloped down through silver birch woods to a stream that had always been called The Water. The bedroom I had slept in from 1929 to 1939 was turned into a nursery, my young man's paraphernalia of sports gear brought out of the cupboard in which it had been stacked away (smelling of Munich and Chamberlain), and inspected by myself with an eye less to its being thrown away than put to future use. There were bats and balls, boxing gloves, old cracked cricket and football boots, rotting tennis shoes, a rusty chest expander, Indian clubs, weights, rackets—tokens of the perpetual-seeming summer in which I indulged my physical aggressiveness under the delusion that I was manfully preparing to get the most out of life, give the most to it, by being fit and even-tempered. The riding crop was there too and in a trunk I found a topee in which I must have sailed from Bombay. The trunk, after twenty years, still smelt of Tradura.

Elsewhere in the room there were pairs of riding boots, ranged in successive sizes like little monuments to my increasing height, the jodhpurs, and the clothes that reminded me of the stage at which I'd first taken care about my appearance—foulard ties with patterns of horses and horseshoes on them, silk paisley scarfs that had been knotted at the throat in open necked shirts bought in Burlington Arcade, polo-necked sweaters. In the pocket of a blazer I found my first pipe and a leather tobacco pouch that still contained a handful of dried-up curly cut. In the shelves of the bookcases were my Henty's, Wren's, school stories, tales of heroism and adventure, and the books from middle youth which brought back to mind the time when historical perspective began to emerge: *The Making of British India*, by Ramsay Muir; Dodwell's *Nabobs of Madras; Echoes from Old Calcutta*, by H. E. Busteed; *The Letters of Warren Hastings to Sir John Macpherson;* and, of course, *A Passage to India*. The books themselves were unromantic enough; not so the choice of them. Obviously I had still expected to arrive, to help these people live better lives, as Mrs. Canterbury and Grayson-Hume had said.

"What a lot to get rid of," Anne said, finding me on my hunkers in the middle of the mess I had made. Except for the books, it was nearly all got rid of. I felt no deep resistance to getting rid of it. The room was stripped, painted and refurnished but eight years later, like an invisible snowball, it had gathered bulk again and bore a certain resemblance to its old self, containing as it did the conglomeration of the boy Stephen's fantasies instead of those of the boy William. By then Anne had slept with three other men to my knowledge and I had slept with two other women. Between whiles we slept with each other and mated with a masturbatory joylessness if we had had enough to drink, which we usually had.

What is there really to say of my life with Anne? It lasted over ten years, one quarter of my life to date, more than a quarter of her's. During it I earned upwards of sixty thousand pounds by exercising a certain shrewdness and native intelligence, owned in succession six cars. We employed altogether ten foreign maids; rode, played tennis and golf, ate, drank, visited Paris, Nice, Majorca, the Costa Brava, Venice, Tangier, Munich, Oslo, Loch Lomond and Aldeburgh; attended at an estimate eight hundred cocktail parties, one thousand dinners away and as many at home in company. I committed adultery in St. John's Wood, Penzance, Rye, Tunbridge Wells and Barcelona; she committed adultery in the Golden Arrow, Paris, Hampstead, Marlow, Wrotham, on Box Hill, on the sheepskin rug in the living room of Four Birches and in Stephen's bedroom. The first six places are guesswork. She admitted to the sheepskin rug and I caught her at it in Stephen's bedroom.

We condoned each other's adultery, took no particular trouble to hide it but drew the line at actually discussing it, except explosively, challengingly, accusingly, in the explosive, challenging and accusing quarrels that were necessary to bring the temperature back from below freezing.

When I opened Stephen's door and saw the man's bare backside bouncing up and down it struck me as funny, even funnier when he twisted around and I saw it wasn't the man I thought was her lover of the moment but a friend of ours who had brought his wife to dinner a few nights before. This put her one sleeping partner up on me. I apologized, explained that Stephen had left his golliwog behind, crossed to the mantelpiece where the golliwog sat, askew, white button eyes staring from above a wide, grinning red mouth, and went out with it down the white-walled, green-carpeted corridor and down the white-walled and green-carpeted staircase to the hall that had been renovated from the pseudo-Tudor of Uncle Walter's day to the Greater London Contemporary of ours, through the arboreal and draughty open-planning into the dining room (teak, real leopard skin and festooned ivy), poured myself a drink and waited for Tony Grainger to come down, which he did ten minutes later, white around the gills and looking a bloody fool.

He stood at the bottom of the stairs and I went out to him, told him that if he wanted to make love to my wife he ought to make love to her in his own son's bedroom. He said he was sorry and then, "I suppose we've got to hit each other."

Grainger and I had quite liked each other. Even now I think it was the hall we most disliked, being trapped in it, and by an absurd situation which had somehow gone beyond the bounds of probability. I told him that if we were going to hit each other he'd better have a drink first so that we would be evenly matched. I poured him one, straight scotch up to the rim. Watching him drink it bored me. I told him to get it down and get out. He got it down. The spirit, on top of the shock, the relief he felt and felt I felt because we hadn't found it necessary to go through the motions of going for each other, made him sick. His cheeks bulged out, a bit wrinkled, like perished but still blown-up balloons. His hand went to his mouth and then he spewed all over the Swedish glass and into the wandering sailor plant, a violent animal explosion that burned up the civilized atmosphere and left us standing there in a kind of vacuum, disgusted with each other because of the several sorts of stinking mess that had been made of things. He made a feeble attempt to clean the sideboard with his handkerchief. I told him to leave it for pity's sake, that Gretchen could deal with it, or Sonjie, or Rosa, or whoever it was who pottered about the house at that particular time in black stockings and piled up hair singing *Chow Chow Bambina*; but he said, no, he couldn't leave things in that state. I let him get on with it, waited in the porch with the front door open while he went to and fro between dining room and kitchen with polythene buckets of water and spontex sponges. Finally there was a smell of pine disinfectant, and he came into the hall, walked past me without a word and down the gravel drive. There was only my own car (the new Jaguar, bottle green) and Anne's personal run-about two-tone Hillman Minx parked near the garage. They must have used the Minx to come back to the house from wherever they'd arranged to meet. It was a long walk to the bus stop for him on a grey, Saturday afternoon.

She was putting make-up on in our own bedroom. The door to the bathroom was open. The bathroom was full of steam and the washed off smell of Grainger. On the candlewick bedcover she had put out the little black dress that had cost her sixty guineas and which carried her over from tea to cocktails and was a symbol of her sexual emancipation. The old window which had been diamond paned in Walter's days had been pulled down some years before and replaced by a picture window, the point of which was lost because lime-green Venetian blinds were nearly always lowered over it, the slats opened when she wanted daylight. The dressing table was a battery of circular mirrors at different heights and angles and built on the curve in the way an executive desk is built to fit the fuller male figure. She sat at it using Helena Rubinstein contour lift on her chin and wearing a quilted housecoat which was dotted with tender old-fashioned roses and virginal green leaves. It was an asexual room, except for the mohair rugs. It had once been my barefoot pleasure to stand on these in the days when she would stand barefooted on them with me.

I asked her whether she had to shit on her own doorstep. Her hand was steady enough as she began to work something into the creases at the edges of her eyes but she was keeping it steady with her little finger against her cheek and the edge of the housecoat fluttered in a way that suggested her whole body was trembling—but with anger and frustration and half-cock intercourse, not fear. She asked me whether it mattered where either of us shat.

I said, "But why the boy's room?" and on impulse, went out, down the corridor and into it with the sole intention of stripping the bed, but having stripped it I wondered how I could leave it at that. The whole place seemed to need to undergo fumigation. For his seventh birthday I had had the room refurnished again, feeling he was too old for a decor of rabbits, mushrooms and funny little men in red coats and green breeches. It was still a kid's room but the fluff had been blown out of it and replaced by things I thought more suitable for a boy. Stephen himself had been as pleased as punch and there was nothing in the plain colour-washed walls, the plain oak furniture which in my present mood I could take exception to, but I looked around at them sensing that they were not simply soiled by the copulation I had interrupted.

In one corner there was a miniature punch bag on a flexible pole and kid-size boxing gloves hung neatly by their laces from a hook in the wall, a bleak reminder of the fact that Grainger and I had not gone for each other. Nothing in the room was out of place. He had inherited my passion for form and order: nothing for show, everything used but with care and kept clean, serviceable. On the wide table along the wall, which Anne called his work top, he had ranged his own boyhood equivalents of tin soldiers: cowboys and Indians on one side, long-range rocket projectiles, tanks, amoured cars on the other; and in the middle the construction outfit he was working on at present.

The walls were hung with pictures of faraway places, of mountains he would probably never climb because they had all been climbed, nomadic people he was never likely to encounter and would find dirty if he did, artists' impressions of planets he stood a good chance of seeing in the heavens only as stars; and older pictures too—the defense of Lucknow, the sinking of the Titanic, the meeting between Stanley and Livingstone. I had obviously been concerned with his sense of proportion and at the same time still pursuing experiences that had eluded me.

In Stephen's room my personality overlapped his. They were my nomadic people and my mountains, his planets, my stars, my Lucknow, my Titanic, my meeting between Stanley and Livingstone, his cowboys, his space guns.

I opened his toy cupboard. Bricks, jigsaw puzzles, boxes of model railway equipment were stacked on the shelves. The old cuddly toys were thrust to the back. He obviously recognized that he already had a past, a period of activity to which he was too old to return but from which he could never wholly escape. Only the golliwog remained on show. He was staying with his aunt, Anne's sister. I had driven him over that morning. He had promised to lend the golliwog to his cousin Drusilla but had forgotten to take it, perhaps intentionally forgotten. "You ought to let her keep it," I told him, "you're too old for it now."

"Yes, I might," he'd said, and pushed his lower lip out in the way that sometimes irritated me, sometimes touched me. I told him I'd drive back and get it after lunch. He said, "Okay," and scowled and stuck his hands deep into his pockets.

I beat him once with a strap for pulling the wings off a fly. He howled the roof off and then wept so piteously, kept saying, "You shouldn't have hit me so hard, you shouldn't have hit me so hard," that I took him in my arms. It was, paradoxically, one of the closest moments that we had together. I tried to avoid the trap of being over close to him because I believed that this closeness would be a gift to myself rather than one to Stephen, a compensation for the distance between myself and my own father. But because Anne was never close to Stephen except vicariously through *Noddy* or *Prudence Kitten* or *Listen With Mother,* there were times when my instinct was to overindulge him to make up for her stoic-matron pose.

His bedroom was proof of the success I'd had in fighting that instinct. It was spartan and masculine. It was also proof of my failure. In the imaginary world for which his room treacherously prepared him there were, masquerading as rules instead of as exceptions, tokens of love, honour, courage, defense of the good against the bad, of the weak against the strong, the things, no doubt, he thought his parents stood for.

If he had been in the house that afternoon of Grainger, I would have brought him upstairs, shown him the stripped bed, explained why it was stripped, told him that his father and mother were held together now only by a kind of social inertia, the pretense that they had to stay that way to provide a home for him, a background of security against which he could grow up in the right way. But, I would say, all we're doing is covering up the truth and if the truth is hidden from you in the house you're being brought up in, how the devil can you learn to distinguish truth from falsehood in the world you're going to have to make your way in?

But the idea of "making one's way" struck me that day as simply another of countless misconceptions. Standing in his room I was moved to anger by the books which defined what we meant by honour, the pictures that lay upon the wall like windows giving on to a wide, adventurous world, and the plastic images of impossible heroes, and would have swept them all into the dustbin if doing so had not seemed like a personal revenge on a small boy who had done nothing to deserve such unhappiness but had simply been there on the receiving end of the fairy tales for as long as he had lived.

I expect Stephen feels bitter about me now, and holds to some boyish dream of making things right for Anne, his mother, eyes his new father (not Grainger but a man with whisky eyes and an exploded face) with caution, and is alive to the undercurrents of passion which bind his parent and step-parent and may leave him, sometimes, excluded in a way he does not fully understand so that in passing their bedroom he senses its alienation from what he's wrongly learned to think of as the homeliness of his home. The truth is under his nose but he has never been taught to smell. Where there is blood he will smell roses. He will go back to his room, that symbol of his sex, and perhaps be comforted by its familiarity, the sense it gives him of his individuality, his continuity and his future; or he may be more proud of it than comforted by it if he has laid claim to maturity by throwing out most of what is too obvious a reminder of his father, the man who has let him down, proved himself a rotter, a louse, whatever the word is these days.

I am thinking of Stephen as he is now, a boy of eleven, and not as he was when I said good-bye to him and he stared at me wide-eyed, his lower lip trembling, determined not to cry because Anne would have told him not to. I came away from that parting feeling that every bone in my body had been dried and bleached, that between the bones and the clothes I wore there was neither flesh nor blood. When I got into the car I could not turn my head to see if he had come to a window because there was nothing to articulate it. The picture he will have of me will be of a father who did not even care enough for him to wave good-bye. Of his mother his picture will be that of someone loyal and loving. How wrong he will be on both counts!

Sometimes, in Manoba, the phrase "sanctity of the family" has come into my mind. There was always something mouldy and cryptlike about it, but out here the sun and the white sand of the beach seem to have been at work on it and left it pale, dry and skeletal. In the days after I had said good-bye to Stephen, and Anne and I settled back to watch our divorce go through from our different points of vantage, the phrase "sanctity of the family," coming into the cold-ash court of my consideration, always quenched the tongues of flame that could spring up from the apparently dead fire like evidence against us, like judgments against a decree— tongues of flame which meant what sanctity of the family was supposed to mean but failed to mean because it was smug and protestant and could not exist alongside of the memory of Tony Grainger's backside going up and down— or of my own, for that matter, in Barcelona.

In the end I taught myself to accept that there was no sanctity in a family that had come into being as Anne's and mine had. The vows Anne and I exchanged in the presence of an old fool who didn't know his soul from his elbow were made blasphemously. We had no conviction about them. The marriage service was no more than a formal step to the bedroom and the joint account. On such a basis Stephen was illegitimate and my offense was no greater than it would have been if he had been born recognizably out of holy wedlock and then provided for by the man who had fathered him. Stephen was the product of my lust for his mother and of her lust for super-tax status and it was better for him to discover it too late than not at all.

But he won't have discovered it yet, and will probably

never do so. What might have been a hot gust of truth will have been cooled down before it is allowed to penetrate that citadel of his bedroom, that fortress, that prison in which he prepares to launch himself into the second half of the twentieth century wearing the straitjacket of nineteenth century compensation fantasies; as I did.

Stephen's hair is fair, like Anne's, but he looks more my child than her's. In certain lights he has a look of my father too, although his face is going to be square, like mine, whereas Father's was pointed and narrow. "You're like your father, Stephen," people used to say to him, then turn to me and add, "but he's got Anne's colouring."

It is largely a question of the tyranny of the genes. I think of them as working their silent, invisible, counter-revolutionary way into the rebel stronghold of our privacy, of what we imagine to be our privacy, imposing and re-imposing on us thoughts and behaviour that ought to be dead and done with. That look of my own father which I sometimes saw in Stephen is a look I feel I have left to grow stronger in him now that I have deserted him.

I did not see my father die, but Cranston saw his. He said the flesh fell away from his bones, his father's bones, and yet his own bones too because he saw in the shape of his father's dying face the shape of his own living face, saw it more clearly than he had ever seen it in life. He said that he no longer felt entirely alone in what he thought of as his strengths and weaknesses and was moved by this too-late revelation of how it could have been possible for them to have felt more friendly towards each other.

It was in prison camp that Cranston told me this about his father and because, so far as I knew then, my father was still alive I made a resolution at least to try to end the estrangement that had grown up between us if I ever saw him again. We met again, indeed, and I realize now that I had a certain opportunity but wasn't ready for it, and he died alone, as I

think he would have wished in any case. If I had been with
him when he died I don't think I should have seen what
Cranston saw, but if he had lived much longer, long enough
for Stephen to grow up and watch him die, I think Stephen
would have caught a glimpse in the changing structure of the
old man's face, of what was firm and fixed in his own.

2

I HAVE never discovered anything about my father's early
life that provides a solution to the puzzle of his eventual behaviour towards me. As a young man I never really looked. I
was too youthfully bound up with the effect it had on me to
spare time and effort smelling out the cause.

  In those days, when I first went to live there, the interior
of Four Birches was the then equivalent of what it was in
Anne's and my time too: upper income-bracket middle-class
domestic home-counties English. Between 1930 and 1939 it
looked not much different from the interiors of those hotels
in market towns to which motoring associations award stars
as symbols of merit—cream-washed walls, fake beams,
warming pans, copper pots, wing chairs, sofas dressed in
plain oatmeal-coloured covers and Jacobean patterned cre-
tonne curtains. There was a parchment shade with a Span-
ish galleon painted on it on the lamp that stood on the
oak sideboard in the dining room, and the standard lamp
which spread a warm, theatrical pool of light behind the
sofa in the drawing room was decorated with silken tassels.
These especially vulgar touches were Aunt Ethel's work. I
accepted them as I accepted certain mannerisms like standing indoors with her arms folded, small uncertainties in
vowel sounds and shyness in front of my friends sometimes
degenerating into embarrassing overfamiliarity, as proof of

what Aunt Sarah had warningly described to me before I
left Tradura as Aunt Ethel's "not having had our advan-
tages." There were Sanderson Wells hunting scenes on
the walls of hall and landing, Russell Flints in the dining
room and a seascape featuring a clipper in full sunlight over
the fireplace in the drawing room.

It was the house of a well-to-do commuter without roots
or with roots different, anyway, from those he was born
with. When Anne and I at last inherited it, and everything
that was in it, I saw how it reflected dead Uncle Walter's
detachment from his own family, a detachment amounting
to exile. Like a son who received no portion he went into the
world of the city, started from scratch and made a modest
fortune. I never delved into his private affairs, his personal
history, and in a typical Conway manner he seemed content
to cover his tracks. He seldom spoke of anything that happened to him before the Great War, when he served in
France. Unlike my father, who was his senior by eight
years, and Aunt Sarah who was his senior by four or five, he
was not born in India, in fact he never went there. After
Sarah was born in Darjeeling, Grandmother Conway became
delicate and four years later at the beginning of her last
pregnancy returned to England and a house in Suffolk
which was the old Conway house, bringing her children, my
father and Aunt Sarah, with her, and there she bore Walter.
Grandfather saw out a tour of duty in the political service
on the Northwest Frontier, after which he also came back to
England to be with his increased family and to work in the
old India office. Grandmother Conway died before the children were grown up and then Grandfather Conway went
back to India for a year or two, leaving his three children in
the care of his dead wife's sister.

Beyond that, the only vital statistics I had of Uncle Walter's
life were that he had studied the law, served in France, gone
into the City in 1919, become a director of a firm of mer-

chant bankers and had married "a bit beneath him." Perhaps it was this last fact which, when I was a boy, most inhibited me from asking more questions than I did; this, and the fact that I looked upon Four Birches as a place of temporary exile. It was never home to me when I was a schoolboy. It was the comfortable place I came to during school holidays. There was only one room in it where I consciously put down roots, but these were roots I had brought with me from India. It was only a question of transplanting them.

And I know, too, that whenever I came back to the house at the end of term I sensed with that delicate nerve of superiority which vibrates in children how the house was a bit put to shame by the things I thought Father stood for. On the first of the two occasions he was in it with me, in 1933 when he and Aunt Sarah came to England for a month during his long leave—a month which did not coincide with school holidays and involved me in an exciting dispensation to go home for forty-eight hours—it actually seemed visibly humbled by his presence, even by Aunt Sarah's, and I was overcome by a nostalgia for India, for "our sort of background," which may have been an expression let slip by Aunt Sarah.

"Couldn't I come out next summer?" I asked her.

She said, "Your father couldn't afford it," and smiled in her tired, wan way. Without thinking, I said something about Uncle Walter stumping up the fare. Her bony fingers fluttered above her prominent, getting-on-for-elderly-woman's breast bone in the manner I now recollected as habitual. "Oh my dear," she said and looked about her as though for a means of escape, a phrase and a movement I interpreted as hurt disapproval, as a warning never to suggest such a thing, as condemnation of the way her younger brother lived.

Wandering through the cold, grey February rooms years

later with Anne and a tape measure, having driven over from the flat in St. John's Wood where we had begun our splendid and vital married life, the sight of the furniture, the fixtures and fittings which death had caused first Ethel to abandon and then Walter, aroused my curiosity in a way it had not been aroused before. They had left worldly goods behind them and that was just about all—rather like the chart of an island with no cross on it to indicate treasure. I knew them as cheerful, fond of each other, busy, never at a loss what to do with their leisure (perhaps too much not at a loss?). The old Four Birches was the antithesis of the agency bungalow in Tradura. It was a place where energy was expended. The bungalow in Tradura I remembered as a place where energy was created and stored, as a larder might be in years of plenty. The later Four Birches, with its picture windows, off-white carpets, square splashes of colour from scatter cushions, is somehow not connected at all with the idea of energy, only with the idea of exhaustion.

The old Four Birches which Anne and I paced out and measured (for no good reason, because the work of refitting it as a background for the intelligent and civilized life we would lead together was presently put into the hands of an architect and then into those of an interior decorator), was quite unhaunted. The ghosts, such as they were, glided only down the corridors of the part of my mind that had been awakened by this curiosity. I stood for some time alone in Walter's and Ethel's bedroom which I had seldom entered and fancied that there and only there might be a clue to what they had been inside themselves and to each other; for there, at least, they might have discussed the past, said things which actually defined the way in which they were different from what I had called the rest of us.

Standing in his empty bedroom I tried to think of any occasion when he had spoken outright against my father, and failed. There had never been anything except an air of constraint and my assumption that they had never quite hit it off.

Physically they were quite different, Walter being short in comparison, and fat. Walter took after their mother, he told me, and said that I had something of her look as well. After the war, when Ethel was already dead and he was retired from business, I sometimes took Anne down to see him. Once he said out of the blue, as though his mind wandered but retained a grasp on certain convictions it had been necessary for him to have, "I've had a good life." His heart began to fail and he went into a nursing home. I saw him a day or two before he died. He rambled, thought Ethel was still alive, that she had just gone out of the room. He said, "Tell Ethel not to be long," and later, "They called her Little Ma," which puzzled me until I recalled from far back that this was the way in which Aunt Sarah had sometimes referred to their mother, that delicate woman who could not stand the Indian climate and died in England a few years after Uncle Walter was born.

I don't remember establishing that my father took after his father physically, but I fancy that was the case because Uncle Walter mentioned his own resemblance to their mother as though of the three children, Father, Walter and Sarah, he alone lacked the Conway height and taut, bony presence. I have inherited the height but not the boniness. From this scant evidence I've built up an imaginary picture of my paternal grandmother. It has to be imaginary. If I saw portraits it would have been as a child in Tradura and I have quite forgotten them. There were no family photographs in Walter's house—only pictures of Ethel in cloche hats and ropes of pearls down to her thighs. The imaginary picture of my grandmother is of a woman below medium height, well-fleshed, handsome but growing pale then thin under the Indian sun, a woman whose poor health adversely affected her husband's career.

I see my grandfather torn by that ill health from what he may have loved most, the hills of Northwest India, a craggy landscape of sunbaked stone and wild, blue-eyed Pathans, a country in which he had watched his son, my father, growing in his image, until Little Ma could stand no more of extremes of heat and cold and child-bearing together and fled to England where she bore Walter, a wholly English child quite untouched by Indian magic, an outsider from the beginning not because of what he was but because of what he represented, the single flaw in the crystal of the family's love for Little Ma. There is always something unforgivable in weakness, sickness and debility. However much her husband loved her there must have been beneath his stoicism, if he showed it—and being a Conway I expect he did—a layer of hurt for which at the time he felt Little Ma responsible. Perhaps a healthy, chubby baby Walter was so much salt in a concealed wound.

And then, perhaps, began a business of compensating for his loss, his frustrated ambition and his removal from the scene where Conways had done their duty before him and where he thought his own duty lay. His seeing out a tour of duty before following his sick and pregnant wife to England suggests a powerful sense of it. The short-lived return to India alone when Little Ma was dead provides a picture of a man trying and failing to regain lost ground in the race for power out there where it mattered. Grandfather had sat too long in Whitehall, just too long, sublimating his ambitions through the files and minutes that conjured visions of the place and people he had set his heart on. It would be natural for such a man to see in his elder son a means of vicarious fulfilment and to see in his younger son, Walter, who looked so like his dead wife, the shape and substance of what had held him back from a fulfilment of his own, so that almost from the beginning Walter would be fed and cared for but otherwise counted out.

Poor Walter—and poor Sarah, too, come to think of it—
they were small sunken islands off the continent of their
father's love: she because she was only a girl and plain
with it; Walter because he was Walter, the cause of Little
Ma's enforced defection.

And the elder son, my father? How did it all strike him?
Was he simply obedient, or had he in the brief years of his
Indian childhood also conceived a love for the wild hills
and a sense of belonging to what his father belonged to?
Had he found no comfort in the damp English climate and
the way the water there seems to lie just under the earth?
Was he a boy naturally inclined to rock and aridity? Did he
share his father's frustration and in his heart of hearts
bear a grudge against the green-and-damp-born Walter?
Perhaps there sprang up between himself and Sarah a private code of memory (not unlike the understanding I felt
existed between Dora and Krishi when I joined them in
Jundapur), a sharing of unspoken-of longings and intentions
to go back across the sea, so that years later when history
had partly repeated itself and Father's Louise had gone the
way of Little Ma, his invitation to Sarah to come out and sit
at the other end of the table was a fulfilment of a vow made
in childhood that one day they would live again together
in India, a kind of rakhi-bandan performed in Suffolk and
coming full circle in Pankot.

If the Conways did not have a quality of keeping so much
locked up inside themselves I should imagine a close father
and son comradeship growing and enduring between my
father and his father, a frank, eager exchange of views, a
fine formulation of plans; winter nights passed in the telling
of tales of old India, the man gazing into the fire reminis-
cently, the boy hotly, ambitiously; summer days when the
sun came out of the east and warmed the chill marrow of
their bones with the leftovers of its elsewhere prodigal

heat. But no, it wouldn't have been like that. They were Conways, not given to speaking their thoughts and certainly not to laying bare their souls. It is easier to see my grandfather turning a ramrod back on the stony hills, presenting to the world of sickness, Suffolk and Whitehall a face that looked like the face of a man who took things much as they came. It is easier to see him as a man who had no other way with his passions than to spin a protective cocoon of silken ice about them, who permitted himself no more than a cold blast of pleasure when he saw the same frosty look in the eyes of his elder son and guessed what lay behind it.

When I look from him to this son, my father, my father stares back at me with two faces: first with the face of the boy who wanted for himself exactly what his father wanted for him and moved passionately and icily towards it; then with the face of a boy who wanted something else, a boy to whom an Indian career was a living death, a cold and bitter duty he would support only because the genes had made him prone to the call of duty and had shaped him to endure cold. Either face could be the real face, and although the evidence weighs heavily against the second there are times when it puts in a stronger appeal. I ask myself what it could have been my father wanted in place of a political career in India. But it isn't the impossibility of finding an answer that turns me away from the second face back to the first. It is the difficulty of seeing his attitude to everyone, including myself, as being other than that of a man who was bound up in his work to the point of defending it jealously from any incursion upon its splendour and perfection; perhaps because it had been hard won.

3

AT school in England—and the school Father sent me to was not his own old school but the lesser one Uncle Walter had been to (and this in itself is significant)—I was nicknamed Rajah, a name that stuck throughout my time there and became a term of honour rather than of disparagement.

When Uncle Walter heard about it he said that my father had a nickname too, "Old Very Light."

Old Very Light? The blush that was half-pleasure and half-embarrassment at the way Rajah had slipped out gradually left my face. This moment in the dining room at Four Birches when we sat around the table eating in the light of candles lingers on as typical of other moments I know there were when the ground I was on seemed to shift or to be about to shift and I held myself ready to defend it.

I was a problem to Walter and Ethel, little doubt about that. Being childless I expect Ethel had once had the idea of making me her substitute son, as would have been proper to the fiction of the situation, and had been astonished when she found that in reality neither of us was prepared to give our hearts to the enactment of such a drama. There was a toughness and down-to-earthness about her which I didn't appreciate until I was much older. Before I appreciated it and showed her that I did, I must have been a childish and therefore slightly ridiculous embodiment of all that in the Conways (leaving Walter out of it) annoyed her as a member of a lower social class and hurt her as a woman, an "all" she had direct experience of only with Sarah. She did not meet my father until his 1933 visit. Sarah she had known and probably been snubbed by during Walter's courtship of her after the first World War. Sarah had not been at their registry office wedding in 1919. But whatever her personal experience of the Conway standoffishness it would have been mapped for her by the odd Conway out, her lover, her husband Walter, for if Walter ever permitted himself to speak out against his brother or his sister or his father it would have been in private to his wife, to Ethel.

Ethel knew, perhaps, the truth of what I only deduce and even so no more than the truth as Walter saw it and as she might confirm it for herself by watching Sarah, in dealing with her, and later in dealing with her nephew William, the motherless boy she was prepared to take into the comfortable home that was barely recognized by the Conway world but could be used by Conways as a convenient nest in which to plant their latest Indian cuckoo. It may be that Walter had to persuade her, saying, "Let's have the boy. They've got no time for him really, you can tell that." Together they had probably expected me to turn out to be more Walter's natural heir than Father's and had been disappointed when I arrived with the look of Little Ma right enough but what looked disagreeably like the manner of his brother, properly behaved but locked away to exclude them from what was vital to the relationship if it was to turn out warm and filial.

Candles on the dining room table were Aunt Ethel's idea. I didn't care for them much because they stopped me seeing clearly what I was eating. They were hypnotic too. Between courses, served by the type of maid I had now got used to (at first I was shocked to be waited on by people with white skins) the pointed, erectile flames were inclined to draw my attention so that conversation was more easily strained then ever it was before Aunt Ethel, following the local chic craze, introduced this waxy form of illumination. I had a feeling that the candles were vulgar. How often, I wonder, did Aunt Ethel touch the little nerve in Uncle Walter that would make him aware of having to hold back, of restraining his natural inclination to say, for instance,

"Oh, Ethel—not candles?" I expect his silence was the result of his abiding love for her and of there being too many things about which to say, "Oh, Ethel—not these?" the result of his whole life being committed now beyond the point where he really consciously noticed that it reflected what made them different as well as whatever it was that had brought and held them lovingly together.

This, the night of the candles, and the tale out of school, the giving away of Father's nickname, Old Very Light, is the one that selects itself in my consciousness as the night on which all the threads of my boyhood were gathered, and enveloped me like a net. A few jerks of the truth might have begun a chain-reaction of disentanglement. But who at that table knew the truth? The truth would have had to come from outside, like a wind that burst open the windows and billowed out the curtains, extinguished the candles. In the darkness one of us would have had to cry, "Quick! The light!" and then we would have been discovered there with pale faces and shadows under our eyes, like prisoners who had lived together in the darkness and were surprised less by the fact that suddenly they were free than by the realization that they were strangers.

A Very pistol is used to fire signals—red over green over red, that sort of thing, infinite variations of warning—and to send up flares which, dropping slowly, will illuminate no man's land long enough to distinguish what moves and is alive and therefore dangerous from what doesn't move and is therefore a tree or a bush or a boulder. If you are advancing across no man's land and the enemy sends up a flare you are recommended to freeze in your tracks, even in an upright position, because in the first blossoming of the light anything that changes form is seen and a man dropping to his belly can be spotted and marked for what he is. In the war I had no experience of this but, as a boy, knew about it from books and magazines and from school OTC lectures.

When Uncle Walter said that Father was called Old
Very Light I thought at first he meant he had been called
this at school and I could not see the connection. But no,
Walter said, it was what Father was called in India, and
added, "Or so your Aunt Sarah told me once." He asked me if
I knew what a Very light was and I said yes. Aunt Ethel
said that if she were a man she'd rather be called Rajah than
Old Very Light. I stared at the winking silver. I can remember making traces of four parallel lines with a fork on a
cork table mat and while the rhythm of the episode eludes
me I still have a clear impression of the pauses that pointed
my annoyance at their "sly dig at Father." I think Walter
saw that what he had said lightly had been taken heavily.
What steps he took to put it right only made it worse. Even
the smile on his fleshy, always flushed face, I interpreted as
a sneer, if interpreted is the right word to use to describe
what at the time was a tumbling-over inside me of conflicting emotions; no, not conflicting emotions—none of
them was sufficiently precise to be said to conflict with another.

Uncle Walter had not said enough to force me into the
open to ask, "You don't like Father much. Why?" He had
not said enough but I did not want him to say any more. I
couldn't say to Aunt Ethel when she spoke about which
nickname she'd prefer, "It's nothing to do with you, you
keep out of it," although that probably sums up what I felt
as she regarded me indirectly, with half her eye on Walter,
incapable of saying, thinking or feeling anything quite for
herself, or so I imagined; a rather plump, indeterminately
featured woman whose hair, dyed too fair and set in waves
too rigid, alone expressed the self-assertiveness she never
displayed in company.

There is so much that I don't know about all that happened to guide and shape my life up to the moment that
found me sitting in candlelight resenting the imagined

slight to Father—a boy of what? fifteen? sixteen?—that it is difficult to see myself, really see myself, sitting there in the full bloom of my ignorance. Thinking myself back into that seat I have my present face on those shoulders. I see that boy almost as a total abstraction, representing different things to different people, including what he now represents to me, the shadow of a former self that sometimes falls in front of me when the sun is on my back. Walter, plunging on into waters whose depths he may have judged exactly or not judged at all but taken as they came, said that Father was called Old Very Light because he seemed to have that effect on the places he was sent to. However turbulent a condition a state or group of states was in, it became calm almost directly he arrived, as if people froze in their tracks at his approach. He said that, of course, it was a bit of an exaggeration but that it had happened often enough to make the Political Department notice it.

"According to your Aunt Sarah, anyway," he said. "She was awfully taken with it."

The night of the candles fades off now into that odd blue-black oblivion that is rather like the blobby darkness that descends the moment you close your eyes. Neither Walter nor Ethel ever got round to asking me why I was called Rajah and I never mentioned Old Very Light to Father. I had, of course, few opportunities. But I knew how double-edged a nickname could be. In the beginning I was called Rajah because I tried to lord it over other boys, assumed that my slight familiarity with the courts of princes gave me special dispensations in the communal life into which I was thrown. I grew wiser and older and the name, still sticking, changed as I changed and in the end I think it would have worried me to discover that the newest new boy did not know of Rajah inside a week of his arrival. It was a nickname I lived up to, sometimes intentionally, sometimes accidentally. It received official, if sarcastic, recognition. There was a man called Bates. He taught us history. In the course of a lesson he quoted words attributed to Mountstuart Elphinstone. Speaking of the princely states and their preservation by the British, Elphinstone referred to them as sinks, cess pits. "We must have some sink to receive all the corrupt matter that abounds in India, unless we are willing to taint our own system by stopping the discharge of it." These are some of the few words I have ever committed to memory. Having read that passage Bates said, "Well, now, Conway, you're our expert on Indian affairs; your comments please." We had not always been wise, the old Gray Hum had said, we had not always been kind. I said, "I think he must have been a bloody bounder, sir," which provoked stunned silence and on Bates's face a look of shock or amusement; I never did know. He took the dignified way out, addressed everyone but me. "One was forgetting. One has, as one might say, made a gaffe. One should not ask such questions of a Rajah." At the end of the lesson they carried me shoulder-high. On bonfire night that year the effigy of Guy Fawkes was labelled Elphinstone. Only the Rajah could have got away with saying bloody in class.

But whatever Old Very Light's later meaning, I couldn't avoid looking at it as a nickname that had begun as mine had begun. It sounded unfriendly, too close for comfort to the truth about the effect he had sometimes had on me and which I suppose I had always tried to ignore. I decided that the nickname was given to him by a man who had served in France and come back to India, the kind of officer whose exodus from the Political Department to rejoin his regiment had left one of the vacancies that were filled by ICS men, men like Father (ah! that!), professionals whose careers in the Indian States might never have blossomed at all if the war hadn't come along. You did not enter the Political Department directly but came to it by way of the ICS or the Army. It was a plum. The most my grandfather could have done for his son would have been to put him through the ICS and pull what strings he could. If, as I think, my father burned with the same political ambitions that had been frustrated in his father the Great War probably came like the trumpet note that shattered the walls of Jericho. Men who had fought in France and returned to India to find no vacancy in the Political Department perhaps had cause to sneer gently at those who had taken their places.

I wish I could feel again the authentic twinge of disappointment I know I used to feel as a boy in England whose new friends had fathers who had "fought in France" but whose own father had not; feel it again, exactly as it was, so that I could judge the actual degree of its intensity. I know that whenever the subject of war service came up and the inevitable question was asked I described my father as, "Oh, ICS, India," and if pressed for an interpretation, "Government," an explanation which I believe always satisfied and even impressed the inquirer but increased an inward wariness in myself, an instinct to protect myself from some kind of stain that wasn't in itself a stain but could be made to look like one by a too simple examination of the facts and a too literal presentation of them. "Government," was inaccurate, a lie really, but it enabled boys to see my father as I saw him and as I naturally wanted them to see him. It put him beyond reach of accusation and into what my loyalty conceived of as his rightful place. At least, he had not made money out of munitions. If he was not covered in warlike glory he was not covered in shame, he was not labelled "profiteer."

And there was always Uncle Walter to push forward to fill any gap there might be in the thin red line of my pride; Major Walter Conway whose campaign ribbons and Mention in Despatches I should have known nothing of if I hadn't come across his old field-service uniform behind some sacking in the potting shed at Four Birches about a year after I went there to live. Yes, I could always push Major Conway into a breach, but just as I protected myself against the poison of disappointment in Father so I protected myself against the poison of taking too much pride in Uncle Walter. To do so was not difficult.

I was puzzled that a man could leave his uniform to rot in a potting shed like an old gum boot. I let several days go by before I mentioned it and then was equally puzzled by his casual remark, "Oh, is it still there? Better burn it." So much off-handedness about what was important was peculiar. The questions I asked about the ribbons probably sounded surly, but my curiosity had to be satisfied and the scene of its satisfaction is still clear enough. I can still recapture the smell of creosote and the sight of the motes of dust rising in the beam of sunlight that came through the dirty, cobwebbed-over window of the shed as I stood there with him and watched him go through the pockets to make sure they were empty before he put the uniform on the bonfire. Perhaps the creosote smell, drawn out of the wood by the sun, reminded me of the bungalow at Pankot, of Mrs. Canterbury talking about the mutiny, wearing her Edwardian straw hat, and filled my eleven- or twelve-year-old breast with atavistic longings for the brave sight of scarlet and pipe-clayed pouches. I made some excuse not to watch the uniform burn. I wonder whether Uncle Walter thought, "The little tick! Damn him for his disapproval. He's a real Conway," and treated me ever afterwards with a reserve I hardly noticed through the thickness of my own?

There were other subjects, apart from the First World War, which caused twinges of doubt or disappointment; and they too were met with lies, small fictions. "Did you do much shooting?" someone might ask. At first a shrug would answer him, together with an, "Oh, a bit. Of course it was the Maharajah's land and he was a bit stingy about permits, but the last year there we bagged a tiger." Later, bolstered by extra years and reputation I would say, "No, not really. Actually there's not much sport in cornering a tiger on elephants and then popping off at him." By the time I took that line I don't think there were any boys with Indian experience old enough to challenge me on it and I don't think I should have minded if there had been because by then I had acquired a contempt for blood sports, the result partly of a further flowering of the childish intimations I had had of the Kinwar tiger's perfect right to be there in the clearing, and partly of adopting as my own an attitude I had worked out defensively as Father's attitude. I had worked it out to explain away the doubt, to balance the nagging memory of what Krishi had said that made me fight him.

It wasn't until I was at school in England, nicknamed Rajah, the butt of other boys' searching questions that the real hurt, the real import of what Krishi had said, began to work in me. I don't mean that it worked in me constantly or that I worried about it. I was a happy, extrovert boy. But when these questions were asked: What did your father do in the war? Did your father bag much big game? they seemed to be questions about a stranger and I think I was aware of the danger of Father becoming a stranger to me, a man who might, if you didn't defend him against it and keep reminding yourself that he was your father, reveal things about himself which made him a stranger and made you, as his flesh and blood, to that extent a stranger to yourself.

The difficulty was that it simply wasn't possible to admit that the questions, stripped of all politeness, meant: Is your father a man? Has he got spunk or is he a coward? and that upon the answers was going to depend an off-the-cuff assessment of yourself. All this was implicit. If it had been made explicit it would have called for a punch on the inquisitor's nose. Question and answer were balanced on a tight-rope one false step upon which would have tumbled the speakers into an act of violence.

My honour was involved, and my father's honour, and in Tradura they had never been involved. They had existed and had not been questioned except once by Krishi and that was so isolated a case, my going for him so instinctively immediate, that they had been saved almost before the threat to them had sunk in. In England it was different altogether. The questioning was slower, subtler, more insinuating, and I had to stand up to it quite alone, not only because I was alone but because the questioning was also taking place inside me. And there I was answering it with jealous and more determined love. "I suppose you saw lots of tigers and things?" Aunt Ethel said in the early attempts to establish accord during the first few days after my arrival at Four Birches. "There aren't many left," I answered, "and we're against shikar."

It was the illusion of Father that I loved, the concept of him as an embodiment of what I was to be, and this is what I defended whenever it seemed to be in danger. The night of the candles marks the beginning of the end of this phase. Behind the line lay childhood, ahead of it youth and manhood and as I grew older, felt myself grow smaller in a world that grew bigger, so too I felt my father grow smaller, saw him in my mind's eye shrink into the actual mould of being a human being, the bottle from which as a child I had caused him to rise like a genie.

The night of the candles, the nickname Old Very Light, probably came at a moment when certain wounds were exposed. I might have recently received one of his letters, which would make it a night near to Christmas or my birthday or early on in my long summer holiday. These were the occasions when he wrote me brief letters which began "Dear William" and ended without greeting, "Father." A rhythm of correspondence had established itself. I wrote him letters early enough to enable him to reply in time for these major events of my year. Between whiles I wrote and heard from Aunt Sarah. It was Sarah who established the rhythm, early on, by taking it upon herself to answer the frequent letters I used to send him during my first year or two in England. "Your father and I are glad to hear—," "Your father and I were amused by your account of—," "Your father is away which is why I'm answering your letter to him—," "Your Uncle Walter will be giving you a bit of money to buy something you'd like. It comes from your father and me with our love for Christmas (or your birthday, or your summer holiday)."

The infrequency and brevity of Father's letters also caused those twinges of disappointment; and in addition to the natural disinclination a boy has for writing letters, this not hearing from Father made me see letters from other people, Aunt Sarah, Mrs. Canterbury, Dora and Krishi, as poor substitutes. Correspondence with Dora and Krishi was the first to dry up. It can't have lasted for more than a year or two. For a bit longer than that I answered Old Mutton's epistles but when she left Jundapur for another pupil in another part of India that correspondence ended too, although right up until just before the war she sent Christmas and birthday cards. It was Father who was India to me, from Father I wanted to hear. When his brief letters came I used to try to read between the lines, read questions into them, questions like: Well, how are you shaping? Are you nearly ready? Do you understand, really understand, what you are in for when you join the service?

Other boys whose parents were abroad were luckier. I knew one boy who went out to India twice to join them for the summer, but then he was older and I told myself, My turn will come. That I only found the courage to mention it once, to Aunt Sarah ("Oh, my dear—"), shows how little

I must have believed it likely, in my heart, where I defended an illusion by a progressive toughening of its skin.

The stream that wound through the birch woods, bubbling and singing over its stony bed, the stream we called The Water, was, I suppose, my youth's equivalent of the childhood place of rhododendrons, but although I was not eleven years old when I first saw it I never played there, never took off my shoes and socks, splashed and mudlarked in it. I sat on its banks, or fell asleep by it on drowsy afternoons; or in that moment between sleeping and waking saw it through half-closed eyes tumbling down into the heart of a river that flowed gravely to the open sea. I launched upon it slow, dreamy boats of recollection and swift, thrusting boats of ambition and expectation; but whatever kind of boat it was its voyage ended on an Indian shore. Exile is hard to bear without some link nearby. Depending upon my mood, to wander down to the banks of The Water was an excitement or a sadness, but always a connection. Appropriately enough it became the scene of the last prod, at the end of the narrow path, which sent me sprawling, through the invisible columns of arrival into the world of reality. Stephen plays there still. I have sat there with him, naming trees, identifying birds, sharing his lust for life, sharing his imprisonment. It wasn't the scene of our parting, and sometimes I wish that it had been, as much as I wish that I had prepared him for the future when we were together there, had had the decency to say, for instance, Don't be taken in, one day while we're here the odds are I'll say or do something that will crack your little world straight up the middle. There would have been a tidiness in that, the kind of neatness both of us appreciate, because it was on the banks of The Water that my father, on his second visit to England, in 1936, when I was seventeen, told me, who had expected to discuss the approaching maturity of plans for following in his footsteps, that he was making arrangements for me to do what he called "going in with your Uncle Walter."

At first I didn't understand. When I understood I blurted out, "But I wanted an Indian career, sir," and then looked closely at him, studied him as if to lay bare clues to the pattern of his astonishing betrayal. He had come a day sooner than he had announced, without Aunt Sarah, who had told Uncle Walter (for yes, it was she who wrote the letter of arrangement) that she had been a bit under the weather recently, and didn't feel up to the long journey. Was she reluctant to witness the blow he was going to deal me? He had come on a glittering, burning August afternoon which had found me sunbathing, giving my body to the too often clouded yellow disc, so that at least he should find me looking fit, ready for anything, any task, even any penance within reason for my years in the smug, suburban world of Four Birches which I thought only his necessity had forced me to endure but which I hoped had not touched me.

Lying on my belly, browning my back, Four Birches had been in my line of vision whenever I opened a lash-teased, sweat-smudged eye to disrupt the great slow waves of peace and lassitude that had been set in motion by future expectation as well as by heat, and consider the prospect of yanking myself out of such idleness to go inside and dress and get down into the town to swim at the new open-air pool.

And there he had been, a tall stranger, crossing the lawn with Uncle Walter; and nudged then by a different spur I had got to my feet, embarrassed by the expanse of bare belly and breast I had to present to him. Now, dressed, the embarrassment long since over and in its place a youthful hope that he was pleased to find his only son grown straight, we were made strangers by his announcement, and I saw, coldly, that it required only a fractional elevation of my eyes to meet his and that this, with my extra pounds of weight, dammed the flowing outwards from him of judgments and decisions that could swamp me. His long, thin face had changed. The texture of the skin looked thicker, drier, as if it had been smoked and toughened and made insensitive by extremes of climate and experience. He was too old to understand the needs of my blood. I had to make him understand. "But I was to have an Indian career, sir."

Aunt Ethel had long ago laughed me out of the habit of calling Uncle Walter "sir" which she had thought "cute but stuck-up." I never called my father "sir" in India, but I did so now, automatically. The "sir" gave substance to the shadow that had fallen between us; fallen between us long before we met on the banks of The Water, but only noticed now.

"I suppose you think it all eyewash?" he said and for a moment I thought he meant that calling him sir was eyewash; which is probably why I remember the actual words we used. But that is not what he meant. He meant that he supposed I thought the periodically declared intention of the British to lead India to independence nothing but eyewash. He pointed out the likelihood of there being no career for me in India if things moved fast, the possibility of my career being brought to a premature end if things moved at a more reasonable pace.

"I thought," he said, "from your rather prolix letters that you were making a close study of Indian politics." I was quite outclassed. Words and the variable uses to which they could be put were the tools of his trade. He had browbeaten princes with them. I felt loutish, tongue-tied. All my study, learning and reading had resulted in a shallow knowledge of affairs that counted for nothing when ranged against the knowledge and opinions of a man who had spent a lifetime dealing with them.

"You'll be better off," he said finally, "earning money like your Uncle Walter," and, drowning, I clutched that straw. I tried to explain why I shouldn't be better off and in the course of explaining also caught hold of the idea that Father liked the decision as little as I did myself, couldn't afford the expense or was being too cautious, too wary for my future. He heard me out, unsmiling, as he must have heard old Ranjit Raosingh out on the subject of the succession, and when I was finished said, "I repeat, William. You think it all eyewash?"

He stayed two days. That night my Uncle Walter said, "Well, so you're coming in with me," and touched me kindly on the shoulder. I said, "Yes, Uncle," and looked at him not as my uncle, which after all I had seldom done, but as my future employer, and wasn't sure I liked what I saw. The fleshiness of his good nature might prove to cover bones stuffed with shopkeeper's marrow. If Father's decision against an Indian career was a surprise to Walter he probably looked at me with much the same thought at the back of his mind, saw me not as his Indiaman nephew but as his new office boy whose head was crammed with ideas that would have to be knocked out of it. At that moment all my bitterness towards Father resolved itself into a sullen contempt, not unmixed with fear, of Uncle Walter. He said something like, "You'll be all right." He took the line that my father was right, "sensible as always," that I was young, had fifty years of active work ahead of me, that in less time than that the only Englishmen in India might be tourists and commercial travellers. He reminded me I had another year at school, time to get used to the idea, to the disappointment. When he used that word, "disappointment," I reserved judgment on him, discarded the angry notion that he was behind the whole thing and had taken advantage of Father's comparatively thin purse to agree to help me, but only on his terms.

I've often wondered since whether Uncle Walter knew or guessed that when I was older Father would turn thumbs down on me. I've even wondered whether he secretly hoped that this would be the case and saw in me qualities he wanted to get his hands on like a man getting his hands into clay. I've wondered from time to time whether it gave him little pricks of satisfaction to see another Conway exiled from the Conway inner sanctum as he himself had been exiled years before. But I have long since absolved him from the suspicion I entertained at the time, that he took part in a battle with Father that was fought over the ground of some past quarrel, ground which it was my bad luck to be rooted in by the chance falling of Father's seed, my fate to be snatched up from by the winner, along with the rest of the spoils, whatever they were.

This suspicion was not entertained for long. He showed no signs of victory, went out of his way to give me a good time. "You'll be all right," he said. And later, "For God's sake, Bill, it's not the end of the world," and he gave me a fiver because, as he himself put it, "that's all I've got to give you, isn't it, old man?" and after some hesitation, I took it and, not in return, for such a thing I prided myself couldn't be bought, consciously gave him, youthfully grudging and late, some of the affection my father had left lying ungathered like the leaves that fell that autumn from the silver birches. I gave some to Ethel too, not for what she said or did, because she said and did precisely nothing, but for treating me as if it could never enter her head that I wasn't man enough to take knocks and be content not to chew the rag about them.

But this didn't prevent me from entering a year of secret hope that Father would change his mind, return to India and think, Good God, the boy was serious, wasn't he? Daily I expected a letter. Young Englishmen were still sitting for the ICS examinations, still planning to do so three and four years hence. Nightly I pondered the wisdom of sending a letter to him to say I would prefer to take my chance of having a career cut off; and then of talking to Uncle Walter, man to man, as now seemed possible. But no letter came and I wrote none; and when I rehearsed the kind of things I could say to Uncle Walter I saw how like it would have sounded to a snotty kid howling for his lost balloon. In those weeks following Father's visit, Uncle Walter's detachment from the family and from India acquired depth, revealed the possibility of there having always been density below the surface of random thoughts and impressions such as those I had had that he didn't like Father much, that he was the kind of man who rather let the family down by marrying women like Ethel and by not worshipping the family Gods, nor any gods unless they were the gods of money, which he more seemed to live on terms with than worship. I was inclined to look at him now as a man who might have intentionally cut himself adrift from the firmly anchored tradition of service in the glittering heart of an Empire because he saw it not as an anchored tradition but as the hung-on-to balloon I was trying not to yell for. Perhaps he had decided that the bad in India far outweighed the good. The good had been held in trust by men like my father. It had been part and parcel of the illusion of him, but now the illusion was breaking up, losing all its protective skins as my eyes bore into them and peeled them away to get at the reality of the unsmiling man who had watched me not through corresponding eyes which revealed my likeness at its root but through splinters of ice that revealed nothing, unless it were distaste.

On the banks of The Water I measured that distaste, measured it against what had been my love but wasn't love any longer. I told myself that it wasn't simply in this one case he had let me down. He'd never thought anything of me at all. I measured the years of exile against the fortitude with which they had been borne, for of course in retrospect I saw it as fortitude. The fortitude had been for nothing because the exile had been intentional. I measured my old expectations of arrival against the reality of journey's end, and shrugged at my expectations. I had been made a fool of. I'd been led by the nose to act out the part of an old-fashioned flat-wagger. The whole of India could sink into the ocean and I wouldn't care. The guardians of a sacred trust were whoring imperialists and the nation they enslaved was a nation of snivelling fools. And Mountstuart Elphinstone had had the right idea about the princes. My father had wasted his life and was ridiculous because he didn't know it, was old, dried out, quite out of touch. I might, of course, not go into Uncle Walter's office. I could go to sea, or join the army. How, I wondered, did you become an explorer? Probably by being a geologist first, something technical and rather dull like that. If I went into Uncle Walter's office it wouldn't be for long—only long enough to put some money by and then fend for myself.

An inborn sense of discipline is strong, hard to recognize for what it is, easy to mistake for the virtue of determination. I thought, "Life's not half bad," added, "No thanks to Father," and threw my first grown-up cigarette into the stream where it bucked and twisted for a few seconds and then gave itself to the irresistible current, was lost to sight where the banks of The Water curved into the denser wood.

And, in youth, when the blood boils, when body and spirit might dare anything, there are snares whose sharp teeth we give ourselves to gladly. There is one inheritance, at least. Later we might lash ourselves for lost opportunities in life, for indolence, weakness, and indecision, for letting ourselves be swept up by the flashing, bubbling stream which proves to lead so quickly only to the dull, grey sea. But at the time it is different. It was different for me, then. The bubbling stream was the torrent of life itself; indolence was energy; weakness, strength; indecision and lost opportunities, no less than taking life by its scruff, living and enjoying it to the full.

On a week end in the early autumn of 1937 when I was eighteen, I lost my cherry, an event which tended to confuse even the simplest aspect of the question of liking or not liking working for Uncle Walter. The loss was sustained in a place that smelled of pine cones, French Fern, and petrol: the smells of love outdoors.

At eighteen I was five feet eleven inches in stockinged feet. I shaved, more often than absolutely essential, but I shaved. I sang a splendid baritone in the bathroom. I drank beer and smoked a pipe on Saturday and Sunday, applied myself assiduously but less seriously than before to the business of fresh air and exercise. But I still had this cherry of mine and it weighed. There was a girl called Lilian whom I met on the 8:15. She lived in Ashtead and wore net gloves. After evenings with her, after the good night kiss, a business involving the knees as well as the lips, I drove back from Ashtead too fast, went to bed trembling and impatient and made love to the sheets and pillows, which relieved the pressure and induced sleep but exacted payment in the morning in the shape of the evidence in my pyjama trousers and an aggravated sense of the absurd and irrational.

It wasn't Lilian who used French Fern. It was a friend of hers called Betty Mitcombe. There was a roadhouse called The Wallace. It had a swimming pool that could be floodlit at night from underneath as well as from on top. The sun umbrellas were tartan and on the walls of the neonlit lounge there were little plaques, clan insignia. The waiters wore white monkey jackets and tartan trews. There were pots of heather on the tables in the dive bar. The dive bar was called the Bonnie Prince Charlie. There was a snuggery called The Kiltie which the manager looked after. He wore a kilt and used to emerge to collect glasses and obvious comments.

Where the road from The Wallace joined the main London road a quarter of a mile away there was a history of accidents. The junction was known as Scots Wha ha'e fra' Wallace bleed. It was as we approached it one night that Betty Mitcombe, sandwiched between Lilian and myself in the front seat of Uncle Walter's car, put her hand in the fork of my trousers and said, "Watch your step, Bill." It was dark and Lilian didn't notice Betty's action, only mine, when I swerved to avoid a ditch. The next day was Saturday. Lilian was spending it at home. I rang Betty Mitcombe. She agreed to go for a drive and picnic lunch. She said, "Bring a mac in case it rains." I couldn't believe she meant what I thought she meant. I checked my wallet for the contraceptive that had been pressed in it like a flower between the pages of a book for something like six months, but as an emblem of optimistic anticipation rather than of fond remembrance. The ring of grime and the circular bump on the packet which I had grown used to, now alarmed me. Could it have perished? The makers recommended a lubricant to go with it. It sounded messy and sordid, but the idea behind it remained compelling. There was a curious aroma in the room, the odour of animal secretions caught and held in warm cotton cloth. Outside, in the sunshine, the air smelled of ether.

The jobbing gardener Uncle Walter employed was cutting the half-moon of grass that sloped down to the tree-lined road and, in the spring, sprouted clumps of daffodils around the four silver birches. The mower was wet and the grass arched thickly from the blades to the box. It would have been almost the last cutting of the year. I got out the red MG two-seater Uncle Walter had given me on my eighteenth birthday on a pay-back-from-salary-as-and-when basis, and as I eased her down the gravel drive there was this sensation I had of the whole situation being transparent, and this, in itself, like the ride to save Dora from the wheeling horsemen on the other side of the maidan at Tradura, had no ending to it. It cannot have existed for more than a few moments. I remember its beginning, as the gardener turned his machine with his nut-brown forearms, faced me across the distance that divided him from the slowly moving car and jerked his head in a general approval and a particular greeting, but I don't remember its ending, I don't remember coming out of the strange transparency back into the unique secret of being a private person who needed only to reveal what he wanted to reveal, and this, I think, is because the sensation of transparency had not at all to do with the fact that I was on my way clothed in an ignorance and an innocence to a meeting at which both were to be lost forever, thank heaven, but with the sharp attack, explosion really, of joy; not joy in prospect so much as joy that was there, existing there, and having to do with what was clean and natural and had a purpose of its own: the glittering, lacquered red bonnet of the car and the swanky leather straps that held it down, the way the grass was wet and the bark of the birch trees was mottled grey-brown and silver-white like the hide of a strange, nobbly species of giraffe, the sound the car wheels made on the thousands of brown and yellow pebbles, each of which, picked up and inspected, would have displayed a miraculous diversity and variation of shape: some smooth, some sharp, all pounded out of larger stone and cascaded from a tip-tilt lorry, perhaps on a morning such as this when light, air and sunshine caught the polished black curve of a sensuous-to-the-touch steering wheel, the conker colour of a leather toecap, whorled grey worm-casts in the lawn, the furrow-straight and alternating dark and light green swathes left by the man-pushed mower, the tough, fibrous stems and bulging ostrich plumes of dahlias, the woodsmoke smell of early yellow chrysanthemums that had been brought on under panes of summer-heated glass—the whole joy of being man-in-environment. It is this that

was transparent, this that had no ending. It is always coming
back to me as a sensation outweighing all others. It is here
with me in Manoba, now, as I write, actually at this moment. The bulbous yet slender pen, expensively yellow with
its gold, the perspiration from my hand that dents and
damps the woody paper, the smell outside and inside of
decay which is as well the smell of life, the sudden slicing of
the air by Melba at her singing and shouting; the acid
green and Vandyke brown shadows, the potentially scarlet
air—scarlet because today it is very hot, scorched, and the
air might at any moment achieve spontaneous combustion
and produce a conflagration that would feed on the sap of the
forest and belch flame into and over its undergrowth: all
these and countless other large and small manifestations of
physical existence conspire to make me as happy as I was on
that long-gone cherry-fall morning, at peace in the full sens-
ual consciousness of being alive and uncommitted to anything except my body and what it is surrounded by, what it
can pick up, hold, see and touch, what can press over it,
against it, or lie outside it and touch my sensibility with an
exactness, an actual duplication of its beauty or its ugliness,
whatever it is, the work of man in factories, at benches, or
of the elements which tickle the earth and make it throw
up green arms, or of the beasts who—like the Kinwar tiger
—stake out their claims, leave tracks, keep watch from cover.

BOOK THREE

The View from the Terrace

"Some few were brought to me the same day they were caught and I had an opportunity of examining them in all their beauty and vivacity. As soon as I found they were generally brought alive, I set one of my men to make a large bamboo cage with troughs for food and water, hoping to be able to keep some of them. . . . They drank plenty of water and were in constant motion, jumping about the cage from perch to perch, clinging to the top and the sides, and rarely resting a moment. . . . The second day they were always less active . . . and on the morning of the third day they were almost always found dead at the bottom of the cage, without apparent cause."

(*The Malay Archipelago:* the land of the orang-utan, and the bird of paradise. A narrative of travel, with studies of Man and Nature; by ALFRED RUSSEL WALLACE: Vol. 2. Macmillan & Co., 1869.)

1

In 1945 Aunt Sarah who was then sixty was, when she stood, a bit out of true. A plumb line suspended from her nose would no longer have found a point of vertical rest between her feet but one a few inches in front of them. She was far from being a bent old woman but there was this just notice-able need of hers to incline herself forward from a point near the base of her spine as if it were there that the first weakness of old age had set in; and yet, in this, nature was kind to her. What she lost in bony uprightness was offset by the new look of almost lively curiosity which the forward-poked position of her head gave her. To get a sideways-on view of her as she stood on the terrace and watched the malis at work in the Residency garden, to see her bring one thin hand up to her chest and flutter the fingers on the now even more prominent breastbone was to forget momentarily that she had ever been preoccupied with plans that never came to anything much. The garden she was watching, if you knew no better and took into visual account only the enquiring profile, the overseeing-foreman tilt of her upper body, the fingers drumming as if only the best would do, might have been one whose rich blooms and sparkling lawns drew ex-clamations of admiration from all who saw them. It was nothing of the kind.

When she faced you, or sat down, this picture of Sarah as a rigid perfectionist was lost. She sagged a bit as though in late

middle-age she had begun to put on weight for the first time
in her life, a fattening at the onset of which her bones, accus-
tomed for so long to supporting next to nothing, had cringed
in protest and so discouraged and halted the fat before it
had really taken hold, so that now in her thinness there was
a looseness, a certain anatomical disorganisation that made
you think of her corsets and clothes as essential to the business of keeping her held together in the rigid manner she
required. But here again nature had been kind. The looseness suggested a faded feminine softness and roundness. The
looseness hung on her face as well and because of this and
because the bones of her face were still marked, there was an
idea to be had that she had once been a handsome woman.
Her hair, colour-rinsed to keep uncompromising grey and
silver at bay, thin at the temples and along the line of her
forehead, had a fading lustre in it that falsely suggested a
hey-day shine. Her grey-blue eyes, veiled always by the ob-
scurity of her personality and which I had only once in my
life remarked as glittering with excitement—on the night
she left the agency bungalow at Tradura for the banquet in
Ranjit Raosingh's palace—were now misted over, and a
stranger might have seen the mist as that of a tranquillity in
which much experience, much happiness and some sadness
were being recollected towards the end of a full and fruitful
life.

When Dora—herself a grown woman—said to me that she
remembered my Aunt Sarah as having been "a nice grown-up
to kiss" I said something like "Was she?" and thought of her
from the point of view of the boy who hardly ever kissed her
and of the man who kissed her not more than twice, when we
met after the long separation of the war and when we parted
—forever as it turned out. The sensation these recollections
of mine and of Dora's give me of Aunt Sarah having been
two people, one who responded to Dora's affection and the
other who did not seem to want affection, indeed protected

herself from it by wrapping herself into the self-sufficiency of her vagueness, remind me of how on the Residency terrace she frustrated me by her refusal to be drawn into a single focus. At one minute in standing profile she was this elderly but still active woman who looked incapable of giving any but clear orders and straight answers; at another, facing you, sitting opposite you, giving out these hints of old warmth, tenderness and wisdom. But when she spoke, the temperature of human intercourse dropped at once. Sometimes I felt that this was because she had no contribution to make to it, at others that she used words as sponges to absorb your thoughts and wring them out like someone whose duty it was to go through life mopping things up against the day when something of value might put in an appearance or because nothing valuable was anticipated and the place had simply to be kept clean and tidy and undistracting, like the lavatory, the flower beds, or chests of drawers whose contents might at any moment have to be packed into suitcases.

How little I remember of what she ever said to me. "What a grisly old game—"; "Oh, my dear—"; and after I had told her something about Pig Eye camp in Malaya, where I had been imprisoned by the Japanese for three and a half years, "Well, it's over now, William. And you're looking better."

The meeting with her in Delhi should have warned me I was expected to accept my imprisonment in Pig Eye as something that was over, as something that had fallen to my lot because the odds had been stacked that way. On Delhi station, where she had gone to the trouble of meeting the train coming in from Calcutta, I made the awful mistake of putting my arms round her. I could not help it but it was a mistake because she had no armour to withstand the onslaught of a grown man's sentiment, and I should not have subjected her to it. Seeing her standing there, dressed in white skirt, yellow blouse and short white coat, holding a stick but not leaning on it, surrounded by the awful hullaballoo of an Indian railway arrival, I was not absolutely sure that it was she, for I hadn't set eyes on her since 1933, but I hoped it was because there was a staunch, gentle but rocklike look to this elderly woman whose face was shaded by an old-fashioned, round, white linen hat with a brim designed to shield her eyes from the sun and not to flatter her face. She stood, a white pillar, undeterred by the press of coolies, passengers and luggage, secure in a long experience, or so it looked, of the respect accorded to her by strangers and the unlikelihood of harm befalling a lone Englishwoman of her age and frailty.

Drawing nearer to her but kept from reaching her directly, my eyes at last met hers and then I was sure that it was she. Her face was composed into an expression of acceptance. It lacked sadness, it lacked joy, it lacked recognition. Perhaps this is the expression all of us wear who stand on platforms knowing whom to expect but not what. But once our glances met they did not part and when I was separated from her by only one pair of shoulders she raised her hand in a gesture of inquiry and greeting and said one word.

"William?"

The hand she raised remained there and got pressed between us when I put my arms round her. It was not a barrier so much as an entanglement and it may for all I know have distressed her to have one hand taken up with her stick, the other trapped against her chest, and no means to respond spontaneously to my embrace. She may have learned to accept it as her fate to be incapable of initiating a display of affection and to be caught at this kind of disadvantage whenever a moment proper to such a display arose. But when I drew away from her, noticed that her hat was knocked a bit awry and moved to straighten it, something stopped me; an instinct not to meddle with her because to be touched puzzled her and knocked her off balance. At that moment I don't believe she felt the discomfort of the crooked hat, only felt that momentarily she did not know who I was or who she was or what she had to do about it all when things became clearer. And this was nothing to do with being annoyed or embarrassed by the sudden contact. It was because she had neither armour to withstand it nor weapons of love to return it. My embrace had not been accepted, nor had it been rejected, it had just gone into the void where it died of inanition.

My memory has lost the details not only of the journey from Pig Eye to Delhi but of the second journey, from Delhi to Gopalakand where at the end of his career my father had returned as master of the palladian mansion in which I was born. These high spots remain: walking across Mingaladon airfield and, in Delhi, embracing Aunt Sarah. We were no more than a few hours there before catching a train that took us overnight to Gopalakand. She shared a first-class compartment with three other women and I shared a first-class coupe with another man who took one look at my prison face, nodded, and buried his own face in the *Reader's Digest*. But was it before we left Delhi, or over breakfast at an early morning station-halt, that she told me Uncle Walter was well, but Aunt Ethel was dead, killed, stupidly enough, by a buzz bomb in the local high street? And was it to tell me that she elected to meet me in Delhi, so that I should arrive in Gopalakand uncluttered with the obligation to be told something, so that the arrival in Gopalakand should be Conway-clear and Conway-crisp, as uncharged as possible with emotional shock? It didn't occur to me that this might have been the case until long afterwards. I think she told me in Delhi, in the hotel where we rested and had a meal between trains, but even so Aunt Ethel's death didn't register with me as a close personal loss until Christmas drew near and, under the impact of the brassy Indian sun, I thought of

Four Birches under snow and of Ethel's high-banked, lower-middle-class fires raging in its hearths.

There was a car to meet us in Gopalakand. The station lay in the goodsyard no man's land between town and cantonment and when the car moved out of the yard, there was the Residency clearly visible on top of the hill, two miles away. It was lost to view in the cantonment by the curve of the road and the height of the trees, the general built-in-ness of the shopping centre. Aunt Sarah told me that the road we were driving along was called Residency Road and that later it became Residency Hill. It was about five o'clock in the afternoon. Some shops were open for the evening trade. There were horse tongas drawn up. Two white women, climbing into one, paused when they saw the car and "moved" to the resident's sister by inclining their heads. Aunt Sarah "moved" back to them by inclining her head and raising that questing, querying hand. Beyond the shopping centre the broad avenue of Residency Hill opened up, paved, treed, walled by the gardens of substantial bungalows, and just about here the Residency itself came back into view, a miniature Buckingham Palace at the end of a climbing, miniature Mall. There was a statue of the White Queen, Victoria, orbed and sceptred in the middle of the road where it forked for its lanes of entrance and exit into and from the Residency grounds. As the car slowed for its turn there was a sudden shout and clatter, the unmistakable sound of armed authority. The nerves in the back of my neck and the small of my back frisked me of all sensation other than that of waiting for a blow, and I leaned back, knowing that we were only being slap-butt saluted, but tucking my fist into my mouth because the relationship between what was going on visibly and what was going on invisibly wouldn't be sorted out. A nervous reflex started me laughing, and as we drove in past the ramrod soldiers whose bodies must still have been vibrating with the shock waves from leather stamped on concrete, I turned to Aunt Sarah, like that, with my fist stuck in my mouth, making a noise in my throat that was a cross between a man's laugh and the cry of a trapped animal, and for one second I thought I saw behind the mist of her eyes a look of complete, utter and devastating understanding. I had never seen it before. I never saw it again. The odds are that it wasn't there at all.

When the car stopped a servant opened the door. We were at the bottom of a flight of steps. Aunt Sarah got out and then I followed her and, looking up, saw my father emerge bare-headed from the dark, monumental, laid-back entrance, and come to stand above me on the topmost step of all. We had not met since 1936. We had scarcely exchanged letters between then and 1939. From 1939 I had not written to him at all. In Pig Eye this had weighed on my conscience.

I was grinning, breathless. I opened my mouth to say, "Well, come down, say hello to me," but all that came out was an inane croak. He stayed where he was, smiled, extended his hand and I walked up to take it, no longer a boy, taller than he, a large, gangling skeleton, returned to the museum where I had been born to adorn the pages of history with accounts of my courage and wisdom at best, my simple dedication to humble duty at worst.

He said, "Hello, William," studied me while retaining a grasp of my hand, then added, "You're looking fitter than we expected. Good." Then, placing one hand on my shoulder and, I think, the other on Sarah's shoulder, he turned us around and walked us into the Residency. We were salaamed by several Residency servants and, at the actual doorway, somehow got mixed up with each other's feet, perhaps because we were all looking at the ground and our feet tended to converge upon the central line of advance.

. . .

I had a sensation of being clearer-sighted than ever before. I seemed to be able to make out details of landscape that would have escaped me previously. I thought that this was the effect of my being free to get up and walk to whatever point on the horizon caught my attention and that may have been a contributing factor, certainly. But there was, in the world, so much to see. I think the sensation of clear-sightedness was due to the fact that I felt you couldn't afford to be slack about seeing it.

I used to embarrass Aunt Sarah by trying to save scraps of food from my plate. The sight of anything going to waste made me gently hysterical. I knew there was no actual need, knew that the motive of keeping some back as if you couldn't be positive that there would be more where it had come from was without reasonable grounds; but there again, there was so much of the stuff, more than you could get rid of at a sitting, and just by being there, tempting, tasty, full of proteins, vitamins, carbohydrates, and calories—utterly amazing really—it had earned the right not to be squandered.

"My dear, it's no longer necessary, you know," Aunt Sarah said once when I covered a chappatti with a napkin, a casual movement made more to save them embarrassment than to enable me later to transfer the chappatti to my pocket without being seen. I told her I knew this quite well, perhaps better than they did because they had never been hungry and so understood less both when it would be wise and when unnecessary to save scraps.

"It's only a gesture," I said, "a gesture to the food," and smiled at her and then at Father who was drinking water from a glass misted over with cold and marked with earlier prints from his now sallow, dry and blue-veined fingers. When he put the glass down on the polished mahogany table it made a mauve, filmy reflection. The silver cutlery was dulled by a faint, yellow veneer, a threat of tarnish upon a worn surface. I was fascinated by the relationship that existed between inanimate objects like dark red wood, transparent glass, heavy silver forks and spoons and animate objects like the flesh that acted as a cushion between the bones of fingers and whatever those fingers touched. I used to stare at the naked feet of the bearers and the pug marks they left on the tiled floor, and was a lot taken up with the way the feet gave, spread like tiger or camel pads, when the whole weight of the man was put on them; and I liked the clean pillow-case look of their starched baggy white trousers, which were caught up at their brown, scrubbed ankles; ankles on which, if you looked closely enough, you might spy blemishes—a pinkish yellow callous, for instance.

Above the table a three-bladed fan revolved slowly. Sometimes it reminded me of the rhythm achieved by the revolving doors of an hotel a few seconds after someone had gone in or come out and so I was intrigued by the fan's apparently perpetual motion: no one going in, no one coming out, but always chugging gently round as if but recently set going by such an impact. At other times I could ignore the blades and concentrate on the down-pointing Damoclean spear head with which the shaft was decorated below the hub. It annoyed me because while the symbolism was quite unintentional it was too obvious to ignore and, being symbolic, suggestive of fate, destiny, of the things that happened to men and women but not to things, it raised the relationship of fan, room and people to an unnecessarily complicated level.

But what I liked best about the Residency was the view from the terrace. Quite flat and unexciting at first glance and never at any glance approximating to the landscape of a country I had known as a child but not seen since, it yielded hundreds of fascinating details if you sat there long enough with open eyes and a receptive mind and didn't allow yourself to be confused by any except a pictorial consideration of what men, women and children happened to be doing in regard to that view, in the grounds, or far beyond the invisible wall of the grounds, in the fields. Some of the fields were given over to rice. At this time of the year they were flooded. On a dull day they looked like rows of oblong, milky mirrors, but on a sunny day they melted into one to form a distant, gleaming lake.

The Residency—grey stone, Anglo-Indian palladian like the palace at Jundapur but on a larger, grander scale altogether—was built on the flattened crest of the only hill for miles around. At the front there was a courtyard of pink and white gravel, iron railings with gilded spear heads and a set of main gates that gave directly on to the metalled road that led down the northern slope of the hill between an avenue of trees to the cantonment. Beyond the cantonment, only a few of whose white, European buildings could be seen amongst the neat, garden-suburb foliage, the town lay open, flat, plastered to the plain in irregular shaped cubes of brown, yellow and pink. In the far distance a wood, and lights showing through the trees at night, marked the Maharajah's winter palace. But at the back of the Residency, seated on the terrace there was, as I have said, at first glance nothing but this flatness, this distance, this immense plate of land, edged on one sector of the horizon by a long bruise that might have been the low blue shape of hills, and actually was although you had to wait for a really clear day to be sure about it. The wall of the grounds was invisible from the terrace because it lay below the crest of the flattened hill and so, although there was a kind of breaking line in the perspective from terrace to horizon, it seemed as if you were stuck there in complete isolation, quite unfenced, completely unrestricted.

Immediately below the terrace there was a formal garden: flower beds in squares, triangles and semicircles; but these would be so parched during the hot weather, unshaded as they were, that you felt the business of growing flowers as a serious pursuit had been given up fifty years before, or a hundred, or never even begun; and in October 1945, when I was there, and the rains had only just fallen off, the flowers already had a drowned, grudging, spindly look, which may have been Aunt Sarah's fault more than theirs. There were bare patches of drying mud in the grass of the walks between the beds, where some of the dozen malis employed at the Residency stood with hoes in hand encouraging without interest the few plants she had directed should be planted there to shoot a few green shafts from June to September and die a decent death when the sun began to burn the swimming rice fields.

The garden itself yielded little of real concern to the eye, but beyond it there were so many things. I remember that there were many things because I sat for hours in the shade of the wide, colonnaded terrace, pretending to be asleep but in actuality plotting the coefficients of the natural graph of the fields and pathways which extended as far as could be seen, with only an occasional eruption of trees and smoke to mark a village.

The land was full of minor mysteries. You needed time to work on them. For instance I remember the pimple that became a blob and then turned into what must have been a wayside temple, although I could never organize the light to fall on it in a manner that would have identified it beyond question. I also remember the bicycle that emerged one day from nothing, moved slowly along what I had taken to be a narrow bank between fields but which must have been a broad raised dyke with a pathway. The bicycle was carrying a man and a raised umbrella on its back. It was a gradual, voluptuous progress, silent and distant but unmistakably mechanical, the kind of glide that could only be achieved by a machine, a contraption on wheels, propelling itself upon its natural element of land as a seal propels itself in water. Only the man who rode the bicycle's back was a disturbing

feature. Even the umbrella had charm, a pleasantness of intention, a rather silly but clever ability to shoot up and hold
itself curved and rigid to keep the cool in or the wet out.

At four, when I was on the terrace, one of the boys
brought tea, placed the tray by my side on a stool made of
writhing strands of wicker which were caught in at the middle and made into a waist by a girdle of plaited straw. Top
and bottom were made of discs of rough-cut, unpolished
wood with the bark intact. In one of these discs there was a
knot hole branded at one edge by a lighted cigarette that
had been placed there and forgotten. The arrival of tea was
a sequence of sounds, smells and actions: bare feet slapping
flagged floor, a whiff of garlic that strengthened when the
boy leant forward to put the drumlike stool in position; the
rattle of a spoon, the clunk and chink of a loaded tray softly
and safely landed; then silence and the slow-drawn-up metallic aroma of hot water standing in a silverplated pot, the
buttercup smell of milk exposed to the open air.

Closely inspected, the exterior of the stone walls of the
Residency revealed scars like the scars on the weathered
body of a man who had lived long and hard in savage country. When I thought about the stone, watched it, contem-
plated it, I became fond of it. My hand, touching it, I took
as a proof of my survival. It was the proof of my survival
mirrored in them that drew me to objects that could, it is
true, have been destroyed but had no life to lose, that made
me in those first weeks in India following my release and
rehabilitation from Pig Eye, wary of people, if wariness is
the right word. The wariness did not come as a shock because shock, being a violent sensation, could not be felt by a
body ticking over at low pressure and concentrating inside
its visible ribcage on the simple muscular effort of pumping
blood. It came rather as an observed, as distinct from an
acutely experienced, surprise, and more of a disappointment
than a surprise, a disappointment in myself because I hadn't

had the stamina to rise to an occasion. During the days of the initial break-up of Pig Eye the expectation of reunion with my closest kin had been like an electrically charged wire that ran through the centre of my body from the top of the inside of my head down to the belly and branching from there in twin strands, one down each leg, right to the back of the ankle. Head, stomach, knee-caps and ankles tingled with it. Such high tension couldn't be sustained. Once I had come face to face with Father and Aunt Sarah my body sensibly took charge and left me with not much more to do than examine, in the inertia of sudden freedom, all that the eye alone could see.

The irony of it! In Pig Eye I had wanted badly the opportunity to make things up with Father but now that it was here, the need, the wish to make things up was temporarily suspended by the almost total consumption by the body of those fuels which in less lean days could have been expended on emotion.

There was an English doctor, a civilian, in the cantonment down the road. He used to come and see me. I don't recall his name but remember that his face was fleshy and slack, particularly around the mouth where it got in the way of his teeth. He was always pulling a handkerchief out of his pocket to dry his chin or, surreptitiously, the chess board. He was a keen chessman and thought the game relaxed me. I suppose it did. The carved pieces felt good to pick up and put down. I invariably lost, though, being more interested in the invisible and visible patterns we made when we moved the pieces than in the threats and openings the moves represented.

He said, "Come on, wipe the board with me this time." He wore spectacles. He was about fifteen years my senior. He was a doctor but wasn't a bit like Cranston, the Pig Eye doctor who saved my feet from going gangrenous, saved me from being a cripple, perhaps saved my life. I began one day to talk to him about Cranston. He said, "Sounds an interesting fellow, white to play." He wanted me to get involved in the game, to forget Pig Eye, to feel the thrill of plot and counterplot. After I had lost yet again he looked at me over his glasses and said I didn't care, did I? and oughtn't I to make an effort?

I asked him what kind of effort he meant. He said he meant an effort to feel things again because it was bad for me to sit on the terrace staring into space. I said that I wasn't staring into space but looking at things and didn't he sometimes think it surprising how much there was to look at, surprising that there were probably one thousand different things to look at in the immediate vicinity alone?

He said yes, he supposed there were, and that it was, but that there were even more things outside the Residency and why didn't I circulate, why didn't I try an evening at the club? He did not add, Forget things for a while and start looking at people. I believe his not saying this was due to a natural inward grace. If he had said it I should have been forced to say that people were all right and I'd get around to them when my body could stand the strain but that in Pig Eye there had been nine hundred and fifty three people counting prisoners only, that I knew the exact number because Cranston and I were virtually the last to leave. We had the sick-bay to clear up and we helped the prisoner-of-war commission people to compile nominal rolls of men repatriated from the camp and the nominal rolls disclosed this total, nine hundred and fifty three. If you added to it the numbers of dead, the total number of people I had been thrown in with over the last three years and a half exceeded the fifteen hundred mark, which put me several up on him in social intercourse, I imagined.

I think we both saw the word "people" dangling like dangerous bait between us and that it would have been a dreadful embarrassment to us if one of us had taken it and established—there on the terrace over the chessboard where my white king stood checkmated in his invaded and ruined court—a situation stultified by cliché. So when he said, "Try an evening at the club," without adding, "and meet some of the members, talk to some people," I just told him that I'd certainly do that as soon as I thought there was nothing new to look at from the terrace. I thought for a moment that he saw what I was getting at, that he understood it was not really a question of disliking people from having been in too crowded contact with them for too long, but of putting first things first, of using unaccustomed freedom to observe the world into which I had, in a sense, been born all over again; to rest the body so that it could heal itself and waste none of its rationed fire to set light to the emotion you always had to burn once you became involved with others; to keep my stock of by no means exhausted emotion stowed away until the bones of my body were fleshed properly and blood could be spared for the brain to think with and the heart to feel with. If there was anything sick in this it was only that having survived physically my continued physical survival stood supreme in a list of priorities. It would have been a waste to go under now.

But he hadn't understood after all. He took off his glasses, cleaned them with his handkerchief which was already pretty limp from his having been bowed so long over a game of chess, dribbling down his chin. People who habitually wear glasses are curiously blank-faced when they take them off. The light seems to drain them. But equally they are disturbingly sharp-looking when they put them on again, momentarily to be watched out for. When a man or a woman for that matter puts glasses back on I fancy them to be in that split second or two capable of anything, as a savage might be who has just finished painting his face. I saw that this doctor (what *was* his name? Taggert? Tangmere? Tan-

field?) would go straight in to Sarah and say, "The boy needs
a lot of care, I'm not really happy about him," and Aunt
Sarah would nod absent-mindedly and say, "Come again
soon. I'm sure the chess is good for him."

Dingy Row was still the ruler of Gopalakand. I referred
to him right at the beginning of this record as Sir Pandirakkar, but of course he only received his knighthood in late
middle-age. He was now an old man like Father (who was
sixty-four and but for the war would probably have retired).
I never saw Dingy Row. I never went to the palace. I was
excused from paying my respects because of my state of
health, my "experience at the hands of those bastards," as
Dingy Row's eldest son and heir put it. This son came to see
me. He had been educated at Harrow and, in 1945, was just
relinquishing his emergency commission in the Indian Air
Force and returning his attention to cricket, polo and politics. I liked him a lot but understood only half of what he
was talking about. He made me wonder what had happened
to that other young prince, young Krishi, but wondering is
as far as I got. In all he visited me three times, lounged
democratically on the terrace, called me old boy, was about
forty, his Rajput leanness mellowing and softening towards
a typically Hindu plumpness. He wore European clothes and
suède, crepe-rubber soled boots which he called brothel
creepers, having served in Cairo for a time. He had a high
opinion of the then Viceroy, Wavell, who, he knew, would
"sort out these chaps Nehru and Jinnah," and wouldn't "sell
the states down the river."

At the time I couldn't take in the contemporary complexi-
ties of Indian affairs. They hardly impinged. Gopalakand
was an island that stretched to the horizon on all sides and if
there were clouds building up beyond it, why, they had no
practical significance. "We've stood by the Crown," Dingy
Row's son said, "and the Crown'll stand by us. The jackals

aren't going to feed on us. Wavell will see to it. So shall we.
So will men like your father."

By jackals he meant the Indian politicians of British India
whom he described as "at each other's bloody throats, carv-
ing up the country and getting rid of the princes if they get
the chance." I got the airy impression he saw an advantage
to Gopalakand and her sister states in all this business of independence for British ruled India, which had suddenly,
with the advent in the United Kingdom of the Labour administration become as *de rigueur* as a war aim; like uncon-
ditional surrender, the Beveridge plan and the Nuremberg
trials. Sometimes he talked about Gopalakand's age-old
treaty with Britain, the paramount power, as one might talk
about the deeds to freehold property, secure in ancient
lights, as a piece of sacred paper setting down inalienable
rights and obligations, one that would protect Gopalakand
through thick and thin, leave her free, independent and
benevolently autocratic if British India became free and
independent and what he called a sub-democracy of pseudo-
intellectuals, fat bannias and religious maniacs. There was,
in his talk, always an underlying note of jocularity. It did not
puzzle me because everything he said and the way he said it
only lapped around me like water around a stone embedded
in sand in a place beyond the reach of even a normal tide—
and it far from puzzles me now when I recollect it; nothing
about him or his carefree attitude puzzles me, although
sometimes when I have skimmed through the books that
have been written about this period in Indian affairs I have
paused, been puzzled *then* by the sense of crisis they communicate, and the lack of remembered crisis on the terrace
of the Residency which wasn't only due to my state of partial
detachment, but was in the air and the stone and behind the
brown, happy, extrovert eyes of Dingy Row's son. Independence had been a goal for so long that it had achieved a mythical quality. It could not stand up to the solidity of that

palladian mansion or the straight Roman road down to the cantonment, the town and further, to the palace where Sir Pandirakkar sat on the gaddi in the kind of security kings must feel when under the friendly, protective eye and influence of another more powerful king. The weight of aspirations was always outbalanced by the greater weight of history and of things as they were.

"Stay on here," Dingy Row's son said to me on his last visit. I asked him what he meant. He said he meant there in Gopalakand, because there would always be a job for a chap like me providing I didn't mind a contract of service with "one of us potentate types." Beyond "contract of service" he was vague about what I should stay on for. He mentioned their defence services, their local chamber of commerce, what he called their legislative assembly which, I think, was made up of court dignitaries, land-owners, prominent local merchants (a touch of real democracy about that) and Dingy Row's relations; certainly it was a nominated and not an elected law making body. Father had been responsible for its development although not for its initiation, for it had existed in some form or another for twenty years.

I thanked him, said something about not being sure what I was going to do, and he left it at that, quite content, quite untouched really either by his offer or by my rejection by implication. He was going visiting in Baroda, or Mysore, or one of the other important states. There was at this stage, so I have gathered since, a kind of tentative solidarity, the leftovers of earlier attempts at federation between the princes— a bit late in the day for anything to come of it because their days were numbered. A month or so after I had gone back to England the Viceroy assured the Chamber of Princes that in attempting to form a constitution for a free and self-governing India within the British Commonwealth no changes in the princes' relationships or treaty rights with the British Crown would be made or even initiated without their consent. I imagine there was no real sense of urgency. Perhaps independence for British India was looked upon by the princes as a kind of forthcoming attraction, an arena spectacle for which they must book seats, jockey for positions from which they could view it to their own best advantage. A few months later the British cabinet mission had to explain that independence for British India would mean the end of paramountcy, the end of treaties the British no longer had the means to adhere to. The states would be free to make their own arrangements, which of course meant cut adrift to fend for themselves. Even then I have the feeling that on the terrace of that palladian mansion the air (and it would have been hot, being May) struck the cheek not much more hotly. What, after all, was independence? Maybe still only a carrot (coloured pink like so much else in an apparently unchanging, unchangeable world) which the "jackals" were expected to fight over until Kingdom Come.

It is possible that there were subtle winds blowing which carried political and emotional scents so new and foreign to me that I did not detect them for what they were, but I believe the restlessness that presently came to plague me was set off by the absence of any such winds, by the stillness in fact, the stagnation, the sense of a long and perhaps endless imprisonment imposed by something old and dead-handed which had nothing to oppose it.

When I had seen my thousand things in the immediate vicinity I turned at last, again, to people I knew and the people who lived in the Residency with me, but as a stranger coming to them refreshed. This would have been about the middle of November. Coming to people again I came first to Cranston, from Cranston to Aunt Sarah, because it was she who had assumed the role of my caretaker, the looker-after of the daily needs, the small amenities for my bedroom-dining-room-terrace existence, and there came a day, obviously, when some hunter-home-from-the-hill look in my eyes encouraged her to say, "Tell me about this Dr. Cranston," which shows I had mentioned him in a way that made her mark him but resist him, store him away until she deemed the time had come when the memory he invoked would hurt nobody.

When she said, "Tell me about this Dr. Cranston," I told her something, not all. It was not being able to tell her even the all I could be articulate about that aggravated the restlessness. I can now only set it out in the way it applies now, which isn't quite the same way it applied then, but is the relevant, the within-context way. And it is no easier for that. The edge, the cutting-edge of Pig Eye, was blunted permanently during the days on the terrace when in an older, tireder way, I reaffirmed the youthful belief I had acquired on the banks of The Water that life was "not half bad," reaffirmed it by acknowledging the interest and fascination of what I was surrounded by and could not afford to be blind to.

2

It happened like this:

I went to sleep in a place where native rubber-tappers had worked before evacuating to the south. I was dirty, exhausted, but a free man. I woke when the Japanese kicked me in the backside. They shone torches into my eyes and shouted. I looked to see what I could of my own men but I was alone with the Japanese. I called out to my sergeant, a man named Treffewin, and got my face punched. They bound me by the wrists and put a guard on me where Sergeant Treffewin had left me saying, "Get some kip, sir." In the clearing beyond the trees there were lights, torches. There hadn't been any firing. I heard Treffewin's voice. "Captain Conway! Sir!" He sounded frightened. I sang out,

"I'm here. Are you all right?" but got no reply from him, only another blow from the guards.

In the morning they showed me Treffewin's body and, separately, his severed head. The rest of my depleted company had already been marched away but their rifles and equipment were still lying around. I had been used to counting men. Automatically I counted the rifles. In the last few weeks the battalion had suffered.

We were a West Country territorial regiment. I had joined it in England in 1939 and later been commissioned into it. Our record was neither glorious nor inglorious. It didn't exist. We defended beaches at home from 1939 until we went to Malaya six months or so before the Japanese cut through the country like wire cutting through cheese. The battalion had hardly fired a shot. Our casualties were from bombs and artillery. Our minds were blank from lack of sleep and information. We didn't feel, as someone once grumbled to me, like pawns in a game of chess; how could we when we couldn't see the board? The trees got in the way. We felt more like an expedition caught up in a tribal battle whose combatants we never quite clapped eyes on.

I saw my twenty men later that day when the Japanese took me to Sungei Kelong. This was a village where battalion had had its last headquarters. My men were roped together by their wrists and ankles. They were being made to hobble around in a circle. The Japanese were pricking them with bayonets. I got the impression that they had been going around in a circle for a long time. My arrival was the signal for something else to begin. The youngest, a fair, good-looking man called Bracegirdle, was cut away from his companions, stripped, held by the shoulders and ankles and sexually assaulted three times. After each man had finished with him he was jerked upright, twisted around and made to look at the man whose turn was coming next. When there seemed to be no more comers they let him go. He tried to stand but kept falling to his knees. He started banging the trodden earth of the compound with his fists.

They took him away then. As they dragged him past me he saw me where I stood fast manacled and tight gagged. He said, "Oh, sir, help me." I closed my eyes, having seen where they were taking him and the two Japanese NCOs waiting for him. I could close my eyes, but not my ears to his whooping shrieks when one of them finally achieved what must have been more than superficial penetration.

In the evening their officer arrived. I was taken to him. He apologized for what had happened to Bracegirdle. He said that his men had expected to find women in Sungei Kelong and had been angry to discover that the civilian population had melted away. Melted away is the expression he used. He spoke excellent English. I asked him whether the men who had assaulted Bracegirdle had been punished. He said that they would be. I didn't believe him. I asked permission to visit my men. He said he would give permission as soon as I had given him a bit of information. He asked me to explain the tactical situation that had led to the remnants of the company being in the Sungei Kelong rubber estate where his own men had caught us napping. I went through the fiasco of giving him only my name, rank and number. I couldn't have explained the tactical situation even if I had wanted to. I didn't know it. Nobody knew it. "Stay there, Bill," the adjutant had said, "until we pull you back." We had stayed there. The perimeter guard must have gone to sleep. I blamed myself. I felt disgraced and filthy. I knew the names of the flanking units but that was all. I knew the Japanese officer would come to them. He did.

He left the room to give the guards elbow room for what they had to do to me. Halfway through I thought: What is this for? I couldn't think that it was for anything, only perhaps for somebody, Bracegirdle and Treffewin. I should have stayed awake. I should have guarded the perimeter my-self. Presently the guards changed their technique, took off my boots and socks and lighted cigarettes.

When I visited the men I had to do so on all fours. They were still roped together, herded into a kind of stockade from what I could make out of it in the dark. My guard shone a torch onto me when I spoke and onto them when one of them replied. Bracegirdle was asleep or unconscious. Someone had thrown some sacking over him. I asked them how he was. They said they didn't know. Most of them were Cornishmen. I had always found them slow and dreamy as if they had been hypnotized from childhood by the sound and rhythm of the sea.

I told them to hang on. It was all I could find to say. I said, "Hang on if you can, lads." Most of them were older than I. I was always coming up against that sort of thing. One of them said, speaking for the others, "Hang on to what, sir?" Even in adversity the habit of politeness stuck. I said, "On to your lives," and wondered later whether I shouldn't have said something more suitable, like, "On to your cour-age." But that is all fable. The guard grabbed my shoulder and shouted. My time was up. I guessed I might never see them again. I said, "Good luck," and a few of them said, "Good luck," in return. One of them called out, "Don't let them bash you again. Tell them everything. We did." Crawl-ing back to my own little kennel I heard myself whimper-ing: not for broken security or their lost honour or my useless, silly silence, but because the pain in my feet was becoming unendurable.

I was sent north by lorry and train and then on foot (my arms slung around the cracking shoulders of two compan-ions) to Pig Eye. There the prison doctor, himself a prisoner, this man, Cranston, saved my feet from going gangrenous.

I was twenty-three then and Cranston would have been

thirty-two or thirty-three. He was of medium height, thin—
the kind of thinness through which you can count the nob-
bles on a man's spine when he stoops. His hair was thin too,
mousy brown, hanging in a lick over his pale forehead. He
was always pushing the lick back, trying to get it to stay put.
When he had pushed it back, he had another habit of flicking
the tip of his long bony nose, sniffing and saying, "Right!"
When he was feeling pleased about something he pronounced it "Raight!" rolling the "r" and isolating the "t."
He has lost the mannerism since but you can still see daylight through his fingers. His arms were long and skinny and
the veins coursed through them like overloaded electric cables. He had flat, broad wrists, a grip like a vice, a hairless
chest.

There were nearly a thousand men in Pig Eye then. The
Japanese were turning it into a base depot. They used the
prisoners to build an aerodrome and a system of roads. The
Indians were kept separate from the British. The camp was
divided into three, Indians, British, sick-bay compound.
After a while a lot of the Indians were suborned and formed
themselves into a unit of what was called the Indian National Army which was inspired by Subhas Chandra Bhose.
I never really found it in my heart to blame them. We had
done a poor job of protecting them from their enemies. This
INA unit was enlisted for guard duty. Those Indians who
refused to join the unit were sent away, but some of them
came to the sickbay to be treated for injuries; mostly for
burns from being held over a fire, or ruptures, or internal
lacerations caused by sharpened bamboo stakes. At first we
thought the Japanese had tortured them but a Rajput sube-
dar said his chief torturer was his own Havildar Major who
had assumed the INA rank of lieutenant. He said his orderly
also suffered, had been beaten to death with leather belts.
He said, "Sahib, I wish to die." He was ashamed of his own
people.

By now I was getting around on crutches, helping Cranston.

The sick-bay was a long, low structure of upright posts roofed with atap thatch, walled with rush blinds that rolled up and down. When I first arrived it was some thirty feet long. In the end it was three times that length. The earth of the compound was raw red against the emerald green fronds of the banana leaves. Beyond the compound were the Japanese; beyond the Japanese the British and Indian compounds; and then the plain, red and green. Beyond the plain were the hills. Whichever way you looked you saw hills. Pig Eye was the flat bottom of a shallow saucer and trembled all day with the sound of aircraft. So long were we there that once when a lone American bomber flew high above it someone said: "That doesn't sound like one of ours."

On the roof of the sick-bay there was a red cross worked from squares of parachute silk. This was an outward sign of the neutrality Cranston carried inside him as a doctor and as a man. Returning to the compound from an errand to the outside world it got that you could sense it. In the sick-bay compound the air came differently on the cheek. After a time even the Japanese acknowledged it. Cranston was called one night to look at one of their soldiers who had complained of violent pains in the stomach but who, Cranston suspected, had been kicked back on parade. He diagnosed an acute appendix. He said he would operate himself because the man would never stand the ten-mile journey to the Japanese military hospital. He sent a message to the sick-bay and I collected his bag of instruments and a precious bottle of chloroform. He operated on the man, using the scrubbed top of a mess table, in the light of kerosene lamps, and saved his life.

As a reward they gave him the red silk for the cross. He had asked for it regularly on the first of every month. In the early days he had been beaten for asking; then it became a joke. The guards outside the commandant's office always knew what Cranston had come for when he walked up to the white line and bowed. They laughed. The commandant got into the habit of coming to the head of the steps leading from his veranda, shaking his head, laughing too. Even Cranston laughed. He stood there having made his bow, grinning. When the red silk was finally hauled onto the roof it seemed as if the whole camp came to watch. You could hear the laughter thrown back across the plain from the echoing-board of the hills.

Cranston was a Quaker but there was nothing mealy-mouthed about him. In the early days when he was still try-ing to save my feet I cried out once. "For the love of God, stop." He stopped. Opening my eyes I found him watching me. For a while we stared at each other. He said, "Well, I stopped. Oughtn't I to bloody well start again?" And he threw me his own handkerchief so that I could bite on it.

The camp had literally grown up around Cranston and his one-man mobile dispensary. The British had built a fair-weather airstrip in Pig Eye in 1941. When the Japanese took it over during their victorious sweep down the Malayan pen-insula they found Cranston there with a truck for which he had no petrol and a score of badly wounded men who had been left to die, whom he had discovered by chance, whom he had refused to abandon. At one time, between the evacu-ation of the area by the British and the arrival of the enemy, there had been some hope of the wounded being taken out by air but no aeroplane came. Cranston, who was a civilian and whose work was purely voluntary, saw it as his duty to tend the sick, succour the dying and await capture.

It had once puzzled me why the Japanese had let him stay once they got to Pig Eye. He said that he just refused to budge and that then they used him as a collecting point for the halt and lame. He looked after some of their own soldiers as well. He thought the fact that he was a civilian doctor helped. If his presence hadn't happened to coincide with the Japanese commander's decision to turn Pig Eye into a base depot and use p.o.w. labour it would have been a different story, but it was good for morale to ignore the factor of coincidence, to look upon Pig Eye as grown up there because Cranston had disallowed the Japanese to plant it anywhere else.

In the three and a half years Cranston and I were at Pig Eye we had three commandants. There had been a fourth but he had gone before I arrived. The camp was called Pig Eye in his memory. The first commandant I knew was Pig Eye's successor. We called him Sanitary-San. He was a hygiene fanatic and went about with a fly whisk accompanied by two orderlies armed with flit sprays. He used the whisk to swat men as well as insects but smiled when doing so. There wasn't much harm in him. He was there throughout the time that I was bed-ridden and through the period when I trundled around in a kneeling position on a little wheeled and padded platform Cranston had got one of the men to rig up for me, which I propelled with my hands and which was called Conway's Chatanooga. Sanitary-San was there, too, during the period of the crutches. I had been walking fairly normally for about a month when he was posted away.

When the incoming commandant inspected us I was standing next to Cranston.

"So you are doctor," the major said to Cranston, pointed his cane at me and added, "Who is he?" "He's my assistant, also doctor," Cranston said. "Two doctor," the major said. We were wearing nothing but trousers. He made us turn away. He hit each of us across the back with his cane. He made us turn round again and slapped each of us in the face. "Doctor," he said, "see pain but not often feel it." He walked off between the line of makeshift beds. Cranston made to follow him as if to be on hand to answer any questions about his patients. One of the new commandant's retinue who had been friendly in the past placed a hand on Cranston's chest and said, "No, no, no," but Cranston pushed him away, telling me to stay where I was and look after things if necessary. The commandant moved slowly, glancing from one bed to the other. He knew Cranston was following him but ignored him. When he stepped out into the sunlight he made a sign and Cranston's arms were taken by two of the NCO's. He was sent back to the sick-bay in the evening. His eyes were black. "I'm sorry," he said, "I may have got you in for something. He doesn't like doctors."

I knew that he had described me as his assistant in order to help me. I thanked him but reminded him that my wholly military identity must appear in the camp records and that it was likely, with the new commandant sorting us out, I should first be punished as a malingerer and then sent back to work on the roads or the aerodrome. Cranston never considered such boring administrative details as records. For him facts spoke for themselves. The facts in this particular case were that from the beginning of my convalescence I had worked as his assistant, had been accepted as his assistant by Sanitary-San and his staff. I worked as his assistant because I wanted to help him, repay him for saving my life or for saving me from being a cripple; also because it was more comfortable than working out in the sun. I was conscious of that at the time and have to admit to it now. Night after night he talked across the narrow space between our beds, describing the pathognomonics of the diseases whose progress we tried to arrest during the day, and during the night as well. We took it in turns to sleep, but I often had to wake him to cope with problems beyond my amateur capabilities. I was a willing listener, an eager student.

Cranston was the first man I ever envied. He communicated a sense of burning purpose. He had the courage of

deep-held convictions. He was not a fake. What he was doing
in Pig Eye struck me as the only worth while thing there was
left in the world to do: save life, ease suffering. Perhaps it
was my obvious and flattering attention to his work that first
made him select me from a score of other men to stay on and
help. I used to hope it was something deeper, his recognition
of me as a man in whom the war had revived the old sense
of impending duty but turned it into something else: the
need to contribute something of value.

Within a few days of his arrival the new commandant im-
pounded the medical supplies. "When you want you ask," he
explained to Cranston, and smiled.

Cranston's nightmares began. He moaned in his sleep and
said, "Dane. Watch it Dane!"

"Who's Dane?" I asked him when he woke from the first
of these dreams. "Dane?" "Yes, Dane. You were talking to
someone called Dane, telling him to watch it." "Dane's what
I called a man called Daintree," he said. "I dreamed the
Japs had got him too."

Once Cranston stood in a downpour, in the open where
the new commandant had told him to stand. He stood for
four hours with his palm held out. At the end of four hours
an orderly walked out of the camp headquarters hut and
placed two aspirin tablets in Cranston's hand, told him he
could go. Cranston came back, dazed, his hand still out-
stretched, the aspirin disintegrating in the rain and warmth
of his palm. I scraped what I could into a tin mug of water.
A patient died. The aspirin would have done him no good.
The attempt, the gesture, was all. "I'm a coward," Cranston
said. He said Daintree wouldn't have stood it. Daintree
would have stormed in. "Daintree would have beaten the
major over the head. He'd have got aspirin. He'd have got all
the drugs out of that little white cupboard."

And while I wasn't looking Cranston went back to camp

headquarters, returned an hour later with a whole file of tablets and some quinine, but sweating, grey in the face. His shoulders were brick red and welted from the blows of a rattan. "It's what I have to do," he said. "Each drug has its price." Swallowing my fear I reminded him that there were two medicos in Pig Eye. He looked at me for a long time and then nodded. For a month we took it in turns to earn the drugs the major kept hidden, which he meant to sell in Penang on his end-of-tour leave but which he was prepared to sell there in Pig Eye in return for our submission to his sadistic pleasures. When he had gone and his successor proved more tractable Cranston said, "We added a new dimension to the Hippocratic Oath," and smiled in self-deprecation.

I had to squeeze Cranston's life story out of him bit by bit. I needed to do this. It was essential to me to know in what way it differed from my own. As men we had something in common, or so I felt: a demon of unrest, a disturbance of the spirit which in his case seemed to have been harnessed to the business of healing the sick; in mine, to nothing.

From the day in 1936 when Father said, "You think it all eyewash," I had virtually cut him out of my life. As a soldier I kept my letters for Ethel and Walter. Now, in Pig Eye, and although he had met my silence with his own silence, this estrangement weighed on my conscience. I tried to talk about it to Cranston but the way I told him left him simply not knowing what my problem had been. He saw it all as cut and dried. My father, for his own reasons, had decided I shouldn't follow him in the service. What more did I want, Cranston asked, a blue print of his complexes, or a blue print of my own?

I said I wanted neither, no longer even wanted a blue print of his reasons, only the answer to a question. Was he, behind that Political Department face, fond of me? Had I mistaken an acute shyness, total inability to show affection, for indifference? In Pig Eye I was a lot taken up with a concern that someone outside it, someone closer in blood than Walter and Ethel, should care a damn what happened to me. It was softness, pure p.o.w. sentimentality, as compulsive an idea as the word home was, then, a compulsive word, always slipping out, not in talk so much as in singing when there was permission to sing.

If Cranston had not been in Pig Eye I might not have been conscience-stricken about Father. Cranston made me want to clear the decks and once more set a course. What had been bred and nurtured in me as a sense of duty and purpose and then stifled in 1936 was touched off again by Cranston. This man was on fire in the way I had thought of myself as cut out to be, destined to be; and watching Cranston at work it occurred to me for the first time in my life that my father might have disliked his job and only stuck to it because he felt it his duty to do so. Cranston so obviously stuck to his job because he loved it. It was not a job, it was his life. Without it he might stop breathing. I had never met anyone like him before. I had to meet him before I could realize this. The illusion of my life had been that a man should love his job, be dedicated to it, born to it. When I met Cranston I saw that he was the only man I had ever met who did and was. I had not found the City a breeding ground for the spirit of endeavour.

I told him so. He said, "You should have met Daintree."

Cranston's father was nothing. He called him nothing. He slept, Cranston said, and woke and ate and went to the office and, Cranston supposed, made love at least once in his life seeing that he himself had been born. He also made money and survived the slump. The house was empty, what Cranston called empty. He wanted to fill it but didn't know how. Daintree was an old boy at the school he went to. He gave them a lecture when he was home on leave from the East.

Cranston went up to him afterwards and said something like, "Sir, how do I become a doctor?" Daintree asked him why he wanted to be one. He replied, "I want to feel that I'm alive." He was sixteen. Daintree said, "You fool boy. You bloody fool boy," and cuffed him quite hard on the ear. He was what Cranston described as a huge bear of a man. He told Cranston to qualify first, then write to him and he'd tell him how to become a doctor then.

Cranston qualified but he did not write to Daintree. He didn't write to Daintree for three years. It took him three years of work in a hospital to feel that he was not a doctor. For a time he felt like God. Feeling like God turned him, he said, to God. He took Catholic instruction. The priest told him one day that he was nearly ready to be received. The phrase, heard often enough before, suddenly appalled him. He did not like the idea of being received. He told the priest that if he had to be received that meant he was an outsider at the moment. He did not feel like an outsider. He became a Quaker as what he called a more practical exercise in humility and wrote to Daintree. Daintree replied from Java, briefly, saying in effect: "Come and take a look at this place where a man's life expectation is thirty years as against three score and ten."

As soon as he saw Daintree in Java he gave up everything to work with him. He worked with him for nothing for two years until Daintree kicked him out, saying, "Beat it, Cran. Find your own burnt offering."

I asked Cranston what Daintree had meant by burnt offering. He said he'd taken it Daintree meant a job that could be offered up like a sacrifice.

A sacrifice to what, I asked.

God knows, Cranston said, and smiled his oddly sweet and innocent smile so that I could take it either way without embarrassment.

There was a technique, Cranston said. You found yourself somewhere remote where nobody in his right mind wanted to go. You shoved the flag in and said, Well now, this is it, the altar. Where you'll make your burnt offering. Daintree stuck his in isolated communities which suffered from yaws. Cranston stuck his in the floor boards of a mobile dispensary after Daintree had wheedled the money out of the foundation Daintree worked for. Cranston went out to Malaya in 1940 and toured what he called the backwaters. He said that the medical missions hated him, that the doctors in the hospitals despised him, that they all envied him a bit because they knew he was "onto something, closer than they were to what medicine was all about."

"What is it all about?"

"Going out to look for the sick," he said, because sickness was misery, often too great a misery for the sick to go looking for a cure.

Whenever Cranston exaggerated I felt he did so to point some kind of moral. In Pig Eye I didn't see fully what he was getting at, but I was hungry most of the time, thinking with my belly and my heart and not with what I was given to think with. But my belly told me Cranston had something to say to me, so I stored him away, piece by piece, day by day, with the magpie habit of a prisoner who is not sure where his next meal is coming from; and added the idea of a burnt offering to the complex of ideas that made up the past and the future. He made me feel that everything was before me. This was an achievement, considering the circumstances. When I recognized that this was what I felt, I saw how much it resembled the feeling I had had as a boy in Tradura where everything and everybody conspired to point me, like a pony at a jump, to a life of high service in order to be worthy of my father and of what he represented. In Pig Eye, with Cranston fighting the diseases of beri-beri, malaria and dengue fever, and feeling myself inflated by little puffs from the winds of fulfilment that blew about in his wake, I forgave my father and asked his forgiveness, thinking that doing so I'd be right one way. Being a prisoner and having no idea whether I should live to see any member of my family again, this was something it was necessary for me to do.

About a month after his arrival I was sent for by the new commandant, the man who succeeded the sadistic major. Like Sanitary-San there wasn't much harm in him. He was elderly and given to outbursts of vindictiveness you felt it didn't take him long to regret. Mild-tempered as he fundamentally was, he found it wearisome to sustain reigns of terror begun during these fits of anger. But his lieutenants went in awe of him and he must have impressed his superiors with the efficient way he ran the camp and got results from the labour because his rule extended right up until our release. We called him Rice-Kraut. He had a Prussian air, a square head and close-cropped hair that sprouted at the back of his crown like the business-end of a scrubbing brush. I admitted I wasn't a doctor, expressed surprise that anyone should think I was. He sent me into the British compound to follow the life of an ordinary prisoner.

I've forgotten how long it was before he sent me back to work again with Cranston in the sick-bay—three, four, five weeks; but on every one of however many days it was Cranston asked for my reinstatement with the same determination he had shown when asking for the red silk with which to make an identifying cross. In the end Rice-Kraut had him standing out in the sun for half-an-hour at a time. Even then, it was said, Cranston shouted upon arrival and upon dismissal, "Commandant, where is my assistant?" or, "Commandant, give me back my number one." He wore Rice-Kraut's resistance down, wore down his bad temper. Rice-Kraut was decent enough. If there had been more food for us I don't think he would have kept any back.

I asked Cranston whether I was too old, had left it too

late to study medicine after the war. He said, "You'll know when you get out." He didn't throw cold water on the plan, encouraged me in many practical ways, took to discussing theory and to drawing diagrams of organs, cells and tissue. He was prepared to help but was never convinced that the ambition would stand the test of freedom, of leaving Pig Eye and returning to my own environment. He knew that a real sense of vocation for medicine was missing. Eventually he said, "Your idea of studying medicine's a form of gate fever. Don't criticize yourself later."

Cranston had gate fever too.

The fact is that in Pig Eye, for the first and only time in my life, there was nothing in the physical environment to distract me from contemplation of human misfortune. It was all damnation and no magnificence. Dora's old woman in rags was there day and night in the guise of hunger, thirst, dirt, the weals left by a rattan, the bruises implanted by fists and boots. The eye fell on nothing, the hand touched nothing that could prompt you to feel life wasn't half bad, or that could give pause to the belief that the present was only supportable in terms of keeping oneself and other people alive for the better future that had to lie beyond it. If you thought there wasn't any future you were finished, because you couldn't have shrugged it off, you couldn't go out on a drunk, or even have a drink, you couldn't tuck a good breakfast under your belt, smell aromatic coffee, get pleasure from the satin-texture of the pages of *The Times* folded into four. If you thought the future held nothing for you you succumbed and it was the end of you. You had to have gate fever to come through it at all. Without Cranston and Cranston's work my fever might never have set in even if I had recovered without his aid from my burnt and suppurating feet.

In Cranston the fever took the form of wondering and worrying about what had happened to Daintree. He told

me recently that not a day had gone by that he didn't worry
about him, because Daintree was getting on and might not
get through an experience like Pig Eye if he were in a
Pig Eye of his own, which was likely. To find Daintree and
to make sure that he was still alive had been as important
to Cranston as my half-formulated plan to study medicine
had been to me. He said that in a way Daintree had been
with us in Pig Eye, that Pig Eye wasn't over for him until
he'd tracked Daintree down.

I had no Daintree to find. Pig Eye was over when it was
over; but there are gaps in the picture of its actual ending.
I remember the senior British Officer coming into the sick-
bay and saying, "I've been talking to Rice-Kraut. It's finished.
We're taking over." There had been signs and portents,
false alarms, but his statement carried quiet conviction—
there wasn't any doubt this time. Emotionally we were
ready for it but after the initial waves of hysteria a physical
inertia settled. There was, you see, nowhere to go. There
had been no aircraft on the strip for a month and overnight the depots and stores had become virtually deserted
by both men and transport. There was left a bare handful
of Japanese troops and these kept out of the way during
the operation the senior British Officer conducted to take
over the administration. There were, it is true, parties got
up for what was called scouting around. There was nothing
to scout for, nothing to be gained except the important
pleasure of walking out of the camp and down the road for
a mile or two, free men in a free but uninhabited world.
The parties drifted back. It was several days before a jeep,
driven by unfamiliar jungle-green clad British soldiers
brought us into contact with our old, our natural selves, and
then the freedom we had was light-headed, heavy-footed.
We felt we couldn't tolerate the drawn-out process of jour-
neying from Pig Eye. We wanted to go home but only in

the sense of arriving there. In my case, by home, I meant India where Father was.

One of the men in the jeep was a medical officer. Another was a war correspondent. The third was a soldier. They had clothes and miraculous equipment that made us feel like pygmies in a dark interior. They smelled of clean, stiff canvas and of that peculiar metal-pineapple stink I always associate with wireless sets and the pilots' cabins of aeroplanes and which must be a combination of the smells of rubber and cellulose spray. Except for the war correspondent, the pink in these men's cheeks looked artificial, almost unhealthy, like tubercular flush. They handed around cigarettes and chocolate but it was difficult to catch their eyes for more than a second or two. Their eyes were very clear, the whites startlingly white. I suppose they were filled with curiosity and ashamed of being so. The soldier left in the jeep that evening. The nearest liberating unit was miles away and he had to go back to them. A rumour went round that in the morning two squadrons of Dakotas would touch down at Pig Eye and carry us to Kuala Lumpur or Singapore or Rangoon. No one slept. The war correspondent came into the sick-bay. He was lean, poker-faced. He sat on beds and said, "Is there anything I can do?" He had the look of being withheld from himself in order that he should not be biased, too much or too little impressed. In later years I came across his name over articles about Korea and China and the United Nations, but for a long time now I've not heard of him at all. I thought I saw him once in Fleet Street, looking much the same, hands in overcoat pockets, expressionless, committed to his day, his age, moving across the bottom of its ocean like a blind, tough, enduring fish feeding on the invisible plankton of world affairs.

He came to me presently and said, "Is there anything I

can do?" I said what every man had said, jokingly, "Sure, get me out of here."

He asked me where to. I said India. He interrogated me gently. I recall getting into a tangle, or rather getting him into one, being clear in my mind that I wanted to go first to India to see my father and Aunt Sarah but being unable to find the sequence of words to express this idea to him properly, to clear up the confusion he was in, faced with a man who lived in England, had served in a British regiment that sailed from Liverpool direct to Singapore, but who wanted to go to India. The truth was that I did not actually trust myself to use the words home, Father, Aunt Sarah, Tradura. I was using a verbal shorthand to keep the conversation sane and level. I think he saw that this was so. He changed the subject, talked about Cranston, the camp, of what was close at hand and only on rising and because I followed suit, so changing the centre of gravity in our bodies, returned to the question of why I wanted to go to India. He had spent a lot of time in Delhi and Calcutta since the war in Burma had folded up. I talked about things a bit, then.

He had talked to scores of men. He must have had a prodigious memory. He never brought out a notebook in front of us. It may have been his habit not to do so or in this case due to a delicacy of feeling for our own feelings who had been so long reduced, in one sense, to identification on paper only. I think he took some steps about me and sorted out the strings I had to pull in order not to end up in Singapore shipping for home and played some part, without my ever knowing it, in getting information about my father's whereabouts to the authorities who supervised my journey and whose plans to send me to England I stubbornly resisted.

He left us the day after he had talked to me. Three days later the evacuation of the camp began by road for the

fit, by air for the sick. By the end of the week Cranston and
I and a few other men were all that remained of Pig Eye.
We were to go by road to a collecting point. And this is
where the details are lost, irretrievably, because Cranston
is as vague about them as I am myself. Cranston thought
that we set off together and that at the collecting point we
were separated. If either of us could fix a picture of the collecting point in our minds that would be a help but he, too,
remembers nothing clearly after the moment we stood together in the swept-out and empty sick-bay.

The sick-bay struck me as an unfitting background for
what had happened there. The thatch, the bamboo posts, the
poles—the whole engineering aspect of it was ruinous, it
was true, but it could have housed happiness as easily as
affliction and in that sense disappointed me, who was in-
tent on briefly reliving its miseries in order to savour my
luck better. Luck had lighted on our shoulders, released us,
and danced away because it had done its job and the rest
was up to us, as it always is.

I can think of no other experience in my life, either past
or to come, that has matched or is likely to match the experience of being delivered from Pig Eye, but it would be
wrong to forget or ignore the fact that at the time it was an
experience that eluded me. It eluded Cranston too, eluded
most of us, I imagine. There was a moment before it, when
it approached us, and afterwards a series of moments when
in a practical way it was with us but in a significant way
already gone. It was an experience without actual substance
and Cranston and I were probably seeking its substance
when we stood in the deserted sick-bay. It would be nice
if I could reconjure something symbolic, like a piece of
paper, something discarded, left there, a fragment of cloth
or an object one of us had used time and again but had
no further use for. But no, there wasn't anything like that.
I had my hand around one of the bamboo supports. I

was making marks on it with my thumbnail. I thought: How many times have I had my hand here, on this actual post, in this actual place? But you cannot say good-bye effectively to a room, a house, a place; you can only say it to another person. Unless the answer comes back: good-bye, good-bye, your farewell is never taken. To say good-bye in such circumstances is to try to commit yourself to what has no hold on you, to try to make it have a hold, to try to invest it with powers of release, blessing, redemption or whatever it is you feel is owing to you. It would be wrong even to say that the sick-bay was inscrutable. It was simply there, empty, a rambling, man-made construction, pieced together, lacking on the one hand the durability of stone and devoid on the other of the growing powers engendered by sun and water in the stout bamboo trees that had been lopped with choppers, slithered by flashing knives, in order to erect it.

I think it was in a Malayan kampong several miles south of Pig Eye that Cranston and I said good-bye to each other. A jeep was involved, one that I was getting into and he was standing by the side of because he wasn't coming with me to wherever I was going either to pull strings when I got there or because I had already pulled strings that had produced the jeep, the first of a series of jeeps, trucks, lorries and aeroplanes that took me to Singapore, Rangoon and Calcutta.

I left, I know, without knowledge of my final destination. Someone, perhaps prompted by the correspondent, sent a signal ahead of me. I think it was in Rangoon that I heard where Father was, although it may even have been in Singapore; but I plump for Rangoon because I seem to remember that the sandy red earth of Mingaladon airstrip reminded me, as I arrived, of the maidan at Tradura and made me wonder whether I would find Father returned there. Mingaladon was, in fact, nothing like Tradura, and

I had no real expectation of finding Father back in the district whose highest political office he had already held, but Mingaladon was a landscape closer to what I remembered as an Indian landscape and pointed what had been a bit of a let-down in Malaya when I first landed there as a soldier in 1941. I'm sure, too, that it was the sight of Mingaladon, its vague familiarity which suggested endurability, that ended my fear that Father might have died in the last year or two. Be that as it may, Rangoon or Singapore, there was an office, a man sitting at a desk who handed me a signal. My father was Resident in Gopalakand. He had returned as master to the house I was born in. He was now Sir Robert Conway, K.C.I.E.

3

I was an inch taller, almost as thin as Father. Now our positions on the banks of The Water were reversed. It was a fractional elevation of his eyes that was needed to meet mine. It made me feel when I had come out of my contemplation of the thousand things that could be seen from the terrace, that he had to justify himself, prove for instance that his work had been as valuable as Cranston's.

Aunt Sarah's remark, "Well, it's all over now," I interpreted as dismissive of Cranston. "Tell me about this Dr. Cranston," she said, and I told her as much as could be told, as much as was needed to convey the respect I held him in. And then she said, "Well, it's all over now, you're looking better," and went away to prepare cards for dinner places, or so I suspected, and I continued sitting on the terrace, smiling a cynical smile and thinking that it wasn't over because men like Cranston were never over, only things like bloody Residency dinners reached the stage when they

were over. The smile was cynical because I knew already in
my bones that I could never follow Cranston, that he had
been right when he hinted I had no similar vocation.

The landscape receded; the thousand things it contained
lost their individuality; the men and women who moved
in it began to worry me. I would think: Now, what's *he*
doing? Why's she doing *that?* From the terrace, India lay
in front of me, a land full of fragile people clothed in
cotton and moving sedately to their own mournful music.
I stopped sitting there, wandered through the grounds and
the rooms. The windows giving onto the section of terrace
where I had always sat were the windows of the ballroom.
The ballroom was long, narrow, empty, echoing; a parody,
in a sense, of all the ballrooms that ever were. Chandeliers
constructed of hundreds of glass pendants hung from the
high ceiling. Little chairs, gold-painted and red-upholstered,
lined the panelled walls. I heard the distant music of
Tales From the Vienna Woods and *The Blue Danube,* pictured the gyrations of scarlet sahibs and white memsahibs
and could not tell whether to think of it as a dance of the
dead or of the unborn. In the drawing room there were
gilt couches, tapestry chairs, alabaster busts of blind gov-
ernors, dark portraits of soldiers and statesmen standing
amidst rocks and trees, with dogs, and dead game, and
native servants at hand who were about to do their masters'
bidding. And there was a larger-than-life portrait of a
Rajput Prince, looking like Sir Richard Burton with mad
eyes and black moustaches, surrounded by peacocks and
murky shadows.

Once I sat on a chair by the marble imitation Adam
fireplace and thought: My mother sat here pregnant. Then
I moved to another, lowlier chair because I remembered
that in Gopalakand she had been the wife of the assistant
and may have entered the formal drawing room only on
sufferance. According to Sarah, in those days my father had

had rooms in what was called the East Wing, meaning the side of the house that faced east. She probably thought I wanted to see them, particularly the one I was born in. I never went up to them. I was waiting for Father to mention them. I should have liked to believe that his return as master to the Residency awoke tender memories but I did not want to invoke memories by referring to the past and this was because I suspected they might not be tender. I did not want to see him exposed in any way. I no longer wanted the answer to the question that haunted me in Pig Eye. I was afraid of it. The bare inch which gave me this physical superiority over him might have made me want to challenge him to prove that, as Old Very Light, he had hung incandescent over the terrains of feudal kings and scorched away injustice, but I shrank from the idea of using the physical superiority to force him into any kind of confession. I did not want him imposing himself on me as an embittered old man. I was at pains to preserve an illusion of the illusion of his one time magnificence; I suppose because I had seen too much unhappiness in Pig Eye, and resisted, by drawing back from them, the signs of unhappiness and discontent I expected to see at any moment blanch his face.

For the icy splendour had gone. He seemed to me to be diminished by his surroundings, by his knighthood which somehow squeezed him in between its Sir and its KCIE; by a manner towards him of Aunt Sarah's which occasionally looked like indifference. Now, when he happened to walk into a room or out onto the terrace, there was quite often a fractional hesitation, a strange jerky little movement of his head from left to right, a fleetingly blank look in his paled eyes, and you had the feeling that he thought: What's this? What am I doing here? His long, narrow face had hardly changed since last I saw him except in the sense that it had even more the look of having been used for a

long time, and had lost what I tried to recall as its special
quality but could not fix satisfactorily in my mind; the
closest I could get to what it had been was to acknowledge that it was no longer there and that its absence revealed how underneath it there must always have been this
texture of fleshy vulnerability.

There was nothing that we could say to each other of
importance, and to that extent nothing had changed. The
change had come about only in the reasons for our silence.
To talk to him, I mean really to talk, I should not have
been able to keep from asking questions: Why did you shut
me out? Did you never get over your Louise's death or
didn't you fundamentally care a damn? Is the dim picture
I have of you sitting by her death bed at Pankot with a ramrod back and your head covered by your hands, your elbows resting on your knees, a picture of a man overcome
in his stoic way by a grief deeper than *I* have ever known
or is it, as it sometimes struck me, the picture of a man
using the time to memorize some instrument of policy lately
come from Delhi, or rather from Calcutta, as it would have
been then, in 1924? Do you love me or do you hate me?
If you hate me, is it because I lived and your Louise died,
or because both of us were a threat to your splendour and
isolation? Was marriage to Louise a contract you embarked
on with your heart, or with your head, a duty you recognized a man drew near to in the course of his career and
then went through with, making as little fuss about it as
possible? Did you watch, in alarm, or in bitterness, your
Louise grow pale and delicate, and remember Little Ma and
the damp house in Suffolk? Were you afraid, from the day
I was born, that one day she would force you to turn a
ramrod back on Pankot? Was that the reason you shut me
out, or have you always shut out the world of the flesh? Why
did you have me whipped so hard, so hard that I carried the
marks for a year, longer than ever I carried the marks of the

Pig Eye major's rattan on my shoulders? Was it because I was flesh of your flesh and had lusted after the blood of a tiger, gone lusting after it in the company of little Dora? Why have you needed such isolation? Is it only Sarah you love? Has the isolation been worth it? Do you find Gopala-kand a fitting end to an immaculate career, or has Gopala-kand opened your eyes to how empty your life has been? Has your life been empty, Father? If not, how, inside yourself, have you really filled it?

When there were guests I usually ate alone, not only for my own sake but, having tried it once, for the sake of others, too, because I saw I was a kind of embarrassment sitting there with the marks of Pig Eye still on my cheeks; and after these solitary meals I had the run of Father's study, would sit there reading, whisky to hand, glancing up every so often at the hunting trophies of past Residents which stuck their heads inquisitively through the walls and sometimes reminded me of Aunt Sarah in her inquiring, sideways-on position. And one night, hearing the door open, I looked towards it and found Father had come in. He apologized, said he only wanted some papers, rummaged in his desk. The light, falling full on his head, showed the sparseness of his hair. He seemed to lose interest in the desk, stood up straight and for a second or two stared across the room in so striking a manner that I recollected the idea I had had of him, when a child, quelling a mutinous crowd with a look, like General Gordon. He seemed almost to have consciously pulled himself together, saying: This won't do, pull up, man, and squared himself into that heroic pose to face up to the shadows which glowered beyond the reach of the study light.

Moving, his eye fell on the chess board that I now some-times played with by myself, and then fell on me and for a few moments we did what perhaps we had never done in our lives before, stared at each other with minds cleansed of prejudice and misunderstanding, although not, in my case, filled with anything more forthcoming than inquiry.

He said, "Give you a game if you feel up to it," and crossed over, became lost in a contemplation of the predicament my white queen was in and the cunning stations taken up by my black queen's bishop and black king's knight.

I said, "We'll set it up again."

He drew a chair across to the table while I reset the pieces. I told him to take white. I wanted the opening move to be his. He advanced queen's pawn two squares. I blocked it. Then he moved queen's bishop's pawn one square. I followed suit. He brought out queen's knight and I brought out king's knight and the game was on.

Within the hour his king faced death; the white pieces I had taken were lined up along one side of the table, temples of misfortune on the road to his defeat. Only three pawns and his unbowed king's knight were left to defend their monarch from the *quietus* planned by my black queen and her remaining minions. I suspected him of having deliberately allowed me, up to this point, to win, but now that the end was near he proved stubborn. In his place I should have said, "Well, I resign!" but he kept on, not I think with any actual intention of making me lose my head (and my knight, as I did in the impatient business of chasing him round the board) but because his powers of concentration, now that he was cornered, were so tight-wound that only the movement of his checked and checked again king into a square where it would discover itself petrified, clearly and uncompromisingly, would have been enough to make him raise his head from the support of his left hand in an admission first to himself and then to me that the run for my money was over.

"Your maharajah's had it," I said. "Old Dingy Row's had his chips."

The symbolism of the game was striking. My black pieces were what Dingy Row's son had called the jackals—the Indian politicians of British India; and the white court these same jackals opposed and brought to disintegration was one of the feudal courts which men like Father had lived for and sometimes, like the agent in Ranpur who was murdered in the 'thirties, died for.

My queen got in at the back and mopped up the remaining pawns, one by one, until only the king's knight, my father, was left to defend his monarch.

That's *you*, I thought. King's knight, rajah's knight, impotent, beaten, but stubborn as hell. Stay on here, Dingy Row's son had said to me, but as what he hadn't been sure. All he had been clear about was that his princely father and his princely father's peers had stood by the Crown as always, all through the war, that the Crown would stand by them and not let the jackals feed. Wavell would see to it. So would men like my father.

But Wavell wouldn't be able to see to it. Neither would men like Father. They were pawns dressed up as knights. Logic demanded that one day we should say to a land we had loved and hated, bled and bled for, felt in our cold northern bones as a source of warmth and in our God-rotten souls as a burden too hot to handle: Yes, we will go, we will go on such and such a day. Logic demanded that we add: And on that day we are finished, the princes are on their own, it is up to them to whom, if anyone, they pay tribute. Logic demanded that at last our strange dichotomy of principle should be exposed, that in the end the King-Emperor's crown should be revealed as sitting as crooked on his head as Aunt Sarah's hat had sat on hers after I had kissed her on Delhi station.

There was, after all, only one player at the chessboard: a man like Father, in whose tall and frigid person were vested the richness and power of a crown that played two-handed chess, moving the black pieces in a direction which had to threaten the white pieces his other hand zealously protected and moved too slowly, ah—far too slowly—in the direction which might, in time, have led to a perfect integration of the whole; so slowly that it was difficult not to see the laggardly pace as deliberate, as part and parcel of a bloody-minded game of divide and rule.

Did Father see it so? Did he see the situation like this, at all? Was it the illogic of the situation which appealed to him? Did it spread for him a faint, ghostly glow of improbability over every phase of his career and give him scope for observing from his sublime and natural position of detachment the ridiculous contortions men got into when they played a double game?

I leaned back and watched him, waiting for him to give me best. There was no expression on his face. You are dead, I thought. You have been dead for years. The dead feel nothing. I moved, restlessly, thinking of Pig Eye, and he looked up then, his thin lips twisting at one corner. "It looks like the end," he said. "I gave you too much rope in the beginning."

Too much, too little—what did it matter how much? It had bound me as a child to a house of the dying and now, looking around the room, it was a house of the dead, and I was not bound. I was bound to nothing. I had to get away.

I said, "I shall go home, soon, Father," and wondered whether the word home, which had slipped out, would have wounded him in any way. He was putting the pieces into their box, carefully, neatly. Presently he said, "I understand." I pondered the lingering echo of that casual remark, to judge what inarticulate disappointment might have been betrayed in it. I detected none. We sat on for a while in the kind of silence that falls when two people are in a room and the only sounds that would fill it are the sounds of words they have grown unused to forming with their tongues.

That night, next day, soon after, I don't remember exactly, there was a letter from Walter. The silence was filled then with the distant sound of muffled drums. He did not mention Ethel. He said, "I'm glad to hear from Sarah you've come through it. Don't rush things, that would be bad for your health, which must be precious just now. But I look forward to your return, old man, even if you elect not to come back into a world of affairs which at the moment must seem pretty remote to you."

Two years after that game of chess, when Father was alone in the world, Aunt Sarah dead and buried in the churchyard of the Protestant cemetery that lies at the foot of Residency Hill, the career he had followed for forty years came to an end more abrupt than the official and delayed retirement that coincided with it could have made it. Gopalakand, like all her sister states, was forced to surrender her autonomy to the province of the new self-governing dominion that bounded her frontiers, bounded all that flat plate of land that had seemed in my days there to be boundless. For the dominion had no romantic notions about princes.

I was in England when the end came; I was meeting Anne, holding her cold hand, trying to get my arm around that narrow little waist, the blood pounding in my neck, and between such stirrings there were these other stirrings, little proddings in my chest and behind my forehead of a wish to do well in the City, to make something of a name as an able young man who figured more and more in board room discussions. Like the world of the maharajahs, the old Conway world had gone. For me it had been buried in Pig Eye. Cranston had kept me alive. There was no more I could do to repay him. I could repay Walter for his understanding and repay myself in commonsense for what I had squandered on the dead. I had a flat in the Marylebone Road because Uncle Walter had stumped up the key money; I

spent week ends at Four Birches and at Anne's parents'
house in Esher; lunched at the Carlton Grill, Simpsons,
Pruniers, with other men who were scrabbling in that grey
post-war world for money, influence and power, and discovered I had this knack for the intricacies of investment,
for the expertise of dealing in figures and not commodities,
in goodwill rather than in goods, for bringing together men
for whom I cared little but whose coming-together profited
Uncle Walter and his partners and earned me tax-free bo-
nuses; and, in this gulf-stream warmth of embryonic prosperity, dealing always with shadows, never with substance,
I entered a new Elizabethan Age of merchants who sailed
the seas by cable and telephone and sat at mahogany desks
with their feet on crimson carpets, forgetting their youth.

This was the background against which I intermittently
followed the end of the British Raj, watched the revelations
take shape in the narrow spaces between the lines of news-
papers, and smiled because I was not part of it and preferred every so often to forget that I had wanted once so
fervently to be part; smiled because I was still young and
what was going was going because it was old and should
have gone long before, and yet, still, had the power to
nudge an old ambition if I walked down Whitehall, or,
back from the House, the long way around through St.
James's Park and up the steps past the statue of Clive whom
I utterly despised as a braggart and purse-liner but could
also envy and always saluted with a swing of my furled un-
brella onto my dark blue-suited shoulder.

And reading the accounts of this new decline and fall,
I was lost sometimes in admiration of the way we English
could twist an essential retreat until it looked like a voluntary advance, could seem to shrug our shoulders in paternal amusement at the antics the jackals got up to and tap
our feet in the background as if we had been waiting for
thirty years and not three months for them to decide what
to do about their freedom, could lop the chain of para-

mountcy and take the attitude that only the badly ruled
states would suffer. And I was a bit admiring of myself as
well, of the gaunt, shadowy-eyed shell of myself who two
years before had seen it all prophetically written in the
moves of black and white chessmen on a black and white
squared board.

Father wrote to announce his retirement, his change of
address. He had retired to a bungalow in the hills at a
place called Dhooni, where in the later years of his career
he and Sarah had become used to spending the hot weather.
He bought the bungalow when Sarah was still alive and his
retirement was always looming, always being delayed. Now
he lived in it alone and for this I was sorry because I no
longer needed anything from him. Our correspondence became heavier than it had ever been before: an exchange of
letters four or five times a year, but brief. In one of them,
in answer to my question asking him how he spent his
time, he said he was making a record of his career "in
case there may be some still interested in a closed chapter."
I sent him pictures of Anne which he thanked me for but
did not comment on.

He used to write on thin blue paper that smelled faintly
musty. His handwriting was old-fashioned, rounded, oddly
gentle. Towards the end I thought I detected a hint of
desolation in the bleak, clear-cut sentences that told me he
was well, thank you, that the weather was a shade cold for
the time of year, that he planned to have "one more look at
Kashmir, and perhaps Tradura and Pankot," and in the
last letter but one, which, with the last, I found when sorting
papers at Four Birches after Anne and I had finished with
each other, both of which I preserved and have continued to
preserve, he wrote referring to an invitation to Gopalakand.
He didn't say from whom. Dingy Row's son had succeeded
to the gaddi, but a gaddi divested of its authority. He said
he had declined the invitation, "not feeling quite up to
it," and commented:

"The old Maharajah is dead of course, I fancy killed by that business as I anticipated and could not ward off finally. It was for the son I did what I did, forgetting momentarily in the press of events that Gopalakand was no Hyderabad."

To this, I remember, I replied saying politely but without interest, "What was it you did?" which may have warned him that for the first time in his life he had opened, if by no more than a fraction of an inch, the door behind which he lived his private, secluded life. Perhaps he saw the warning as proof of failing faculties, and such proof as a sterner warning still. The letter that followed and in which he made no further mention of Gopalakand ended like this:

"I am not a rich man as you know, or if you have not known, always guessed. I had left my whole estate to your Aunt Sarah. When she died I changed my will of course, since you were then my sole surviving kin, apart from my brother, since deceased. Provision has been made for the upkeep of her grave and for my own which will lie next to hers and therefore need not bother you in any way. The bank, up there in Calcutta, are the executors, and would communicate. What little there is will come to you although it can't make much impression."

The letter was dated in the July of 1950. A month later he was dead. Anne read the Obituary Notices in *The Times* for a few days and said "How odd," when presently only a short, formal paragraph was printed. She would have liked larger public proof of her connection with a Knight Commander of the Indian Empire. The bank sent me an inventory of his effects and asked for instructions. In reply to my inquiry about the record of his career they reported that no such document appeared to exist. Perhaps he never really began it, or destroyed it before he had finished. With the proceeds of his estate Anne bought a coat of Persian lamb and we wintered in Majorca, installed Four Birches with central heating. From his coldness, as Anne remarked, there came this kind of warmth.

BOOK FOUR

Against the Wind

"I have never seen one alive, my love . . . They build in trees and feed on insects and berries, associating in flocks of forty or fifty, and flying always against the wind, as otherwise they would be buried in the abundance of their beautiful plumage."

(*Investigation or Travels in the Boudoir*, by CAROLINE HALSTED, 1837)

1

THERE are no tiger in Manoba: pigs and rodents which I've seen and the birds of paradise which I haven't seen. Accompanied by two Manobaon lads who were more upset than I when the promised display failed to materialize, I crouched for hours in a natural hide of trees high on a hill above the tribal valley Daintree had brought me to at last. We waited for most of one whole afternoon and again the following morning, watching the dawn in, and getting cramp. There was a distant wawking noise which the boys told me in sign language was their cry, but it never came closer. We went back down the hill to the outskirts of the village, to the hut where, a few hours before, I had left Daintree snoring over his empty bottle. The villagers rigged up a rough palanquin of bamboo and crisscrossed rope and we took Daintree home in this, one of his arms hanging loose, his white-maned head lolling. It reminded me of the bearing home of the Kinwar tiger; although it was raining hard and there wasn't an acid smell of sudden death.

When he sobered up he asked whether I'd had any luck with the birds, and commented, "They've killed them all off, I expect," and held his hand out for the bottle and glass his boy had hidden. I came back to my own hut and spent ten minutes trying to coax Melba out of her sulks. It was the first time I had left her alone overnight. I didn't trust my own boy to carry her safely from one cage to the other, so I left her in the small cage. I thought she would be afraid of the big cage in the clearing once the light faded and the jungle woke up all around her. She has been a long time in captivity. But she didn't thank me for my thoughtfulness. She resented being left alone. She kept her back to me to pay me out. In the end I told her she could sulk if she wanted to. I put the silk scarf over the cage, although it was broad daylight, and tore the lost day from the calendar Griffin has lent me to mark the running out of my sabbatical year.

Above the thick wad of dates whose flimsy leaves sometime come off in the hand two at a time, there's a sepiacoloured photograph of a ship unloading at a SIAT wharf, under a cloudy, straits and islands sky. The ship's derricks look like stiff fingers crooked to investigate her open hatchways. There aren't any people on deck, nor any on the wharf. It is a day when the ship has been left alone, and she takes the opportunity to satisfy her curiosity about her own cargo. I wonder whether she is disappointed to discover what she's been carrying; or whether she's dismayed to find the holds empty, and interprets this as proof that she had deluded herself, that she has ridden high on the sea in ballast and not, as she may have thought, low, laden heavily to the gunwales.

It is over a month since I added anything to this record. I asked myself the question: Have I been telling the truth? I saw how likely it was that Father, pausing in his own record, asked himself the same question and found that the answer was: No, not always; and so destroyed it. Had I really been like that as a boy? The boyhood attitudes were comically solemn. Had I been like that as a young man, and as a prisoner-of-war? Wasn't the little worm of conscience that forced me to admit it was better to work for Cranston in the sickbay than work on the roads and the airstrip evidence of the reality behind the illusion? Wouldn't it have been nearer the truth to say that I never had much in me at all, but was content to drift in whatever direction the wind blew me? Hadn't I been compensating for the revelation of an empty hold by scratching around for memories of rich, impossible cargoes?

Daintree found the manuscript one night. I was asleep at the time. He'd dosed me up against a bad bout of Manobaon tummy that had given me a high fever. When I woke I thought it was still night because the pressure-lamp was on and Daintree was sleeping, cradling his head in his arms, slouched over my table. I was astonished. There wasn't even a bottle on the table. I thought I must have been very ill, almost at death's door, for him to have sat up. Raising myself on my elbow I took in together the facts that it was morning and that all the pages of my manuscript were scattered on the floor; some face upwards, others downwards showing the red feint-ruled columns of Griffin's printed stores returns which he never uses and gives to me in pads of badly glued-together foolscap sheets. The glass and bottle were on the floor too: my glass and my bottle.

When Daintree woke up he didn't apologize, made no attempt to pick the pages up and put them together. His khaki shirt and trousers hang on him as clothes would on a beanpole if anyone ever bothered to dress a beanpole up. His thin, silvery-white hair reaches to his collar. When he wakes up his hands shake uncontrollably. His face is that of a lion too old and fierce to kill efficiently. He came to the bed, pulled my eyes about to get a good look at the whites. His fingers felt like arthritic, bony butterflies, until they got a good hold of my skin, then they were firm and dry on the cheek, like skinny lizards eyeing their prey.

"You're all right, now," he said. I said that was good, thanked him for looking after me. The alcohol he drinks in such terrifying quantities has an effect of brightening and darkening his eyes instead of filming them over. However drunk he is he never slurs his speech, never throws himself about or has that look of the drunk, that look of wires and cables collapsing under the weight of the body they're meant to hold upright. He uses his limbs violently, but incisively, and in the end he falls abruptly as if pole-axed, and his boy drags him to bed. His body transforms liquor into pure energy. Finally the energy becomes more than even his body can stand. I say even his body, because although he is wasted almost to the bone, his rib cage has the look of having been forged and shaped on an anvil or carved in wood in the Middle Ages by a man working for the church.

"Cran's wrong," he said, breaking the silence. I said, "Wrong about what?" He said he had never cuffed Cranston's ear, never called him a fool boy, never said in Java, "Beat it, Cran." It was Cran who'd said, "I'm off." Daintree had asked him where he was off to. To find his own burnt offering, Cran had said, because he wasn't going to share Dane's. "He got that right, he always called me Dane. It's why I called him Cran." He didn't wait for me to argue but turned and left the hut like an old Goliath resuming his search for David.

Later, collecting the scattered pages together, I saw how Daintree's reading of them had served its end. He had reminded me of the relativity of truth.

Perhaps it is I and not Cranston who was wrong about the burnt offering, but I don't think so. I think Daintree is wrong; although a phrase like burnt offering might have come more naturally to the Quaker. But even if Cranston wasn't wrong about which of them used the expression burnt offering, he may have been wrong about other things. There have certainly been times in Manoba when I've thought Cranston's concern for Daintree deeper than necessary. But that's not quite what I mean by wrong. I mean he may be wrong when he says Daintree is drinking himself to death (I look at Daintree in mid-bottle and see him outliving us all), wrong when he says Daintree can't last, wrong when he says Manoba's Daintree's last stop, the last place of all where the man who made a name for himself in tropical medicine can be kept as far away as possible from the ridicule of a world where Cranston who was once his disciple is now his boss. But Cranston isn't wrong to worry, or to take what has happened to Daintree to heart. Such concern is rare enough. And I suppose the facts can't be bucked. Daintree is dying. One day he'll fall pole-axed for the last time, although I doubt he'll do so while I'm still here. There is still sand in his glass—more than there is in mine—unless, when a particular smudge of smoke appears on the horizon and Griffin sends a lad up to help me with my luggage I send the lad back, go down myself and say to Griffin, "Cancel the passage, Lew."

Another example of Cranston's possible, unintentional misrepresentation, or of my own misunderstanding: the picture he gave me of Daintree when I talked to him before coming to Manoba. It was a picture of a sick and ailing man. That may be how Cranston sees him, having known him in his prime. But he mentioned the silver mane of hair and it could have been that alone which, Lear-like, drew the picture for me. He also mentioned Daintree's experiences in Java at the hands of the Japanese, and this was enough in itself to make me think of Daintree as beyond everything. Daintree was pent in what sounded like something not much bigger than a kennel for weeks—or months. Now that I know Daintree I imagine it as having been for months, because he's a man it would take months to turn into an animal. They made him kneel with his hands tied behind him and drink water from a bowl. They fed him with bones and biscuits. They took him out for execution three times and sent him back to his kennel to crouch there in his fouled trousers. His bowels emptied the moment he

saw the soldiers and prisoners lined up and the officer bar-
ing his sword, because he had seen a man's neck a quarter
cut, and then a half before it got severed. They broke him
in the end. They put a rope around his neck and led him
around the camp beating him to his all fours whenever he
tried to stand up. "I used to hear myself whimpering for
food," he told Cranston (so Cranston said). "If I'd heard
myself bark I should have gone mad." They did this to him
because—as Cranston had prophesied—he had stormed into
the camp office of his own Pig Eye and called the Japanese
commandant a bastard pig dog.

Recently I tried to talk to him about the Japanese, but he
stopped me. He said, "We must forget Bushido and think
only of Sayonara."

My picture of Daintree is different from Cranston's picture of him. When I say Cranston's picture I mean, of
course, my picture of Cranston's picture. It is hopeless trying to get at what we call the truth, but I had to ask myself
the question: Have I been telling the truth? before I could
arrive at what may be the only possible answer—arrived at
it with Daintree's help, because he said, "Cran's wrong."
The answer is that I've been trying to tell the truth about
people as I thought they were and about myself as I thought
I was. Thoughts are not without foundation, although they
are affected by other people's errors as well as by your own
and probably can't be divorced from the place they're
thought in. Manoba and the presence of Daintree may have
coloured mine. If I brought Tradura with my other recollections to Manoba, I must have taken Manoba to Tradura.
If I go into the forest I can, as I said in the beginning, take
the Kinwar tiger with me but in the midst of recollection
my eye must wander. The mind's eye and the real eye
merge. Daintree can ride an elephant in a procession or beg
for alms at the roadside. Anne can climb the hill from

Griffin's bungalow complaining about the heat; Cranston can sit with us flicking his nose on the night of the candles which can be celebrated here in the hut.

That is not real reality; but there is the reality of significance in it and it is where the drama of dull days lies. The arms of a day as you live it are not made for lying in, being hard and angular. Later you can lie in them, and the day is then transformed. You go back to it forewarned, wiser than it. Words that had never entered your head when the sun set on it now give it a substance it never had. You can also pick an old day up, like a shell, press it to your ear and hear the sound of the sea.

There are scenes, places. Not only their conjuration against a Manobaon background links them. Obsessions link them. There is the scene of my last blazing row with Anne; verdigris-green furnishings, scarlet splashes of small square scatter cushions, white walls, a reproduction of the Picasso dove: the drawing room of Four Birches in its final transformation. Here, she struck me in the face. The blow I gave her in return knocked her to the floor where she shrieked and scrabbled with her unpainted finger nails in the hide of the slaughtered sheep that decorated the hearth. To furnish that room and to clothe our bodies, animals had been flayed for wool and leather, teak trees had been dragged out by the roots, elephants had been chained by the foot and pricked by musky-smelling mahouts; the white, fibrous flowers of cotton plants had been plucked, baled, spun and woven, dyed by the secretions of vegetables and the reactions of chemicals; and there in Four Birches we consumed their remains with our eyes and the habit of our bodies.

We were Consumers. This was my obsession. The room confirmed our status as consumers, a status that carried with it an obligation to consume because there was no longer anything you could contribute as an ordinary man. Perhaps there never had been. In moments of ease or pleasure the obsession existed as an attitude that caused wry amusement. I went about my dead Uncle Walter's business doing what every man I knew was doing: manipulating other people's money, biting off a chunk of it for myself, giving as little as possible in return. But in moments such as that of the blazing row with Anne the obsession would burn the marrow out of my bones and I would strike out because it seemed then that quite apart from what an ordinary man couldn't contribute, the out-of-the-ordinary man was up against it too. There wasn't a square inch of earth that hadn't been discovered, trampled on, littered with cigarette ends and Kwikkaffy tins; not a square mile of ocean that hadn't seen the passage of a million balsa-wood rafts; not a social or political concept that hadn't been tried, tested and discredited, not an idea that hadn't been had before and been applied and then disowned; not an instinct that hadn't been written up by Freud or Jung, not a microbe that hadn't been bottled by Pasteur or Fleming; not an act of mercy left unperpetrated by UNRA or Schweitzer.

It had all been done. The moulds were cast. They only had to be serviced, filled with the molten sub-standard iron of inherited good intentions and upended to produce little tombstones of inferior, repeat performances.

Another scene, not the Four Birches drawing room this time, but the service flat I took in the bleak hinterland near Shepherd Market, when Anne and I had finished with each other, had spat each other out like slimy lemon pips. Four Birches was already hers by virtue of an earlier settlement and I was content to let her get away with those particular spoils. It had only been my home, the home I felt as home, for two short periods of my life: the first year of our marriage and the months I lived there alone with Uncle

Walter when I returned from Gopalakand in time for Christmas 1945, having put India behind me forever and left my father and Aunt Sarah within the silence and indifference I thought I should never try to break through again, for once more there seemed to be things to do, my way to make in a world that I still saw as full of things to be done and of people making their way. Uncle Walter shook my hand when I got home and neither of us spoke of Ethel but being Conways, poor emotional actors to a man, we tried to show each other in dumb charade that she was not forgotten, that the buzz bomb in the High Street, unlike the Germans, would never be forgiven; and so Gopalakand faded, and Pig Eye faded; Cranston wrote from Singapore to say that he had found out where Daintree was and was going out to get him; and this was important and yet unimportant. I put back weight. Anne appeared.

I never lost touch with Cranston. He worked in many different places, all over the East. He was in India twice. When we stopped exchanging letters we sent Christmas cards as if to keep a long-distance finger on each other's pulse. I thought of him when I sat alone at night in the Shepherd Market flat. He had gone to a lot of trouble to save my life, or save me walking around on stumps. I pictured him still touring the backwaters, tried to imagine myself helping him in some way, but it was difficult in those surroundings.

The rooms of the flat were painted and carpeted in toning shades of green, the furniture was figured walnut. The bed was covered with a crimson satin spread. White nylon-net curtains, stirred by gusts of air that rose in the inner well of the building, blew gently in above the gilded radiators. I felt that all the rooms in all the flats were like mine because mine did not feel original. The lift was narrow, also lined with figured walnut. It smelt of warm rubber and electricity. The globe of its ceiling light was rose-coloured and whenever I entered it I thought I might be cooked by infrared rays on the journey between the fifth and ground floors. The entrance hall was furnished with a little upright chair with claw feet, and on this sat the brown-uniformed janitor, whose name was George. There was a walnut table whose vase of constantly fresh spiky flowers was reflected in the huge pink mirror on the wall behind it. Entering, leaving, waiting for the lift, coming out of the lift, there was this pink reflection of myself, a man living in comfort in a world made safe for people without faces.

"I shall take a year off," I told the youngest of my partners, a man who had thought Anne a good scout. He said, "Where will you go?" and without thinking I said I didn't know, perhaps to India where I was born.

The telephones began to ring, the boy from Cable and Wireless was sent for and in this way the opening stages of my sabbatical year were taken out of my hands. An itinerary was typed, placed on my desk in a blue plastic folder. During discussions I'd said that India would only be a beginning, and this had been remembered. There were summaries of situations developing in all the top expense-account places from Karachi to Bermuda, situations I might care to look into if I happened to pass that way. I wrote to Cranston, checking his last address in my red leather book. He was in Rangoon. I said, "My firm's sending me out East in a month or two. I'm going to India first and then to Burma. Any chance of seeing you?" The itinerary showed that something of interest was developing in Rangoon so I wouldn't have to go out of my way. The prospect of offering my services to Cranston had receded, had already been thrust into the background by the almost irresistible force of a life I had not chosen but had become committed to. It was a life one did not, for instance, interrupt in order to go out and nurse lepers. You knew the odds were you would get leprosy and become a burden to the nuns.

When Cranston wrote back his address had changed. "No

need to go to Burma," he said. "As you see, I'm back in India again." This seemed like an omen—I wasn't sure of what. Muzzafirabad was a new name to me. It sounded old and yellow, dominated by mosques, full of flies and men kneeling on prayer mats, a predominantly Muslim town, but in India and not Pakistan; not my childhood India, but even older, the India of the great Moghuls. According to the maps I looked at, Muzzafirabad was a day or two's journey from Gopalakand, at least two days from Tradura and Jundapur. I could go to Gopalakand after I'd seen Cranston, and after I'd been to Gopalakand I might go down to Tradura and Jundapur, make contact with that other prince, Krishi, if he still existed. One ought not to waste opportunities to bury the dead. Antigone was right.

First ringing the press attaché at India House to get the style of address of a contemporary maharajah, I wrote to Dingy Row's son, reminded him who I was, told him I expected to be in India round about the middle of April onwards and that although I had some business to do in Karachi, Bombay and Delhi I'd have some free time and should like to see him. I had an idea of looking at Father's and Sarah's graves, but didn't mention this. A reply was not long in coming. It was signed by the personal assistant to His Highness. He thanked me for my letter, conveyed His Highness's regards, and regretted that he wouldn't be at home at the time I indicated. The letter lay on my stomach like stale fish. I remembered another letter, one of the two I'd found and preserved when sorting out papers at Four Birches. Reading it again in the light of the maharajah's, it stirred my curiosity in a way that it should perhaps have stirred it long ago. "It was for the son I did what I did, forgetting momentarily in the press of events that Gopalakand was no Hyderabad." What was it he had done? There was only one obvious way of finding out.

.   .   .   .

I scoured the political history shelves of the public library: *India Since Partition; Betrayal in Delhi; The New Dominion; The Last Viceroy; Farewell to Princes; The Integration of the Indian States:* titles like that. And here at last was the wind of crisis blowing down the palladian terrace whose air had lain on my cheek so stagnantly at the end of 1945. Here was an angry maharajah aiming a pistol at a minister of the new dominion; here were friendly persuasion, disguised and undisguised threats in the course of diplomatic negotiations to force the maharajahs to take their first step as wholly free men, unshackled even by the tenuous chain that had been called paramountcy; first steps that were also steps on to the political scaffold. Here was the historical perspective of events that intermittent reading of *Times'* reports from Delhi in 1947 had only confirmed my preconceived notions of, because I had anticipated the general drift of them.

What the British Crown had taken from these princes— supreme authority in the three matters of external affairs, defence and communication—they were now asked to give to one of the new self-governing dominions. This sounded reasonable enough but it was the thin end of the wedge, just as I had predicted when playing chess with Father. How could a congress-dominated government leave matters there? It could never have been part of their policy to preserve the internal autocratic authority of the men who were descended from the great moghuls and the fierce Rajput warrior kings. The British might lock a politician up without trial but a criminal always got a fair hearing. The princes had dungeons where men languished unsentenced for stealing bread. Now the writing was on the wall, but it seemed that so many of the princes had failed to see it. They actually welcomed the British announcement that paramountcy over the states would come to an end automatically with the

end of British rule. The old musty curtain was flung aside
and revealed a freedom and power almost greater than they
had dreamed of. But not for long. The winds of crisis
changed quarter and blew from colder regions. The maharajahs ate crow. With nearly six hundred of them, they ate it
in different ways, a few eagerly, most reluctantly, some by
forcible feeding. Some threatened to accede to Pakistan even
if geographically such an accession would have been non-
sensical; others were as much coerced into accession by their
own people as diplomatically persuaded by the politicians of
the new India. They had riots in their own capitals, riots
they described as raised by Congress-inspired rabble but
which Congress described as the struggle of their enslaved
subjects for democratic freedom. Sometimes there were
shows of arms by India, as in the case of Hyderabad, the
most powerful of all the states. The maharajahs twisted and
turned and the old Political Department burnt records
like an embassy preparing to evacuate. And in the end there
were only the details to work out, the quid pro quo for the
surrender of ruling powers and internal autocratic authority.
One by one the states were formed into provinces or merged
with provinces of what in our own day had been called
British India. The quid pro quo was the retention of title
and prince's privileges for the ruler and his heirs, whose suc-
cessions to the in-name-only gaddis would be subject to the
approval of the President of the Republic instead of the
Crown Representative. There were to be payments, as well,
an annual privy purse for the upkeep of palace, family,
servants and pensioners. In this way the work of men like my
father was taken out of their hands to be brought to its
logical end.

My childhood in Tradura and my youth in Four Birches
twisted and turned and bulged in my mind's eye beneath the
pages like animals that had fallen asleep long ago as captives

under a net but woke and tore at it as though it had only
just descended; had actually been what woke them.

I never found any reference to Tradura, but in one of
these books there was a reference to Gopalakand. A paragraph was all Gopalakand merited by way of recorded history. But the paragraph was enough. It lit the whole subject
for me.

Old Dingy Row, who had celebrated my birth with fireworks, had been obstinate. He had refused for a month to
sign the first agreement of accession. There was no show of
arms by India but Gopalakand was one of the states where
there had been riots in the capital. Whatever Dingy Row
saw in the future for himself and his state, his subjects saw
his hesitation and reluctance to sign up as evidence of his
intention to keep them in what suddenly looked to them like
feudal bondage. The marches on the palace were resisted
half-heartedly by Dingy Row's police and Dingy Row's
soldiers. In the end he signed and, it was hinted, if not
openly admitted, by delaying did worse for himself and his
family than he might have done.

Gopalakand's month of indecision was by no means an exception and I doubt that it would have been recorded in
ordinary circumstances. I think it was recorded for one reason only, to illuminate what ranked as a side-issue. The account ended: "Gopalakand provided a good example of the
obstruction sometimes encountered when the rulers were
still being influenced by retiring British Residents. The Resident in Gopalakand, Sir Robert Conway, persuaded Sir
Pandirakkar on more than one occasion to go back on prom-
ises given verbally to the States Department; and actually
interrupted a private conference between the Maharajah and
the representatives of the department and threatened to tear
up the draft documents which he described as instruments of
a blackguardedly policy of intended seizure and forfeiture,
masquerading as agreements between free parties."

· · ·

I searched through every other book I could lay my hands on, but found nothing that expanded this half set scene. I wrote again to the bank in Calcutta to ask if Father's record had been discovered. It had not been. I wondered whether he had submitted it to the young Maharajah for approval prior to publication and had had approval withheld or the manuscript torn up. The scene remained tantalizingly incomplete with Father still there, standing at the table, having said his say, waiting for someone to speak, or rise, order him out or follow him out of the room. Ah, which? It is a scene which at the time I first drew it for myself from that lone paragraph I came to wish I had never glimpsed because it showed my father a man in his middle sixties losing all his sense of proportion, making a public spectacle of himself, acting like a fool and—it was fairly obvious, judging by the letter I'd had from Gopalakand—earning the hatred of Dingy Row's family who in the end had had to face the facts of life alone and found privileges harder to come by in the new world of new men, where you could not afford to be labelled an obstinate old dug-out unless you had the wealth and power to make the obstinacy look like firm determination.

"Instruments of a blackguardedly policy of intended seizure and forfeiture, masquerading as agreements between free parties." There was an element of truth in it which like all the elements of truth that usually exist in angry, reactionary outbursts must have stung men who were trying to be fair, patient, but logical. There was nothing logical in the continued existence of places like Gopalakand, and nothing could have saved them once the illusion of stately togetherness was destroyed. That illusion had been created by their preservation and protection under the single head of the British Crown. The illusion vanished with the Crown, and it was too late to create the similar illusion that might have taken its place if the old 'thirties plan of a federation of all the states had ever come to anything. It had come to nothing because the princes had distrusted each other, and British India had distrusted Whitehall. The princes were happier with the status quo which gave them at least the outward appearance of being their own undisputed masters. The only illusion left now was that Dingy Row was free to choose, free to sign or not sign. It was an illusion all of them around that conference table must have been anxious to preserve; all of them may even have been blinded by. Judging by his intrusion Father was certainly blinded by it but the intrusion probably shattered it for the men who stood ready with the blotting paper. They wouldn't forgive him, even if they thought it was only for his bad manners, interference and foolish old man's lack of grip on reality they weren't forgiving him. Wounded, they remembered, and recorded his speech against him. Was the illusion shattered there for Dingy Row too? Perhaps he had just reached the stage of thinking: "It's not much to give away. Conway's wrong." Perhaps he held his hand out for a pen; and then Father opened the door and walked into the room.

Once he had spoken, did he see that he had shattered the illusion for everybody, including himself, and that after all the only reality in that room was the document which embodied the first of several logical steps his own people should have taken years before, so that the land they were committed to return to those for whom it was held in moral trust shouldn't be a land divided? I think it unlikely that he saw this; only later, in the isolation of the Dhooni hills. I think it unlikely, too, that Dingy Row would have felt anything in that room except the wound to his pride in himself as a man capable of making his own decisions in public. In that room, as I conjure it here in my hut in Manoba, and as I conjured it there in the Shepherd Market flat, the chair occupied by Dingy Row sometimes bears, be-

cause I never saw Sir Pandirakkar, only his son who wore
suède boots, the frail weight of old Ranjit Raosingh wearing cloth-of-gold and white jodhpurs. In my imagination
Ranjit Rao sits there restlessly, flicking those sinewy fingers
on one of which gleams the emerald ring. He watches the
others through those pulled-down eyes that fascinated me
as a boy, and sees at last Father's wisdom in not allowing his
son by a Goanese whore to succeed, for what would these
new men think of negotiating with a man who would be
succeeded by a whore's son? The other men at the table are
easy to imagine: middle-aged Indians who had studied the
Law and had probably held briefs in the Congress-
dominated provincial governments; men who dressed with
rather crumpled simplicity, in European suits with wide
lapels, or in homespun cottons and Gandhi caps, carrying
portfolios, polishing steel-rimmed spectacles, forgiving of the
past and of terms of imprisonment for old incitements to
civil disobedience, turning brown eyes to a future that was
as rewarding to have as it was uncertain to contemplate.
That room contained the trinity of the Indian political
power: a Rajput Prince, educated Commoners, and a Guard-
ian of the sacred trust; it brought them together at last, but
in mutual distaste and suspicion.

This then was how Father's career ended and what it
would be remembered for in the few remaining years that
would pass before it was forgotten forever. Perhaps on the
anniversaries of Indian independence, Dingy Row's family
drove down from the winter palace to the old cantonment
cemetery and put hemlock on his grave.

2

WHEN I sit here writing these things down the days of my
life in retrospect seem to acquire a gravity that was mostly

absent from the days themselves; Manoba broods beyond the
window, responding to the rhythmic pulse-beats of my recollections; until I pause. Things get crossed out then, rewritten
in a different way, or I push the papers to one side, light up,
pour a drink and, depending on the time of day, sit relaxed,
eye the bed and perhaps think of Kandy, or go out into the
clearing to talk to Melba or down the track to see Griffin or
play cricket with his boy. Manoba stops brooding then, and
the day is neither grave nor dignified but haphazard as always,
a maze of distractions for body and mind.

Griffin put Kandy my way. She comes over from the mainland where Griffin sometimes goes to spend a night when
he's what he calls "crook with it." The trip adds to Kandy's
expense because the boat people have to be bribed a bit,
or pretend they do, pretend they might lose their jobs, or
licences, whatever it is, or get into some kind of trouble.
One doesn't dare touch the Manobaon women, even if one
finds them attractive, which I don't. Kandy comes pretending to sell buttons, stationery, all kinds of things that she has
in an orange cloth, makes a bundle of and carries on her
woolly head. She is negroid, neither islander nor main-
lander; and her price is high because she has a head for
economics. She understands the meaning of expressions
like scarcity value. She wears a bright green sarong that
comes down nearly to her ankles and has a passion for earrings and bracelets and charms that tinkle. In her bundle,
whenever she comes, there's always something like that
which has taken her fancy across the water and which she's
got on tick and makes me buy for her in addition to paying
her the money she earns.

On her first visit she opened the bundle and made a show
of interesting me in her wares. Then she lowered the sarong
and showed me her dark brown breasts that curve out and
down and up, like scimitars. She laughed and said, "You
like? You like?" She has white, broad teeth and swollen,

blue-black lips. Only when she's gone do I have the time to worry about how clean she is. I think no man could resist her attentions to the deeper secrets of his body or her cunning knowledge of his curiosity in hers. There is nothing between us except this detailed and unrestrained physical connection. Its lack of restraint may be due a lot to the different colour of our skins. The happiness she gives me is heightened by the knowledge that neither of us could fall in love with the other. Nor does the passing of money spoil the happiness in any way. She does not come to the island often and the curious thing is that I seldom feel heat towards her in her absence. God knows how many or what kind of men she serves between whiles. I watch for signs of gonorrhoea and syphilis, tell myself not to be a fool but give her up. But when she returns I throw such considerations away as if I didn't care one way or the other what happens to me. Perhaps this is another aspect of the new obsession I seem to have about the ends that people come to—an obsession which may prompt me to see parallels where none exists.

Muzzafirabad was not old and yellow. It was new, squat, geometrical, white, hygienic and air-conditioned; full of white-coated men and women who had a concentrated look on their faces of being in on the mystique of world health and the battle against the female anopheles. Cranston said, "Of course it's only a beginning," and I thought then that he had changed beyond recognition, had become reconciled to his own role of consumer, ready to consign the Muzzafirabad laboratories—outwardly perfect but inwardly no doubt already short of essentials—to the heap of brand-new rubbish that seems to surround us always. He took me on a tour of the laboratories. The low white buildings were connected to each other by covered walks which radiated from the central hub of the administrative block where Cranston worked,

surrounded by wall maps. The Foundation was proud of
Muzzafirabad and had gone to a lot of trouble to give itself
the right kind of setting. The covered walks had fly-away
roofs supported by the thin steel poles architects are fond
these days of sticking into the ground at a bit of an angle,
which always makes me think of them for some reason as
like knitting needles. I remembered different needles; flags
you stuck in remote ground where nobody else in his right
mind wanted to go; I remembered that you said, Well, now,
this is it, where I make my burnt offering. Pointing at the
knitting needles I said, "You've got a lot of flags."

Cranston said, "Flags?"

Cranston looked much the same. He had more fat on him,
naturally, and that kind of colourless hair goes grey quickly,
but the impression of slightness and wiriness was still there,
and his face was remarkably unlined for a man already in his
fifties. Where he was different was in his attitude of accepting things as they are. The fire he showed in adversity was
now a steadiness in the face of success, a casualness grown
out of experience, and perhaps out of a certain physical tired-
ness. He sat in his central office, a slowly ageing, once pred-
atory and perambulatory spider who had raced through
the jungles looking for his prey: that sickness he spoke of in
Pig Eye that was too great a misery for the sick to bring to
him. Now the sickness was all on slides. His minions
stared at the sickness through microscopes and when you
stood near their benches they looked up blandly, knowing
they were one up on you in international errands of mercy;
and Cranston himself waited in the middle to be fed. All
the same I had to admit that I should have hated to find the
surface Cranston still fighting, still boyishly flicking his nose
with that old gesture of grim determination at being faced
with, or of pleasure at having overcome, snags, difficulties,
cruelty, injustice; admit that I preferred to find the surface
Cranston smoothly on top of his job, but I wanted signs

that below the surface he was just the same as I felt myself to
be below the layers of everlasting compromise.

When he said, "Flags?" as if he'd no idea what I meant, I
said, "Daintree's flags. How is he, by the way?" and his face
closed up. He said, "He's gone to pieces, I'm afraid," pushed
open a door and led me into another of the cool, anaes-
thetized rooms. It seemed that he had no time for Daintree, and that we were both grown into a mould that could
have been cast for us eighteen years ago: that of outwardly
clean-living, liberal minded, efficient and reasonably intelligent men with sharpish senses of humour to convey or
cloak felt duties towards mankind in general but no one
man in particular. It was because Daintree had inspired
Cranston that Cranston was what he was, boss of Muzzafirabad. And it was because of Daintree who taught Cranston
to go looking for the sick that Cranston had been in the place
that built itself around him and became known as Pig Eye.
It was therefore because of Daintree that I was alive and,
being alive, rich enough to spend twelve months doing nothing. I said, "Did he have a bad time in prison camp?" Cranston, pointing at a map that could be lighted up to show the
different stages reached in the antimalaria campaigns, said,
"That's right."

Cranston had said, "Come at any time," and I had taken
him too literally, delayed too long in Delhi on the firm's
business. When I reached Muzzafirabad he was packed for
a conference in Rangoon that would take him away for a
week. We were neither of us at our best. I must have appeared to him as a man who had become used to arriving at
moments convenient mainly to himself and he was in the
kind of hurry a man can't help being in when his packing is
done and there's nothing further to do except presently
catch a plane, but too much time to spend before departure,
time in which odd jobs are remembered and weigh on the
conscience; so that in greeting me, showing me round, the

picture I formed of Cranston as a medical organization man was added to each time he drew a bit away from me to answer or ask a question of a subordinate which could not wait a week to be asked or answered.

We had a hasty lunch together in a room furnished in the modern spindly style. The blue and yellow candle-snuffer light shades on the walls were made of perforated metal. There was a wire construction on a plinth into which was screwed a brass name plate engraved with the construction's title: "The Cure." On the opposite side of the room there was another plinth and on this there was a bronze cast of the Founder's bust. Rubber plants stood erect in corners.

Here I questioned him further about Daintree. Perhaps my voice came out in a tone blanker and more colourless than might be normal to it. On the other hand I have known for some time now that, being a Conway, I lack the gift of naked warm-heartedness and that it is difficult for others to judge the temperature of my feelings.

Cranston made nothing of his search for Daintree when the war was over, and at the time I did not notice the omission. He used expressions like, "He had a bad time," "You could hardly recognize him," "When he reappeared on the scene, there'd been enormous advances in the field of tropical medicine."

There came a point when he stopped, spread butter or poured water, and said, "Did I ever tell you what he specialized in before the war?" I said he may have done, but I'd forgotten. He said, "Yaws." He hesitated, then added, pointing an eccentricity in Daintree, "He was in love with yaws."

Yaws were a double-edged affliction, Cranston explained. They sapped the spirit as well as the body. Daintree had sweated through a score of years and a score of jungles, fighting this disease. It sank whole communities into states of apathy and physical misery. He had most success with an

arsenical preparation. He was still fighting yaws in Java
when the Japanese got him.

Cranston said, "And after it was all over there was this
thing called penicillin. Daintree found you could cure a
bad case of yaws with it in ten days flat. He felt like a man
who'd spent years climbing Everest and when he got to the
top found they were serving hot soup and sausage rolls." I
laughed, and Cranston's face closed up again. There is no
end to the misunderstandings that can exist between man
and man.

Another aspect of Muzzafirabad: one of the two rooms
reserved for visitors which Cranston made available for me.
Zebra skins on a polished pine strip floor; white rough-cast
walls decorated only by a black Zulu shield and long, crossed
hunting spears; a vague smell of scented polish and cold-
storage air; a continuous, whispering draught. The private
bathing cubicle was underwater green. There was an illuminated tank of tropical fish set in an alcove above the semi-
sunken bath.

Here you could live forever, never emerge. No one would
question it. When you were hungry or thirsty you could lift
the receiver of the scarlet telephone and in half an hour,
the tray would appear, a tinkling little city of aluminium
domes. When the fish in the tank died you could scoop them
out and put them down the lavatory, like pages torn from
my Manobaon calendar. No one would notice they had gone.
No one would ever ask questions. No one would come and
talk to you.

The only real understanding there was between Cranston
and myself that first time in Muzzafirabad was that I might
get in touch with him again when he came back from
Rangoon. In not much more than a couple of hours after my
arrival I was alone in the air-conditioned bedroom, staring
at the Zulu shield and hunting spears, imagining them laid

aside long ago by some old African who now squatted on his hunkers, smoked a corn-cob pipe, dreamed of lion and leaping impala and sunned his bones in the doorway of a hut that had a roof of corrugated iron; a foolish, decrepit old man, like Daintree, and like my father who had not seemed to know when the time had come for him to hang up his shield and spears but had come into a room brandishing them as if that were expected of him. He had died alone in a place called Dhooni, and now Daintree was dying in a place pronounced Man'bah but according to the map Cranston had shown me spelled Manoba. Daintree was drinking himself to death, apparently because someone had handed him a cure for yaws on a plate, spoiled his old man's dream of a fight to the bitter end. I pictured him sitting in Manoba, old and sick; and because I had never seen him he had a face that wasn't unlike Father's.

From the window of the African hut in Muzzafirabad I could see India: flat, brown, and yellow, with smudges of hot purple low down in a sky blanched by the sun. I had seen this quite unrecognizable land from the comfort of air-conditioned railway coaches that carried me between stone cities where fans whirled and business was done across shining mahogany tables or in leather armchairs reserved in olden times exclusively for white backsides. My childhood India lay beyond the horizon, a vast oasis of black shade, emerald grass and white palaces, where gravel was hot and sharp to plimsolled feet, the leaves of rhododendrons sweated, (*were they really rhododendrons?*), and a red brick wall hummed in the heat when you put your ear close to it.

I moved away from the window, looked again at the spears. They were probably manufactured and blackened to look authentic and had come from the concrete city of Johannesburg. The old African didn't exist, and whatever Daintree was or wasn't, the last thing my father had been at the height of his career was a fool. I had him to thank for the fact that I was here, sitting at well-breeched leisure, with time on my hands to regret deep down that I wasn't losing my temper with obstinate princes in tarnished silver turbans, or sweating on horseback up and down the Punjab, growing fed-up with petitions from litigious peasants and the stubbornness of old grey heads who said their grandfathers had done things this way and this was how, may the sahib continue long in health and prosperity, they would continue to be done. It was thanks to my father that I wasn't sitting in some God-forsaken dak bungalow, swilling whisky, approaching the end of my tether, developing fixations that in a year or two would earn me the nickname of the Mad Commissioner.

But I was forgetting. Father or no father, I should all the same be doing none of these things, unless I had turned out to be a koi-hai and had gone to seek my fortune in the kind of country where it seemed there would always be a Welensky. That I shouldn't be doing them was what Father at least pretended to have foreseen. Had he foreseen something else, as well? The day, for instance, when, if I followed in his footsteps, I would finally admit that it was all maya, that nothing a man could do with his life would really satisfy him, unless he were a slug and content with the sight of his own slimy wake? There were times, and this was one of them, when I almost believed Father had been appalled by the effect the upbringing he had left to others had had on me, and in spite of caring nothing much for me had at least wanted to save me from discovering in too hard and slow a way that there were no means of matching deed to will, had wanted to put me, early on, on the quick sharp road to this discovery by getting me used to the habit of disappointment, to recognizing the reality behind the apparent magic.

.   .   .

The telephone is a mindlessly efficient instrument. It makes no distinction between past and present, dead and living worlds. I asked the operator to trace and ring the number of the palace at Jundapur. If Krishi still existed he was my only link with the past. I wanted to enter it and kill it off. I fooled myself that this was the point of my sabbatical year. The operator had never heard of Jundapur. This was a promising beginning, suggestive of my whole Jundapur experience having been hallucinatory. It took him five hours to trace a number that was said to be that of the palace, and then half an hour to get the call put through. A servant answered but I couldn't make him understand anything. There was a long wait and then the click of an extension receiver being lifted and a woman's voice saying, "Is that you, Harry?" I said that it wasn't, but was that the palace at Jundapur, and if so could I speak to the Rajah Sahib? The woman said, "I'll get him. Who is it calling?" I said the Rajah Sahib might not remember me and I was assuming the man I meant had succeeded to the title, my name was Conway, my father had been political agent in Tradura, and Krishi and I knew each other as boys. At first I thought the line had gone dead and I said, "Hello?" to stir things up again. But she hadn't gone away. She said, "Did you say Conway?" and then, when I'd confirmed this, "It can't be William Conway though?" Puzzled I said that it was, and again there was a pause. She said, "Wherever are you speaking from?" I told her, and added, "Who's that?" There was a confusion of conversation which was ended by a man's voice: "William Conway? It can't be our William Conway?" I said, "It is. Is that Krishi?" He said, "Good gracious!" and then there was the woman's voice back, saying, "Bill? It's Dora speaking. Do you remember me too?"

Sometimes when Melba is at her singing out there in the ramshackle cage I can hear shouts from Daintree's hut but I no longer need to rush out of my own to see what's going on, or to calm Melba down, because she has become as used to Daintree's performance as I; so used to it in fact that I think both of us know when it is due, just as in the middle of the night you can wake up here and tell that storm-winds have gathered out to sea and are grouping for attack. The island knows. You can feel the palms on the beach below holding themselves in the darkness, leaning away from the calm fringe of water that in an hour will be lashed into white foam by the whining thongs of the wind. In the black sky above the hut, which you can't see, you sense the presence of forked and jagged wires which presently, charged electrically, will glow white and blue in the shape of lightning. It is the same with the rain. You can hear the winds that herald it cutting swathes through the forest and in the hot silence that the last flick of the wind leaves behind it like fumes from an exhaust, you anticipate the deafening hiss that sounds like the sudden turning-on in the forest of hundreds of steam valves.

Although the explosion does not always follow, one of the signs that Daintree is building up pressure is the sight in the morning of patients returning down the hill as one laughing, chattering group. You know then that Daintree has made a night of it and that his boy has had no luck with buckets of water. The patients never seem to mind. They either go home or over to Griffin who has a rough working knowledge of how to clean and dress a cut, diagnose constipation and other homely ills, and we do what we can together, treat nothing we're uncertain of.

It is the lingering smell on my hands of disinfectant, the lingering of the distaste I find I have for touching wounds, the recurring reminder through the morning that I had no vocation for professional medicine, the morning heat and the sense of inactivity on the brow of the hill, that depress me a bit and get me ready for Daintree's outburst, and per-

haps all this communicates itself to Melba, so that she
guesses it's one of those mornings and throws herself determinedly into her Paraguayan love song in order to be
oblivious to it if it comes.

And Daintree must prepare for it too, must drink steadily
from the time he wakes up in the filthy bedroom he won't
let his boy clear up—although the adjacent lean-to dispensary is as clean and tidy as a new pin—and goes un-
shaved in the clothes he slept in to sit in his chair and think
not of lion or impala but of rows of disfigured faces and
bodies which used to be dependent on him for his compas-
sion and his skill. He drinks, on mornings such as this,
deliberately to humiliate himself, because he holds the Daintree who howls for his lost balloon in the greatest medical
contempt. He sees the absurdity and madness of wishing in
his heart that the disease he dedicated himself to eradicate
was still defying all his efforts to control it. There is nothing
you could tell him that he doesn't already know about the
way the means of a man's job can become more important
to him than its end, and even more often blind him to the
fact that the end will either never be reached, or if it is,
reached probably as the result of an accident: an accident
in a laboratory, say, which produces a culture of healing
mould; or of an accidental conjunction of time, place and
opportunity when action grows of its own accord out of in-
action and inertia, and Empires fall; mark the end of duty,
leave some of the dutiful behind to contemplate their glory
and folly, get drunk, or make records of past history and
open doors into private mansions that suddenly look lonely
and conspicuous when they are empty and it is getting dark
outside.

And if Daintree reaches the point when he can stand himself no longer, he storms into the clearing as once he stormed
into the office of a camp in Java, and tries to inject the trunks

of trees and the stems of plants with a hypodermic needle, shouting: "The buggers are leprous! Ah! Cure the buggers! In! Out! In! Out!" or sometimes stands in the middle ordering invisible throngs to line up and bare their arms to the shoulder so that he can stab their illness out of them. Occasionally, stray Manobaons stand on the edge of the clearing and watch him dispassionately; trying to judge what connection there is between his curious behaviour and the tins of Kwikkaffy he gives them for carrying his monthly consignments of Muzzafirabad cargo up the hill from Griffin's go-down where they are stored overnight after they've been unloaded from Griffin's lighter that comes in from the ships that anchor beyond the reef.

"If I were younger," Daintree told me the other day, in a rare moment of sobriety and talkativeness which seldom come together, "I'd throw myself into cancer. But men like me are finished. I mean men who've always gone it alone. Ah, God, if I threw myself into cancer these days I'd still have to be a cog in the bloody wheel like now, pumping stuff into people like a garage hand pumping petrol," he paused, added, "or draining it out of them."

The hunger of such men is always the same: only the kinds and degrees of snarl, the forms of protest, differ. My coming here was meant to be a protest—but I'm a man not given to dramatic actions. All my actions, in the light of Daintree's, are pale and elusive. All my fires are lit these days in dark and airless corridors, perhaps they always have been. Nobody sees the smoke. It chokes nobody but me.

I shouldn't have said nobody. Cranston must have seen it when I went back to Muzzafirabad from Jundapur and said, "Is there anything I can do for Daintree?" At that time I'd not set eyes on Daintree. Cranston didn't answer at once but looked at me for as long as he did that time in Pig Eye when I reminded him there were two medicos to earn the price of confiscated drugs. Eventually he said, "You can watch him die."

I think Cranston saw the smoke. Dora and Krishi didn't. They were both stifled by their own and each other's, exhausted from the business of trying to damp their own fires down.

3

DORA has been going back to Jundapur for years. The only coincidence in our reunion was my choice of month. Both she and Krishi are married, she to a man called Harry Paynter, Krishi to a girl he married at the age of sixteen when she was twelve. Dora told me in confidence that Krishi was ashamed to have been forced by his father to follow such an old-fashioned Hindu custom. The Rani was no longer living at the palace. In confidence, for I had confidences from them both, Krishi told me that the Rani was living in sin with a parsee in Bombay. Did I know about the parsees, he asked me? They were the sect who committed their dead to the towers of silence to be clean picked by vultures. Had I seen the vultures waiting day in day out like rows of shagged-out umbrellas? He wondered whether the Rani would be reincarnated as a vulture and made to eat her own children when they died, hers and Krishi's, two girls and a boy. The children were with the Rani in Bombay.

Dora's husband was in the Himalayas. He had been in the old Indian army, which meant he lost his job in 1947 when he was thirty-two. He had been quite a good climber. At forty-five, Dora said, he thought he lacked the head for heights but usually wangled himself a place as quartermaster on one of the expeditions that got up every year to climb, map, explore. She thought him too modest. He had always

kept himself fit. They lived in Calcutta. He was a public relations officer now. While he was in the Himalayas (she pronounced it Himmahlliuz) she came to Jundapur to see
Krish. (She had taken to calling him Krish.) April and May,
which were climbing months, were hot months to spend
in Jundapur, but it was dry heat, better than the humidity
of Calcutta; and she and Harry could no longer afford the
hills. Years ago they had had a little girl, but she died aged
two of scarlet fever.

I should have recognized neither of them had we met in
the street or sat opposite one another in a restaurant. Krishi
said he would have recognized me anywhere, but Dora wasn't
so sure. She would have thought of me as shorter, perhaps
because she remembered me mostly as overwhelmed by a
topee that always looked a bit too big for me.

Occasionally I play a game of pretend in this hut of mine
in Manoba, imagining it to be the palace in Jundapur.
Through the window of the hut I catch glimpses of Melba's
cage in the clearing, but visualize the Jundapur cage and the
Jundapur clearing. My narrow, wooden veranda, scarcely a
chair's width, becomes the long stone terrace that would
have overlooked the gardens had it not been for the damp-
ened tattis between the columns that blocked the view
and darkened both the terrace and the old Victorian drawing
room, the only room on the ground floor of the palace still
in use. In the subaqueously lit anteroom that divided the
drawing room from the main entrance hall there was a
statue of the dancing Shiva. Near it joss sticks burned. "To
get rid of the awful damp smell," Krishi said. He wore a
brightly coloured Bermuda shirt, pale blue linen trousers.
He was on the short side, stocky, his arms no longer thin,
his stick-insect fingers grown plump and hairy. His face was
plumped-up too, and shadowed under the brown eyes which
Dora described as like those of a gazelle. His nose alone remained lean: a Rajput beak that he had a habit of twitch-

ing the tip of to left and right after each sip of his endless drinks.

When he took me out onto the terrace I had a brief but surprisingly near view of the lake and the island through the two unblocked columns that flanked the head of the steps to the garden; and then he led me to where a middle-aged woman was sitting forward on one of the wicker chairs that were set out around a table with bottles and glasses, close to a standard portable fan whose cable snaked in through the open drawing room window. She stubbed the cigarette into a full tray, stood up, coming no higher than my shoulder, and held both her hands out. I took them and, when we shook, the slack muscles on the outer curves of her upper arms flickered, as if she had recently lost some of the weight she'd reached the stage of putting on too easily. She said in a rather husky, ragged voice, "Hello, Bill. May I still call you Bill? I don't like to think how many years it's been."

Her hair was cut short. It was curly, inclined to be frizzy on the temples and along the line of the forehead. Bronze lights still gleamed in its fading darkness, but here and there were wiry, strayed-sheep strands of grey, warning threads that pointed to her mortality. Her eyelids were dusty with recently applied powder. Crows-feet tangented from their corners. Her make-up clung reluctantly to skin that had suffered from too many years of exhausting heat and sunlight. There were patches of freckling on neck and breast. Standing, she was trim enough waisted; sitting, her legs were good, deserving at the ankles of shoes made on more expensive lasts. She was dressed plainly in a fawn, pleated tricel dress that left her arms bare and a deceptive fullness in the breast. She wore no status symbol apart from her thin gold wedding ring. It was in the grey-green eyes I thought something of my hazy idea of the young Dora might lurk. They were now her main attraction.

Except for the servants they were alone in the palace. Even taking into account the surprise and curiosity of reunion, I got the impression they were glad of a new face, a new voice. They wanted me to stay for the rains which were due any day and were said to bring with them a fine sense of release. Before the moon got up at night and just before dawn, if you woke then, you could see sheet lightning reflected on the southwestern sky. It may have been the distant lightning that made me feel eventually that my arrival had turned them up like leaves showing their pale backs before a storm.

At first I wondered whether they were lovers. I slept in a bed that was brought out onto the terrace. Krishi said he slept on the roof under the canvas awning that shaded a glass dome in the ceiling of the drawing room which I had quite forgotten existed. If he had made some excuse to take me up there to prove it I shouldn't have believed him. But he didn't. Dora's bedroom was distinguishable from the back of the shuttered upper storey by the only window whose veranda was closed in by purdahlike tattis.

From the anteroom where Shiva danced you could hear temple echoes. The servants were old, waited for you in corners, appeared from behind doorways. The drawing room was a Grand Hotel setting for tea and orchestra. The telephone never rang. We ate on the terrace. The food was wheeled out under yellowing, silver-plated covers from some remote kitchen. A bathroom and dressing room on the ground floor were earmarked for me. The porcelain tub was old-fashioned with claw feet and big brass taps. The uneven mosaic floor was as crinkly to the foot as a warm wet honeycomb. Lying in the bath the ceiling looked far away. The light from the single bulb scarcely reached the corners. The walls were glazed white and bottle green, and reminded me of old tube stations, dim subterranean corridors where bits of blown

paper came permanently to rest. From the little dressing room
a red and blue windowed door opened on to a long, narrow,
gothic lavatory whose mahogany throne was set on a marble
dais, almost as long a walk to get to as it had been to get to the
other end of the Durbar Hall in Tradura. A musical box did
double duty as a tissue holder. It played *Schlafe Mein Prinz-
chen* and *Heilige Nacht;* both of which were soporific.

The old bearer who looked after me spoke no English
and I no longer spoke Urdu. Through another old man he
told me he remembered the Burra Sahib, Conway Sahib,
and remembered me as a little boy, playing with the Rajah
Sahib. Once he had helped us look for a lost tennis ball. He
woke me on the two mornings I was there with a pot of
tea and two green bananas: chota hazri, the "little breakfast"
that had always accompanied dressing for the early morning
ride with Grayson-Hume.

The front of the palace which I'd approached in my hired
car along a dust road leading through an avenue of trees had
been familiar as a type of façade rather than as this particular one. The grey stone had probably darkened. The
asphalt of its courtyard was broken. Weeds grew in the
jagged cracks. Two stubby wings jutted out and the entrance was recessed, colonnaded. The interior of the house
was quite unremembered. Recognition belonged wholly to
the back of the palace where the old formal garden sloped
down to the stone steps and the lake in which the island
stood upon its own reflection in dark green water. Beyond
the island the lake got shallower until the bed emerged,
murky, absorbently grey, lightening to hard-packed, dry,
cracked mud up to the farther shore. There, bayonet-sharp
rushes might have harboured water fowl. Was the cage still
there on the island? I asked. They told me it was.

There appeared to be more steps to the water than there
had been and the slimy green moss and weed were hard,

petrified. The rubbery-leaved water lilies had spread and thickened and formed a mass which when you half-closed your eyes looked like the body of a flat green bubbly fish risen to the surface and lying on its side asleep. There were more steps than there used to be because the level of the lake was lower at the end of May than at the beginning of April. The rolling parkland had come closer, but there was still an aspect of it where it met the sky: where the bereft herdsmen who once gave chase to wandering cattle could still be seen in the imagination.

Krishi said, "Old Nannie's dead, you know." I thought he had slipped up, asked him whether he didn't mean Old Mutton. I think he began to tell me this when we were alone on the first evening. Dora must have joined us in mid-story.

In 1933 he went to an Indian college for the sons of Indian gentlemen. He cried at their parting. He wouldn't have mentioned crying in front of Dora. He said "blubbed." Mrs. Canterbury, or Old Nannie as he seemed to prefer to call her, as if a governess to the age of fourteen was retrospectively a permanent source of irritation to his self-esteem, had patted him on the head and told him he mustn't cry. Apparently she said, "My other boy never cried." Krishi commented, "She was always ramming you down my throat as the perfect specimen, old man. She worshipped the ground your rotten old feet trod on."

From Jundapur she went to Ranchi. He thought Ranchi was her last governess' job. He lost touch with her, but she turned up again at the beginning of the war as a writer of letters from Srinagar in Kashmir. She wrote to him, he noticed, on each quarter day as if to commemorate in her own mind the days on which in her working life her salary had fallen due. Had she saved money, he wondered, or was her retirement pinched? Were her last people decent to her? He hoped they'd been decent, worried a bit because he'd never quite got around to looking into it. He thought, look-

ing back on them, that her letters had hinted at kindness
received from others in Kashmir, but not affection; believed
she shared a bungalow, or houseboat with a retired couple,
church people. In one of the letters she said, "Have you not
heard from my other boy?" and added that she prayed God
to bless Master Conway and keep him safe in this dreadful
war in which she was certain he would be playing some
heroic part. In 1944 there was a last letter from Kashmir,
not from Canters but from the vicar of the church in which
she had obviously done good works. The vicar told Krishi that Mrs. Canterbury had always spoken highly of him,
("As 'my young prince,' I suppose," Krishi said, "Or as 'my
little Rajah' ") and because she'd talked about him so often
the vicar thought he would like to hear from someone who
had actually been with her at her sudden end. She died in
the act of decorating the church with fruit and vegetables
for the Harvest Festival, "in the very house of God where,
good Christian woman, she had worshipped regularly."

Krishi shook his head when he told me this, looked
across at the island and the lake and said, "You know, I picture her arriving in heaven loaded with marrows, apples
and all sorts, giving them to St. Peter and saying, 'I'm sorry
they're not very good this year. If only you could have seen
Our stuff at The Palace.' "

And Dora, who had probably come back from one of
those missions which I remember left her face more pow-
dery and strengthened her new scent of clove carnations,
said, "Poor Old Mutton. We never did find out where Mr.
Canterbury got to, did we, Krish?" Krishi said perhaps
they'd met in heaven and Mr. Canterbury had cried out,
"Oh, I say! Not you!" or on the other hand, all differences
between them laid aside, if not actually forgiven, gone
up to her and said, "Mrs. Canterbury, I presume?"

"Yes, I like that better," Dora said, "we must give her a
happy ending," and fell into the uncomfortable-looking posi-

tion that seemed natural to her directly she sat down, leaning forward in her chair, legs crossed at the ankles, her left arm held stiffly with the hand clasped around her right leg below the knee, smoothing the flesh of that arm with her right hand, turning to look at the island as Krishi had done; as she might turn to look at Melba's cage in the clearing if she were truly sitting here in the hut and not only doing so in my imagination, and still I should not know whether the action of smoothing her arm was prompted by a recurring ache or chill there, by restlessness, or by the subconscious need to remind herself who she was through physical contact with her own body.

And she had this alternative habit when leaning forward in whatever chair she sat on, either a chair at a table on which she would lean her elbows or an easy chair when she rested them on her knees: in either case her hands would presently come together and she would begin twisting the wedding ring. Perhaps the ache or chill, restlessness and wish to identify herself with something she had always had, if only her own arm, were all present in these nervous habits. But looking back on them I see the habits really as symptomatic of obstacles she set up against the free flow of her desires, or as signs that such obstacles had suddenly been come up against. Going back to Jundapur may have been as far as she could get or would allow herself to get in an obsessional swim upstream to reach the source of childhood happiness. I fancy the habits were less noticeable when she went back to Calcutta. Perhaps they were not usually so noticeable even in Jundapur, but were aggravated this time by my presence, my appearance out of the blue which unexpectedly brought the three of us together as men and woman who felt compelled in the pauses in reminiscing to watch and listen to the island as if we might hear not the cry of a heron but the distant voices of children playing; but there were coming from the island no voices of any kind—only the inaudible breathing of trees and water stunned by the weight of a sun the approaching storm would lift, and then we felt an equal compulsion to turn back to each other and ask the questions whose answers might sketch histories, conjure other people's times and places, hint at vital information withheld and so help each one of us to see in the half-glimpsed truth about someone else's life the truth about our own.

I wonder sometimes how I really looked to them, because they looked so different from the pictures I had always carried of them—or thought I had carried of them. On the two-day journey by road from Muzzafirabad I realized that their faces had been absent from the pictures for years. When I tried to look at the pictures, the sunlight in which I inevitably stood half-blinded me and young Dora and young Krishi peered at me through heat haze from shadows, just as the pale white peahens had peered from the safety of their nut-gathering shade.

We have lost our nine- and ten-year-old faces: they are gone, gone; so that even in photographs if we came across them there would be a reality of bone and flesh too uncompromising to be acceptable as a well-caught likeness. Even the changing faces that accompanied the growth of Dora's, Krishi's and Old Mutton's histories are absent from them. Only their present faces or the last remembered face can be related to the histories. For me, for instance, Mrs. Canterbury's face, watching me through Traduran and Pankot mists that are only penetrated by the idea of a long nose and flaky lips, is the face that reflects the surprise of sudden death amid the stained glass and church-cooled, Kashmiri vegetables. For me her life had come to a halt in 1929 when she knelt to adjust the belt of my jodhpurs and said, "We may never meet again," and I was afraid she was about to make a scene. Her subsequent letters and cards never made her live for me beyond that point, simply confirmed that she had indeed lived until it and had tried to influence me one way or another. For me her life had been compressed into a span of years beginning with a time that was not really time at all but darkness illuminated by a racial memory which we shared and gave form to later in stories of mutinies and pink satin slippers. This dark evolved into an actual time, although it wasn't the kind of time people grew old in. It marked its own passage in movements and actions like climbing steps and washing knees, and was transitory in relation not only to Mrs. Canterbury and myself but in relation to solid and unchanging objects like Edwardian straw hats, towels, hard buttons and soft bosoms. Only towards the end of this telescoped life of hers could time be seen to be the stronger of the two (leaving me out of it) and in 1929 she was gone, giving her few short years as wards into my memory. But now, even though her face is still the Traduran face, this memory has been enriched by Krishi's and by my realization that I've no idea how well or badly she was treated in the household at Tradura, no idea what Father thought of her, or of how, when they were alone, she and Aunt Sarah talked to each other. There are footsteps on the veranda and the faint caress of a wind that flutters a brown silk dress about thin legs that have come so far to sit at the other end of Father's table, and threaten the maternal authority of a woman whose life is mostly shrouded in mystery.

Similarly, Dora's and Krishi's memories of their own and each other's histories are now part of mine, but it is the faces I saw last year in Jundapur that I connect with them, not the hazy faces of the girl in white and the brown-skinned boy who painted his face blue. When there were three of us, on the terrace smoking and drinking, or eating our way through the long meals that always left me feeling like an Arab who had pitched his tent too well, there appeared to be an understanding that in speaking of the past we shouldn't speak of times we hadn't all three shared. These were the sessions in which throwing our different pennies into a pool dated 1929 we produced a series of similar if not exactly corresponding ripples. Most of these pennies were thrown by Dora and myself: the name of the elephant, what had it been? Ranka? The name of the girl with blonde ringlets and a bottom too fat to fit her terrible pink dress—surely I remembered Brenda Boscombe? The Boscombes were in the Civil and I'd made a dead set at Brenda at the garden party. Even Krishi thought he remembered a girl called Brenda. And so it went; the garden party, the lemonade, "What's *your* father?" getting her under the cedar, Queen Mab from *Forest Fantasies* by Walter Carroll, the procession. Did I remember that old woman in rags?

And when, temporarily, we all grew tired of throwing pennies, or Dora and I noticed that Krishi's pennies were fewer than our own, or we all became too much aware of the way our hushed surroundings had begun to toll their bells for the departed, the subject would change and centre chiefly on our present-day selves, so that you could almost hear the hiss of our separate, secret years being compressed and flattened until they showed no more than their fairly obvious upper layers.

But two of us alone was a different matter; the little magician's wands came out then and we waved them over one another's head—ting, ting—to induce tiny balls of revelational fire that would heat and plump the years up and light some of their dark corners.

When there is a moon I can come back up the track from a night's chess and talk and drink with Lew Griffin and then sit for a while before turning in, without bothering to light the pressure lamp; and so be back on the terrace at Jundapur, with Dora gone to bed, and Krishi and I alone, with all the tattis rolled up and the island stuck like a blue-black velvet cut-out onto silver tinfoil representing water.

Krishi sat with his feet up on the wickerwork table, his Bermuda shirt unbuttoned, nursing a glass of whisky on his bare, hairy belly. It was extraordinary how hairy the delicate little boy had become. He said, "Oh, Christ, this bloody awful heat. Barbaric. Don't you find it barbaric, old man?" In heat like this he was always "quite impotent," everything drooped as if he had been struck down by a form of fowl pest. No aphrodisiac was any use from the end of April until the rains came, not even powdered rhinoceros horn. He said, "This sex business. I'm quite scorched by it, you know. Perhaps Old Nannie had an erotic influence." It was because of his scorching that his Rani had left him, although she was now as bad as he was, living in sin with this parsee in Bombay. The marriage had been a failure from the beginning because she wasn't an educated woman and he found he couldn't talk to her. He never referred to their ages at betrothal but told me that during the betrothal period he sent her all sorts of books, all the great English poets, and then James Joyce, T.S. Eliot, Proust, Kierkegaard, Ibsen and J.B. Priestley, to keep her up-to-date. He found out that she never read them. She was only interested in the Vedas and Tagore, "all that old stuff," and in being a good Hindu wife and mother, according to her lights, which meant gossiping over tea and exchanging recipes, discussing the price of saree cloth. He sometimes thought it was a pity that the English beat the French out of India instead of the other way round because the French took their literature seriously and, just as importantly, didn't see anything indecent in making love in the afternoon. But he couldn't deny that the broken marriage was his fault. When he started bringing women into the palace the Rani had called it a day. In answer to the inevitable question, I had told them both of my own divorce. Dora had said she was sorry and Krishi had said nothing. Now he said, "Is that why your wife called it a day, old man?" and grinned. I told him we'd both called it a day. She had brought men into the house. The grin was held but I think he was shocked, and forgave his Rani a lot at that moment. He reverted to the subject of her. They met occasionally at parties in Bombay, she with her parsee, he with his latest woman. It was all fearfully civilized; Bombay was the only decent place to live in the whole of the sub-continent. He only regretted the Rani hadn't been more civilized earlier on. "I don't come to Jundapur much," he said. "I do it really for Dora's sake." He'd always been sorry for Dora, although when we were children he'd been a bit in love with her, and had had an idea of making her a white Rani. "You were a bit in love with her too, William, weren't you? Remember how we used to bash each other when the jealousy got the better of us?"

I asked him why he was sorry for her. He said, "Can't you see?" but didn't wait for me to answer, instead talked about her past for ten minutes or so and gave me, like that, a picture of her as a young woman to which I fit her middle-aged face or an unclear, faintly stylized face that would serve for almost any young girl of Dora's colouring, but one who had an Indian Army father and (Krishi said) a musical mother. Perhaps Dora had tackled *Forest Fantasies* with more military precision than musical feeling. Certainly she announced the titles of the pieces she played for me in the darkened drawing room of the old agency bungalow in a manner her father might have been proud of, having no son: clearly, but a bit primly, proving her equality with the kind of boys who were taught not to be shy but also her special standing as a girl, who was justified in telling you off if she thought you sneaked looks in bushes. I suppose it was the impression she gave of standing up for herself without losing her girl's delicacy which attracted me to her when I saw her walking determinedly in white organdy in a direction that would lead her on to ground hallowed by and for myself.

This military, musical Dora was sent to school in Europe; not to the English girls' school I would have imagined her going to, but to convent schools in Italy first and then in France. This had been her mother's wish. She returned to India in 1939, when she was nineteen and then, after years of "old stone, nuns' habits and quiet cloisters," (Krishi had this odd notion of a convent-school education) her whole traumatic experience of British-Indian military life fell over her like a flag draped on a general's coffin. Music was laid aside. Perhaps she laid it aside as a girl might lay aside a talent for fine embroidery together with its needles and threads and work-in-progress, wrapped in silk and scented with lavender, to be brought out to pass any tranquil hours that might be spared from the hours of living and loving, tranquil hours which finally never came; or, as Krishi thought more likely from hints she had dropped and from the fact that she could no longer be persuaded to play the old black concert grand, which stood in the Jundapur drawing room with its lid open showing white keys stained as yellow as teeth with nicotine and brushed by the sharp fronds of an indoor palm, she laid it aside because she was a bit ashamed of having taken it seriously, of having "succumbed to decadent, artistic Europe," as Europe must have struck her retrospectively when the trauma smothered her and she found herself surrounded by eligible young subalterns who treated her piano-playing as they would treat a girl's talent for water-colouring, making her see it like that herself.

There could be some truth in both these interpretations. It is difficult to tell. When I asked Dora if she still played she said she hadn't done so for years, had "lost it," but in any case hadn't really had the gift, not the professional gift. She preferred nowadays to listen to recordings by Lympany or Moisevitsch or Cortot. And this sketches another picture for me of the young Dora in Italy, still wearing

white organdy, but with her face hidden from me because
she is bent over a keyboard suddenly hearing the un-Cortot
sounds she makes, and feeling a stiffness in wrists and fingers
which accounts for some of it, and warns her anyway that she
will never play professionally (as her mother had hoped?).
And then I see her having a straightforward weep to herself
and closing the piano lid with a sniff of resignation Major
Salford would have approved of.

But Krishi was dead-set on his own picture of Dora in the
grip of trauma. In his opinion she lost her head completely
and simply married the handsomest of the eligible subalterns in her father's regiment. "You can picture Harry
Paynter, can't you?" he said. "Blond, little moustache, pink
cheeks." And so, that night, I did picture him. Dora had a
portrait of him in her bedroom, a black and white photograph that she brought down and showed me the following
day. It was an old photograph. I saw what Krishi meant.

Could anything have been absurder, he asked, than our
Dora falling for a chap like that with nothing to him at all,
the sort of chap who made the British so often disliked as
individuals? And yet Dora had obviously been knocked for
a loop. Paynter had represented everything she felt she
had been exiled from, growing up surrounded, as she had
been (and momentarily Krishi forgot the nuns and the
cloisters), by all those Italian wops and French dagoes. I
remembered "wog" and tried to judge from his moonlit
expression whether he was subtly punishing me by dragging
the dark memory from its burial place in the island across
the water, but he looked quite unconscious of the sudden,
ghostly emergence, continued to explore one of his own obsessions—Dora in the grip of this trauma; Dora on the night
Harry proposed, dressed in something white and flimsy,
leaning out of her window gazing at the Indian moon and
watching a whole imperial procession of scarlet tuniced
Harrys leading sabre charges, or Harry alone, tunic torn,

head bloody, coming first through the gate of a relieved fort where she had been besieged for months, and saying "Hello, old thing." But now Harry probably opened the door of their flat in Calcutta, threw his brief case down and asked why the bloody fans weren't working.

The Paynters visited Jundapur in 1940. Krishi wasn't the Rajah then. He didn't succeed to the gaddi until 1946, but he thought that the palace and staying at it, as man and wife, completed their circle of Indian marital bliss. He said Paynter had been disappointed that there were no strings of ponies whose mouths he could rough up, no elephants, none of what Krishi called all that old rajah-razzamattaz, but there was the lake and the island and a boat to drift in under sunshades, the fable of Krishna, a rajah (Krishi's father), Krishi himself and his young wife who would one day be rajah and rani; and if the palace ran up debts to entertain the young sahib and his pretty wife the Paynters never knew: it was all part of Rajput jannu, and it was better to run up debts than levy an extra tax on the microscopic population, which was the kind of thing he said used to happen in Tradura. Goodness knew, for instance, how much Shikar Week had cost the Traduran peasantry.

"She was crazy about him," he said, "quite blind to defects that stuck out a mile." Paynter was rude to the servants, called Krishi's father "sir" but looked supercilious when doing so. I said, "Perhaps the palace made him nervous of doing the wrong thing?" but Krishi shrugged that off. The post-honeymoon visit wasn't a success. It was 1949 or 1950 before Dora and Krishi met again. She invited herself down because Harry had gone climbing in the Himalayas, "clinging on to his youth and a precipice." It was during this first post-war visit Krishi had begun to feel sorry for her. She looked as if she had lost a rupee and found an anna. The Rani was still in Jundapur in those days, and suspected Dora would become one of Krishi's women because they had always kept up some sort of correspondence. The Rani treated Dora with tremendous courtesy, but gave him beans after she'd gone. The following year Dora invited herself down again. Krishi postponed his departure for Bombay so as not to disappoint her. By now everything was gone, the Rani, the state, Dora's looks, Harry Paynter's military career, Krishi's waistline and most of his natural virility. And the only one of these he didn't regret was the state. "Thank God for integration," he said, "I signed everything like a shot." The other states in the old agency had signed like shots too: Tradura, Trassura, Premkar, Skakura and Durhat; although Tradura only signed like a shot because the political situation there had become very difficult. Tradura had always been in a mess, but it had been the only state of the six that had two pennies to rub together. The Maharajah, Ranjit Raosingh's son, had had trouble during the war from discontented subjects who clamoured for government by elected assembly. There had been meetings, speeches, brawls, beatings-up, sentences of imprisonment. The old jail on the edge of the maidan was crammed. After the war these factions became vocal again. There would have been riots if the Maharajah had shown the slightest sign of wavering, of standing out against Congress when Congress took over from the British Crown. For a long time before 1947 the six states my father had once advised, living on the spot, had come under the eye of an agent elsewhere, a man who was officially only the secretary to the Resident for a larger group of states several hundred miles away. "You'd rather given us up, you know," he said. "We obviously weren't worth bothering about any longer, just a bunch of rotten little bankrupt states that ought to have been broken-up years ago."

In my father's day, there had been an attempt to get the rulers of the Tradura agency states to federate, to pool their resources and administration with Ranjit Raosingh acting as

Rajpramukha. "We were hopeless on our own, too small even for lip-service democracy." Jundapur had been run, he couldn't call it ruled, by the rajah, assisted or hindered by the rani and other members of the family; like a village by a squire. When Krishi succeeded to the gaddi in 1946 he expanded the palace council but it was too late, too little. He had never felt like a rajah.

The federation scheme failed because Ranjit Raosingh was "terrified of his own shadow, eaten up with suspicion and greed and a false sense of values." In the end he and Krishi's father weren't speaking. The Rajah of Jundapur had kept away from Shikar Week, preferring the comforts of his sister's husband's home in Bombay. Krishi said, "And Ranjit Rao's eldest son was no better. They suffer from delusions, that family, all of them, delusions of grandeur." Since integration Ranjit Rao's son, the present maharajah, had shut the Tradura palace up and retired to the hills to sulk. The grandson who had gone to Switzerland to learn the value of time now acted in some smart-alec capacity to the Minister of Education in the provincial government that swallowed Tradura and Jundapur in 1948. The musical box in my lavatory was this son's homecoming present to Krishi.

Krishi hardly remembered my father. He didn't know whether the plan for federation was Father's idea or an idea of the Political Department which Father tried to put into action. Two other men had followed him, each for shorter terms than the five years that were usual for these appointments and by the time Krishi was old enough to take intelligent political notice of affairs he found the state he would inherit advised by the Crown by the old Indian system of a barefoot boy carrying a chitti in a cleft stick.

"We were hopeless on our own, but still wouldn't have been anything together," he said, and repeated, "Thank God for integration," and, "I signed everything like a shot."

When the representative of the new States Department that
had assumed the burden of the states from the old Political
Department visited him he handed Jundapur to him on a
plate, begged him to take it; but the whole business had
lasted months. He had been a fool. He should have led the
other states in the agency in a ganging-up attempt to make
things difficult. He blamed their eagerness to off-load their
responsibilities for the farcical negotiations which followed
the acts of signing everything like a shot: negotiations to fix
the size of the privy purse (which Krishi described as laugh-
able) and negotiations to distinguish between the rulers'
private property and the states' property. In the end he had
dug his heels in and submitted a dispute about "some silver
table junk" to arbitration, as he was entitled, but mainly for
what he called "the hell of it."

"We all became bannias, old man, adding figures, squab-
bling about knives and forks." There were three main
Hindu castes, he reminded me, in case I'd forgotten, which
he imagined I had; the Brahmins who were priests, the
Rajputs like himself who were supposed to be rulers and
warriors, and the bannias who were merchants and shop-
keepers. The whole thing had been an awful bore. A tragedy
too, not that he personally had anything to lose except a
deficit in the annual budget. But the English had thrown
the states to the wolves, hadn't they? You couldn't see the
Political Department for dust when it came to it. All that
stiff upper-lipped business that had ground the real India
down for centuries and left only the priests and the bannias
untouched was exposed in the end. The British showed
themselves bannias too, making up balance sheets and de-
ciding to cut their losses.

There were also three castes in England: the upper classes
who knew they were God, the lower-middle or working
classes who knew there wasn't a God, and the upper-
middle classes who could never forgive God for having ob-

viously got into the act of Creation first: English Brahmins, English bannias and English Rajputs. "We got your
Rajputs out here, old man. That's why it's our Rajputs
who've suffered most." English Rajputs were sannyasi at
heart, weren't they? men and women who sloughed off their
obligations at home and sought nirvana abroad. It was the
climate in England as much as the fact that they could
never be Rajputs at home that was responsible for the
English Rajputs seeking an Empire elsewhere in places like
India and Africa; the British climate and the scenery, no
proper flora and fauna, nothing much more than a rheuma-
tic stag staring red-eyed through Scotch mists, immigrant
cuckoos and shoals of mangy sparrows. The climate was
also why the English Rajputs liked cricket. It reminded
them of the hot summer sun they never had, except trau-
matically through the shades of their Hornby and their
Barlow long ago; all those mythical summers, white shirts,
green grass, nightingales when stumps were drawn and the
poets drinking beer. The wind and the willow.

And there had been a kind of exchange between the
English and the Indian Rajputs. Most of the tiger in India
were now dead and fixed on living-room walls in Chelten-
ham, and men like himself when they could forget they
had become Indian bannias, imagined themselves English
Rajputs. "Look at me, old man. I speak the same language
as you. We laugh at the same kind of things. I don't *ape*
English manners, they were drilled into me by Old Nannie
and the Prince's College. But underneath my princely Indian flesh I have the bones of the serf I always was. And under those layers of liberal flesh, Dora has the bones of the
memsahib she became." He paused. "Old man," he said,
"what kind of bones have *you* got underneath that smooth
expense-account exterior? You see how English I am? I even
recognize the look of the New Englishman who thinks
everybody can be a Rajput on the money they borrow

from bannias who also think they're Rajputs. The world is only safe for Brahmins."

Again he paused. "I'm glad you came," he said, and raised his glass. "There's no one else I could say these things to, old man. Certainly not to Dora. And you no longer count. Which is why we can be proper friends at last. Cheers."

"I'm sorry for Krishi," Dora said. This was on the following morning. Tatti-filtered sunlight that was bright and morning-fresh outside revealed the terrace as the place on which Mrs. Canterbury had sat investigating our games from that point of vantage with her standing-no-nonsense nose. Krishi wasn't up yet. Dora and I tackled corn flakes, eggs and bacon, toast, marmalade and coffee as we might tackle an air-mail edition of *The Times* that had just reached us from perfidious Albion; sharing it between us, knowing automatically that no one else would want it.

Breakfast over, she smoked and played with her coffee spoon. The portable standard fan clacked around slowly, grindingly, and made me feel like one of two lonely weather experts isolated in a metereological station. The disturbed air played with her curls and puffed up the sleeve edges of a tricel dress which this morning was mushroom-coloured. The smell of clove carnations was stronger than ever. I reminded her about the eau-de-cologne. She had had a dizzy spell at the age of seven and ever afterwards her mother refused to let her go out of the house without a dab of cologne on the temples and a sprinkling of it on her little handkerchief. Her handkerchiefs had lace edges, and she quite liked having the cologne sprinkled on them but hated it rubbed on her temples. It was a long time since she had thought of the cologne. I had had a special smell, too—what was it? A nice one. Peppermint. I nodded, not clearly remembering a particular leaning towards peppermint as a sweet-flavour.

She asked me whether I'd never wanted to follow in my

father's footsteps; she'd always got the impression I would when we were children. I said I supposed I had but that he had the foresight to discourage that kind of ambition. As far back as 1936 he'd asked me whether I thought the British policy of leading India to independence was all eyewash. She smiled and said yes, that was foresight, wasn't it, and then glanced away with that little look people sometimes have of controlling an urge to speak their minds. I thought she was thinking of Harry but she said this other thing, "I'm sorry for Krish."

The heat of Jundapur in May was sometimes more than she could stand. It was quite true that Jundapur gave her the only real holiday she and Harry could afford for her; Harry's expeditions cost him money because he had to contribute his whack, but she refused to let him give them up, as he'd offered to, they were the only opportunities he had of living an outdoor life; but the main reason for coming to Jundapur was so that she and Krish wouldn't drift apart. Krish was a very lonely man and she wasn't sure she believed him when he hinted at high life in Bombay. He had been more in love with the Rani than he admitted, or more in love with her than he knew himself. Being made to marry a girl of twelve when he was only sixteen and still at school proved to him that his English-style upbringing had been so much wool pulled over his eyes. He hadn't disliked the girl but what the girl represented—Mother India—and when she turned out to be very ordinary and not even especially attractive when old enough for the marriage to be consummated, Krish had buried his instincts to be kind to her and the marriage was doomed.

Dora saw the Rani twice, once when she and Harry had visited the palace shortly after their marriage, and then about ten years ago. The first visit, with Harry, was something neither of them would ever forget. There was nothing they wanted for. Krish's old father had been so kind and generous. He'd given them a silver tea service with their initials engraved. They still had it, it was the kind of thing you could never get rid of, however awkward things got from time to time over money, and although Harry was doing well enough now it was only because he'd stuck his chin out and got on with it, even taking insults from the kind of Englishmen who thought you were a brainless idiot if you happened to have been an army man and had to learn about business from the ground up at the age of thirty-two.

The second time she saw the Rani everything had changed. Jundapur had been taken over. Krish had got fat and drank too much and hardly talked when the Rani was in the room. The Rani herself was fat too, terribly shy, and kind on the surface, unable to talk about anything of much interest, but sharp as needles underneath. "Do you know what I mean, Bill, about that kind of Indian woman?" No, of course I didn't. She kept forgetting I didn't really know what life was like in India. I'd only known it as a boy. For every emancipated westernized Indian woman there were thousands like the Rani. Sometimes they tried hard to fit in with their husbands' more westernized style of life, but mostly they saw their true role as that of leaders-back to the old matriarchal society which began with doling out rice and flour to the cook from a locked store cupboard and ended with plotting political coups behind purdah screens in old palaces.

It was so silly. Women were in the world to help men and rear their children, not hinder them. Did that sound silly and old-fashioned? Well that's what she was, but in a way she wouldn't change a single thing that she and Harry had gone through together because the things that happened had forced her to look that simple, homely fact straight in the eye. In the old days she hadn't seen Harry as a man who needed help. He had looked marvellous in mess dress. In those days she'd been as brainless and empty-headed as you could imagine. Certainly she knew nothing about life, nothing about men, and looked on men like Harry as not much more than strong right arms and chivalrous lovers who organized the world for her with splendid efficiency. But all that romantic dream business ended quickly enough for any girl, especially if there was a war. Harry had been in Burma. Her father took a brigade to Africa and was killed almost at once. Harry came through all right, but then almost immediately afterwards there was independence and partition and the break-up of the old Indian Army, Harry losing the job he'd set his heart on from as far back as he could remember. He joined the Pakistan Army because he thought Muslims manlier than Hindus and stuck it for the two years he'd contracted for, but he was never convinced that one day India and Pakistan wouldn't get to grips over the Kashmir problem and he'd find himself fighting old comrades. They'd talked seriously of going home to England, facing facts and getting down to it there. During the massacres that accompanied partition they'd seen the trains coming into Lahore piled with bodies of people who'd been killed between there and Delhi, either Muslims killed by Hindus or Hindus killed by Muslims, never British, the British were treated with great courtesy; and for a time Dora thought she couldn't go on living in a country that showed itself so savage just under the skin. But Harry had said, "It's only a phase," and he'd been right. In a way Harry had felt the English were to blame, although he never actually said so. He said we'd got out of the country at least ten years too soon, and that India still needed help. They both loved India. They'd both been brought up there, with the idea of serving the country. Well, she didn't know about herself serving the country, a man felt that more than a woman, but she knew she'd grown to love it. She'd loved France and Italy too, while she was there, but when she got back in 1939 there wasn't any doubt where her affections lay, with

India and with Harry. The things that had happened to
them since had given her a sense of purpose, too; encouraging Harry when he got low and depressed.

She twisted her wedding ring. Harry had started in 1949
as a representative for a firm that imported agricultural
equipment, then he had several different jobs, some in offices,
some as a representative which he preferred because it got
him out and about, one as a personal assistant to a man
Dora described as a drunken Scot who mimicked Harry's
accent at a cocktail party once. Now he was a public relations
officer for an organization that dealt with farm machinery
and chemical fertilizers. They were happy enough, but
Harry was so damned conscientious about chemical fertilizers
it made her angry because she knew that deep down he
couldn't care less about them but had convinced his worka-
day self that chemical fertilizers were what made the world
go round. A man had to think something did. It was probably comic, really, simply bad luck for them that neither
of them had grown up with chemical fertilizers in their nurs-
eries. On the day anyone was born you could judge the source
of their possible future disappointment just by looking
round the room they were born in and interpreting the
family ikons.

And this was why she didn't want herself and Krish to
drift apart. He'd lost much more than Harry because he'd
never *had* as much, if I saw what she meant? Had I ever
thought what kind of an atmosphere a boy like Krishi (quite
unconsciously, she used the old diminutive) grew up in, a boy
whose father was a rajah, and yet not a rajah, because there
was always a white man in the background, a man for
instance like my father, watching everything he did and
reporting back to Delhi or Simla? "Krish was scared of
your father, you know." She didn't mean scared. Scared was
the wrong word. But there must have come a time when
he learned that neither his succession nor his father's right

to continue ruling was automatically assured, but depended to quite a large extent on the good opinion of men like my father. A boy like Krish would grow up to think of the political agent much as she remembered thinking at Marpur of The Brig and The General: as men even her father had to say "sir" to, and treat with reverence. Only in Krish's case it would have been worse. There was nothing her father's brigadier could do to her, but quite a lot that the political agent could do to Krish. For instance, Krish's education had to meet with his approval. And hadn't there been a lot of argument in Tradura about who should succeed Ranjit Raosingh? Had I thought what this had meant not only to Krish who would hear the gossip about succession but also to the rival sons, and of the sucking-up there probably was by both of them to my father? "Krish was scared of you, too," she said, "because you were the political agent's son." And I had been a bit of a bully, if I remembered, very conscious of my physical and social superiority over him.

She smiled. "But you were fond of us too, weren't you? And we were fond of you. We were all fond of each other." This had been another problem for boys like Krish. He would never be sure how genuine his affection for the English was. On the one hand he had someone like Old Mutton trying to turn him into a carbon copy of an English public school boy, on the other he lived in a ramshackle palace and heard his elders saying rude things about the English, but his elders also taught him to treat the English with respect if only because that was the way to get things out of them. At other times he would be told by his elders to remember he was a Rajput, and just as good as the English, and never to forget his ancestors, or his God. God knew how many different ways a boy like Krish would be pulled. And it was no good saying, well, we were only children. The three of us had played the whole adult thing out there

on the island as children. We had had to work hard at being
fond even though we were fond. She had admired me, and
liked me, but had to admit she was also sucking-up a bit
to the political agent's son because he might be Viceroy
one day (he wouldn't have been, but as a child she had
thought so) and she'd had daydreams about being Vicereine
with me. But she loved Krish more, even though she thought
him a bit of a namby-pamby in comparison.

She looked down the terrace. "But then I didn't trust him
like I trusted you. It's what we'd all been taught, wasn't
it? To love, yes, but never quite to trust, not to speak or
even think of not trusting, but to feel it. Can there be love
without trust? Yes, of course there can. Often. But Krish
comes off worst, doesn't he? He doesn't trust himself any
longer. I don't think he quite knows what he is."

And she smoothed her arm, leaning forward in her
chair, one elbow on the breakfast table. I mustn't be taken
in by his cynical western pose. He had got that from the
Bombay international set, which was his latest, perhaps his
last influence. She guessed he hadn't told me about the local
government committees he was serving on for agricultural
and educational reforms, village welfare, local light industrial development. She'd only found out about them bit by
bit over a long period. She didn't think it was done for
effect. She wished she had known him when he was a young
man, within sight of sitting on the gaddi; but apart from
the visit in 1940 with Harry, when Krish struck her as
nervous and shy, that part of his life was a closed book to
her. Occasionally he hinted these days at all the plans he had
had to get Jundapur back on her feet, but directly she
questioned him he assumed what she called his "all that
rot" attitude and grumbled about his privy purse. She
thought it likely that the privy purse was as small as he said
it was because the revenue in Jundapur on which it was cal-
culated could never have been large and of course all the

servants and old pensioners had to be paid out of it. There was one ex-ruler whose privy purse was as little as a hundred and seventy rupees a year. On the other hand, Krish's family had obviously had money of their own which the government couldn't touch. Perhaps he felt guilty about that, especially if the money had been accumulated years and years ago at the expense of the population. And of course I mustn't take Jundapur as typical of what had happened to the princes. A friend of hers had visited one of the larger old palaces a couple of years ago and had said you just couldn't tell the difference, and that even though you knew the gold plate was only held in trust by the maharajah it didn't affect what you felt when you ate off it.

She suspected Krish's plans for when he was rajah involved spending private money for the public good, and that such a socialistic idea was responsible for widening the gulf between himself and the Rani. It was typical of poor Krish that when it came to it (and he succeeded in 1946, a whole year before anyone knew the British were really going to fulfil their promise to leave India) he hadn't done much about it, so far as she could tell. A man like Krish wouldn't have learned much initiative, would he, in spite of the Prince's College and Old Mutton?

She said, "How little we know about each other." Who could tell what really went on in Krish's mind? Perhaps he only like having her in Jundapur because he couldn't break the habit of imagining it was in keeping with his princely status to be on intimate terms with a member of the Raj, the daughter of a brigadier in the Indian Army. And had she ever been innocent of a charge of coming to Jundapur because an Indian prince was not only a socially acceptable member of a subject race but a feather in the cap of middle-class girls like herself? She laughed, and said, "You've kept clear of it all, Bill. Problems like these strike you as quite ridiculous don't they? After all, historically speaking it's all

over." People weren't interested in history any more, anyway. You used to leave it to history to show that something
was obsolete. But in Harry's business, for instance, there
was now a policy for what was called planned obsolescence, which was something to do with gearing demand to
supply. All the same, planned obsolescence or not, feeling a
bit obsolete herself she couldn't help wondering about these
things, couldn't help wondering, for instance, what the
Britons felt like when they lost the Romans, and what the
Romans felt like when they lost Britain.

She referred again to what she had said earlier about how
little people knew each other in spite of all the talk and gossip
that went on day in day out. She spoke of her mother and
father. She said, "You remember them, don't you?" I
recollected Mrs. Salford fussing over Dora, dressed in flow-
ered georgette, and Major Salford's polished boot making
marks in the sand. When her father was reported killed in
Africa her mother couldn't accept it for a long time, hated
being left alone in the bungalow because she always thought
he'd walk in saying, "Phew, it's a scorcher today." Harry
was in Burma at this time, and Dora was doing some nursing
at the cantonment hospital. She didn't do anything but
roll bandages and take temperatures but all the little Anglo-
Indian nurses had to call her Sister. She had wanted to go
out to Bengal or Assam, but her mother pleaded with her
to stay, and had even pulled strings to see that she did. Mrs.
Salford said that losing David like that was the same to her
as if he had left the bungalow for early morning parade
while she was still asleep, hadn't come back to breakfast, or
lunch, hadn't come back at all, had gone without a word;
and after a bit she got this idea into her head that David
had preferred it like that because he had never really liked
her. They had never quarrelled and she saw this as evidence
of his not loving her. After twenty-five years of married life
she believed that there were things about each other they

just didn't know. She had died about four years ago, and
Dora had to admit that towards the end an ageing mother
living on an army pension had been a terrible burden to
herself and Harry, not so much financially as emotionally.
Just before she died Mrs. Salford had said to her, "Have I
made your whole life quite impossible?" Which showed,
didn't it, what odd ideas people got, because she had always
loved her mother, and her mother had never made life
anything but happy and pleasant for her.

"I'm sorry," Dora said, "I'm talking your head off. It's
because seeing you has brought it all back so clearly. Tell
me something that isn't depressing. Tell me about your job."

Dora said she wanted to do some shopping. She always
took back a present from Jundapur for Harry. Would I
take her in the car? Krishi said, "We'll all go." Alone with
me he said, "D'you think Harry brings her a present from
the Himalayas?"

The town was a confusion of narrow streets, open shop
fronts, wandering cattle. It smelled of dung and straw and
hot spiced foods that sizzled in pans on charcoal fires. We
drew up and entered a shop called The Automobile Emporium. There weren't any motor cars for sale. It was a
haberdashery and general store. There were lengths of blue-
striped cotton shirting, lace table cloths, hair oil that looked
like stale plasma in dusty bottles with insecure corks; curling photographs of Indian film stars recommending tooth-
paste. A glass cabinet contained tins of jam, a string of
what might have been dried-up onions or fossilised vertebrae,
and tablets of soap in wrappings decorated with patterns of
lotus flowers and girls looking into pools. The proprietor
was called Hari Janmal. We were shown into an inner room
that had a tiled floor, a brass spittoon and a velvet armchair
that was offered to the Rajah Sahib. It also contained a
wire cage and a green parrot that warned us with its wings.

Dora had gone suddenly, back into the shop. "Where are you, Dora?" Krishi called. "Wurrah— Yadoora!" the parrot cried; which made us jump, then laugh, and brought Dora back to gather with us round the cage while Hari Janmal extolled the parrot's virtues and hinted at a high price.

"I don't think it's quite Harry," Dora said, and held up a yellow neck choker done over in designs of polo sticks as nearer the kind of thing she wanted. "Say Dora," Krishi told the parrot. Hari Janmal wanted the parrot to say "Salaam Rajah Sahib." The parrot arched her wings, opened her beak and rolled her tongue. Now she would sing, Hari Janmal explained. But she didn't sing. I said, "Say— Salaam Rajah Sahib." And Melba looked at me for the first time, swivelled her looking eye round as if she'd not noticed me before. "Salaam Rajah Sahib," I repeated. Krishi said, "Say Salaam Conway Sahib. Conway Sahib. William Conway. William Conway," and jabbed my chest by way of introduction.

"William Conway!" Melba shrieked and bounced up and down, weaving her neck, faster and faster. "William Conway! William Conway!" Then she bent her head, let her wings fold back and began to sing her song of the Paraguayan Hills.

Oh, said Krishi, she'd fallen for me, she'd got it bad for me, I'd have to buy her. "What on earth would *I* do with a parrot?" I asked him, and Dora said, "I expect it's got parrot's disease anyway. How much is the choker?"

On our way out I bought Dora some lace handkerchiefs. When I gave them to her she looked touched and said, "Oh, Bill. How sweet," and for a moment our eyes met and I think we both remembered the kiss. There was a crowd around the car. They salaamed Krishi. "Oh, Lord, all this fearful rot," he muttered, but looked pleased, and talked all the way home along the tree-lined sunlit road to the palace, while Dora, seated between us on the front seat of the hired Vauxhall, examined the seams of the choker and the workmanship of the lace on the handkerchiefs which she said was as good as the lace the nuns had worked for the altar cloths when she was at the convent school in France.

That afternoon, at about five, we rowed to the island to see the birds of paradise in the cage.

The lingam was still there, stonily erect in the grass near the landing stage. We none of us referred to it. Dora said, "We ought to have dressed up, although we're all a bit long in the tooth for that, aren't we?" and freed her neck of the weight of her hair with a gesture of resignation. She took my hand to climb out of the boat. On the far shore the palace was yellow with late sunlight and the sky behind it turquoise green. The rays of the sun, slanting obliquely, were sliced into tubes and funnels by the branches of the trees that surrounded us and lay in pools where they found open ground. The shadowy thickets were indigo blue as if yellow had been drained from their green leaves by the yellowing sun. Later, you felt, there would be lake-water mist binding the feet of the trees with white scarves, but the ground now was tinder dry and there was a mellow resiny scent, like glue spiced with vanilla heating on an open fire. I followed Dora and Krishi along the old track, through one after the other of the slanting funnels of sunlight. Moving through them was like flicking them with our bodies as you flick railings with a stick. The clearing was larger than I'd expected. A white cloth had been laid out and spread for tea. There were blue cushions to sit on. One of the servants waited, tending an elaborate primus stove on which a copper kettle was boiling up. "Char's up, chaps," Krishi said. Dora said, "Oh, Krish, what a nice surprise! I could just do with a cup." We sat on the blue cushions. The pale-green rusted copper dome caught the

sunlight but most of the cage below it was in shadow. I
asked whether the birds really were still there. Oh yes, she
said, we'll see them in a minute. I said you'd have thought
they'd all have rotted away by now. "Oh, but they're going,"
she said, "if Krish hadn't chucked the ladder into the lake
you could have got up there, then you'd have seen." I asked
why Krishi had chucked the ladder into the lake. He said,
"Have one of those sugar cakes."

"He's embarrassed," Dora said, looking at Krishi but
talking to me. The fact was he'd been a bit tiddly, hadn't
he? Oh, more than tiddly, old thing, he said, in fact he didn't
remember much about it and suspected Dora of adding to
the tale every time she reminded him about it. "All I
remember," he said, "was suddenly not being able to stand
the birds." But it began with old Akbar Ali dying, she
said. Did I remember the man who used to climb the iron
ladder and unscrew the birds and bring them down and
do all those fascinating things to them? Well, he died, how
long ago, two years was it? and there wasn't anyone to do
the job because nobody had bothered to learn or old Akbar
Ali had been too jealous to teach them. He used to let her
help though. But two years ago when she came she found
he'd gone and Krishi wouldn't let her climb up and bring
the birds down. He'd dragged the ladder to the lake and
thrown it in so that she shouldn't even try, and then he'd
got terribly tight, and she'd got a bit tight herself. Did he
remember, she asked him, how he'd suddenly appeared on
the terrace with a lighted pressure lamp and a gun and said,
"Come on, Dora, we're going hunting—" She'd thought it
sounded fun. They rowed across to the island and when they
got there she realized what he was up to, that he meant to
shoot the birds down, and she'd had an awful job to stop
him. In the end the gun and the pressure lamp had gone
into the lake too. "The lamp stayed alight for a second or

two," she said. "Wasn't it odd, Krish? It made the lake look absolutely bottomless, somehow."

It was his grandfather's fault anyway, Krishi said. There was a naughty family joke. He hoped I wouldn't mind. Did Dora think I would mind? Oh, no, she said, not *now*. Well, then, Krishi said, the family joke was that the birds in the cage were thought to be like the British Raj, creatures who took it for granted they excited wonder and admiration wherever they went and had no idea that they were dead from the neck up and the neck down, weren't flying at all and were imprisoned in their own conceit anyway. Dora caught my eye. Krishi said that the family joke had misfired, though, because history had shown that it was the princes of India who were dead, in spite of all their finery and high-flown postures. The British had stuffed them and burnished their fine feathers, but as princes they were dead even if they weren't dead as men, and if not actually dead then anyway buried alive in a cage the British had never attempted really to open. Because all that autocratic God Bless the Squire stuff, such as we'd seen in Jundapur this morning, all that was really a prison, wasn't it?

So I saw, didn't I, that when he tried to shoot the birds it was a gesture to history? He was embracing his own destruction like Camus and Sartre. Now the birds would rot and fall one by one and that was symbolic too. "It's like the legends about them only being obtainable dead," Dora said. "Do you remember?" I said I didn't. Oh, but surely I remembered the legends? They were all set out in the glass case with the drawings. Krishi said Dora and I had better go and see the birds now while they were still there, but he wouldn't come himself because the cage always gave him the creeps. Out of earshot, approaching the cage, Dora said in a low voice: "Poor old Krish. I wish he could grow a thicker skin."

The door, or gate, was now rusted into a permanently open position. "Didn't I once see to this?" I asked her; and in spite of her uncertainty at once recalled the whole incident, even the feeling of the sandpaper and oil, getting Krishi to hold the tools while I worked away, entirely absorbed in what I was doing; and leaving him already regretting a scheme that left Dora behind and himself not wholly occupied. Standing at the open gate you could smell an ancient dampness. The rains would always find their way in but, even at its strongest and highest, the sun would cast the shadow of the roof and only superficially dry the cage's floor. It was a plant-house smell, warm and cloying; a smell like that of gum oozing from erectile stalks, the juices from bruised, aromatic petals, the fumes of furry hotwater pipes.

"I always think there should be tortoises," Dora said. "Big ones that come out to sun themselves," and led the way into the cage.

Absurd, fantastic, unchanged; no time at all had passed inside those lattice-work bars, only outside in the place where boys and girls grew taller and changed their voices and their habits; the *Paradisaeidae* flew in the upper air in the total abstraction of their flight to the edge of nowhere.

I peered up at the swooping shape of one of the species of Great Bird whose coffee-coloured body, green enamelled throat and trailing network of orange plumes glowed through the shadows. From the ground there was no sign of decay. I asked her how long she thought they'd last. She said she didn't know, but there would come a time when she wouldn't be able to face coming to the cage because it would be awful when it happened. Our adult voices were out of real earshot, were cast away by the waves of silence that spun down from the roof, spiralling away from the frozen beat of the wings, round and round, down and down, bringing with them a faint, metallic echo of other voices from long ago: *What are they, what's it for, why's it interested in hens, look, those are the females, there, perched on the little branch.*

"I used to get toothache," Dora said, turning towards me, holding her arms crossed like Aunt Ethel, as if to keep out a chill she felt in the cage. "You both laughed at me, so I had to suffer in silence." She didn't get toothache any more, she said, and looked up at the birds again. On her neck, in the soft cavities where the jawbone turned towards the earlobes, there were faint patches of yellow. Didn't I remember this? she asked, turning, crossing the floor leading the way through the tropical bushes. "This" was the cabinet in which the coloured drawings, descriptions and legends could be inspected like old coins under glass. The glass had quite recently been unevenly wiped clean of dirt. She rubbed away the remaining patches with the casual, but possessive movement of someone whose task this was and who automatically noticed evidence of her earlier slackness. "You used to like these better than the specimens," she said; "you said the birds were a bit mouldy and their colours not nearly as bright."

Protected from the sun, because even the slanting rays that would have reached the cabinet were cut off by the thickness of the foliage surrounding the bower, the pictures, although mottled around the edges, were well-preserved. Each stabbed awake a memory almost startlingly precise so that during the initial spasm of recognition I saw them one by one through eyes no older than my boyhood eyes. There was one particular picture, an engraving entitled "Natives of Aru shooting the Great Bird of Paradise," a picture which although only black and white had, I remembered, in spite of never having consciously thought of it since, fascinated me more than any of the others as a boy. Already, writing of it here in Manoba, the detail is going. I know there was a wood, stout-trunked trees with rather stylised curling branches, sparsely leaved. In one, or perhaps two of them—yes, I think it was two—in the fork formed by the trunk and the main branches, one of the woolly-haired natives of Aru crouched under a flimsy hide of twigs and leaves aiming up with bow and blunted arrow at the paradise birds whose orange plumes had had to be depicted as white to get the contrast. Against this whiteness their bodies and opened wings were dramatically dark. It illustrated the story that when the birds congregated in this fashion a great number fell to the hunters before one of them, becoming aware of the smell of death under the excitement and passion of display, took alarm and panicked them all into flight and to temporary safety. In the picture, unaware as yet, they skimmed the treetops and danced in the branches; and in the middle distance there was the first victim lying on the ground, stunned by the blunt tip of an arrow. One of the natives of Aru was picking it up, to kill it by throttling. The arrows were blunt so that the feathers shouldn't be spoiled by blood and the market value of the skin reduced. Closer detail is gone, and I suppose quite soon the whole picture will once more fade from my mind; but if in twenty years I should chance upon it again I think that each mark of the engraver's tool would again strike home, just as it did that afternoon when, like the coloured drawings of the birds, it leaped at the eyes and stripped them of the mists of thirty years, so that at the instant of discovery time was absent from the day. But, the instant over, the thirty years that really separated discovery from rediscovery were sucked back into the vacuum their going had created and seemed then almost too big for it, as if more years came back than had gone.

She was pointing at the pictures and the maps of the islands where the birds were found, reading bits of the legends aloud, commenting on them, laughing, saying things like: "You remember that, don't you? You said something about it, what was it?" She stood in profile, as in the makan on the day of the tiger. The tangential lines at the corners of her eyes, with the yellowing patches on her neck, the husky, ragged, memsahib voice became, briefly, focuses for my tenderness, and acquired beauty as did all the traces left upon her by her years, for her years were her life, and I had loved her as a child.

The bird of paradise, it had been thought, was too beautiful a creature to inhabit the natural world and if further proof were needed that it belonged to the supernatural it was to be found in the fact that the bird was footless. Having no foot, where or how would it perch when tired of flying? And who had ever seen one alive? The bird must be a creature of heaven, although not immortal. It flew from birth to death without pausing, some said into the sun, others that it flew into the teeth of any wind that was blowing to keep its splendid trailing plumes from blinding it in flight. For food it sucked in through its beak the celestial dews that fell each night and morning. Its eggs were laid in flight, onto the back of the male bird whose back was hollowed into the shape of a nest. And when its lifespan was ended it folded its wings and fell dead, down through the airy realms of paradise, to earth where man was at last allowed to see and make use of it.

Men like the natives of Aru who stunned them with arrows, throttled them, cut off the legs, cut out the skull, sometimes cut off the purely functional wings, then dried and cured them and stretched the skins on lengths of bamboo, or alternatively, stripped the dead birds and used their feathers for personal decoration, naturally enough knew the truth; but when it came to bartering the skins with Malay traders and the early European travellers who sailed to the Moluccas to buy cloves and nutmegs, one wondered, Dora thought, how much was done to disguise the truth, how much left to the commonsense of the purchasers, how much of the secrecy that the natives obviously surrounded the birds with was due to their commercial instincts, how much to their own awe and superstition of such unique creatures. One wondered whether they laughed at the traders who for years never seemed to be given the opportunity of seeing one alive, or whether they laughed a bit at themselves for half believing in stories they knew were false, or whether being primitive men they took their myths seriously, used them, perhaps, as a form of worship.

Moved by their experiences in buying the skins of these birds, the Malay traders called them the birds of God; the Portuguese called them birds of the sun; the Dutch gave them their lasting, European name, birds of paradise. At the end of the sixteenth century a Dutchman actually wrote them up as legless, wingless, in constant airborne existence from birth to death. In the seventeenth century an Englishman, who, one imagined, was the kind who would have nothing to do with the idea of legless birds, went sniffing around the Malay Archipelago and was told that the *Paradisaeidae* ate nutmegs, that the nutmegs made them drunk, so that they fell not dead but senseless and were then killed by ants. No one seemed to have been prepared to admit shooting them. No complete specimen was seen in Europe until after the latter half of the eighteenth century when the legend of their having no legs was recorded for all time in the Latin name given to the Great Bird species: *Paradisea apoda*—meaning footless bird of paradise. No one, either, seemed prepared to kill the myth but to let it grow.

I suppose that, as a boy, the legends made no special impression on me other than a general one that the birds were curiosities to the kind of people who couldn't be expected to have known any better because they probably thought the world was flat anyway. For myself, as a boy, there was, after all, the evidence of the stuffed birds, mounted on almost invisible but real enough rods and perched on branches. They had wings and feet, and beaks with which to peck at fruit and berries and drag worms up out of the earth. My boyhood delight in them was in their colour and finery which corresponded to my idea of all natural splendours: sun, shade, nettles, white peacocks that looked like Viking ships and erected their fans if I went too close.

But with Dora it had been quite a different matter. As a child, she said, she was horrified at the idea of their legs being cut off, thought for a long time that this was done while the birds were still alive and still wouldn't swear that sometimes that hadn't been the case. She talked about the time she and Krishi were alone and he shut her in the cage for a joke. She said, "Don't you remember?" and then when I said I didn't, "Krish doesn't remember either." But she was convinced it had happened. She remembered the first few moments, thinking that Krishi was really being an awful bore; remembered rattling the gate and shouting, "Oh, do come and open it, Krish!" She thought he was hiding, then that he had left the clearing altogether, might leave the island and forget all about what he'd done. It would have been all right, she said, if she hadn't begun to think about the legs that got cut off. She knew she'd be missed sooner or later, but that didn't help when she began to realize how the legs would fall, one by one, if someone got at the stuffed birds in the cage. She lost her head, imagined that the legs were actually falling, not spiralling down gently as such lightweight objects might have been expected to, but coming with a heavy plop, one after the other. And when there weren't any more plops and she thought it was all over she found it wasn't. She had to close her eyes and press her hands against her ears because the drops of blood had begun to fall from the wounds. She screamed when she

couldn't stand it any longer. The gate was opened and she
ran out and didn't stop until she got to the stone steps where
the boat was moored.

"Who let you out?" I asked.

"Krishi," she said, using the childhood diminutive again.
"He was hiding after all. I knew it was him and not you
because his face was painted blue for Krishna."

Before we left the cage we stood and gazed up at the
birds in silence. I assumed I would never see them again.
Dora said it was funny, wasn't it, to think that all the time
as kids there'd been that private joke about them being
like the British? Did I think Krish had known about it
then? What had I thought about them? I said I'd thought
them fine and splendid but perfectly natural. She said, yes,
she saw how they would have struck me like that, even if
I pretended not to think much of them. It was a typically
masculine attitude. She'd thought them splendid as well, but
more as omens of all the marvellous things that were going
to happen later, not of the things she was going to do but of
the things that were going to happen to her. She supposed the obsession she had about the birds' legs was really
a warning that the future wasn't going to be all that great.
She laughed, pointed out the three perched female birds.
Poor things, she said, the finer-feathered their cockbirds
were the prouder they were and the higher they tried to
fly, but also their skins were more valuable, weren't they?
They'd get their legs cut off quickest of all.

She put two fingers of her left hand on to her temple
and rubbed, as if she needed cologne there to soothe a
sudden ache. Her eyes had brightened, liquefied just per-
ceptibly along the lower rims. Leaving the cage our bodies
brushed lightly together. Hers felt as hard as flint.

"Krish," she called, "I've been telling Bill about the time
you locked me in the cage, you bad boy."

"I never locked you in the rotten old cage," he said. Behind the hand he had put up to shield his eyes from the rosy-bronze light that was now spreading over the clearing his expression couldn't be seen clearly. "Well somebody did," Dora insisted, "and it wasn't Bill because he never painted his face blue. Did you, Bill?"

We sat on the cushions, in the place where we had exchanged vows to stand for ever in defense of each other. None of us spoke of rakhi-bandan. I couldn't tell whether they had forgotten or felt, as I did, that I at least had made too poor a showing of keeping the vow to have the subject raised. Krishi said, "I saved you from a snake, old man. You remember that, don't you?" I shook my head, told them I only remembered Krishi taking the boat back to the palace shore, leaving Dora and myself alone, until it was dark, and we stood on the steps and watched search-party lanterns bobbing about in the garden. Dora said that it was odd how the things only one of us remembered seemed to be about two of us together, never three. "It is all deeply Freudian, no doubt," Krishi explained. "The island was haunted in those days. Now even the ghosts have buggered off."

The rosy-bronze light was deepening in colour. It might have been on such an afternoon that I squatted in the cage and pretended to be dead after the attack by the swooping, screaming birds, when I clutched the bars and saw my bloody wrists, had the parched feeling in my mouth, and called out for water; a waking dream as vivid still as the ride across the maidan to save Dora from the wheeling horsemen.

Turning from the cage to look at Dora and Krishi I found them sunk into their private thoughts. Thirty years ago, coming to Jundapur, I had found them locked in secrets I thought they shared. Perhaps I was wrong to have thought they shared them. In my mind's eye I saw Krishi walk away, a prince in torn finery, after the fight which Dora had left us to settle because the men in her life were not to be hindered, only threatened later with losing her if they didn't behave. Perhaps her romantic dreams had lasted longer than Harry Paynter had found comfortable while his self-esteem was taking knocks elsewhere. There were things I would never know about Dora and Krishi except that Krishi was sorry for her and she was sorry for Krish.

I hadn't killed the past by going back to Jundapur. I hadn't buried my dead. The dead weren't dead. Everything had grown directly out of the past, undeviatingly; you could squint from the rather blowsy flower down the stem and see the living root; a root which had shaped me to want to ride against the wind but also shaped me to drift with it until it left me in a place like Four Birches with Anne, wetting and lifting my paper finger to confirm my suspicion that it had dropped forever, knowing the world would never blame me because it wouldn't even notice; only I would notice, lash myself sometimes for it, as I did in the cage as a boy, but leave it on the whole to heaven, secure in the knowledge that in reality there was no wind actually to ride into other than a fantasy wind across an open space and a fantasy wind of wings beating in a cage, the wings of birds whose legs were cut off to prove to fools there was such a place as paradise.

"Are you going to have a look at Tradura?" Dora asked suddenly. Perhaps she wanted to go there, comfortably, in the hired car. "You can't get in," Krishi said. "It's all shut up." I told them I wouldn't have the time anyway, that I must be off tomorrow to see this man I had mentioned in Muzzafirabad. Tradura wouldn't be dead either, but I didn't want to see its flower; to find, for instance, that the iron gateway from the agency bungalow looked too narrow for a horse-drawn carriage to pass through with dignity. "Must you go, Bill?" "Won't you stay for the rains, old man?"

The rains, when they came, yes, *they* would be heralded by wind. The leaves would show their silvery backs, and Dora and Krishi would part for another year, he to Bombay, she to Calcutta. They identified me with the rains, I thought, wanted me to stay because they wanted the rains to be with them and release them from each other, float them gently off their May-time sandbank until another year went by and it was time to meet again and watch each other for clues that would explain the meaninglessness of their lives. The bearer appeared from where he had sat apart and began to collect the scattered teacups. "We'd better go. It's time for a drink," Krishi said. We stood, and Krishi and I brushed tiny green daggers of grass from our trousers. "How green you are," Dora said. "Do you remember that game?" and she began to hum the monotonous little tune.

"Is there a place?" I asked Krishi while Dora helped the bearer with the picnic basket. He said, "Anywhere." I walked across the clearing. Returning I found them both temporarily absent, stood by the cage door for a moment and then entered and looked at the birds once more, because there was nothing else to do. In the months or years to come, as the wet and humidity got at them, the birds would slacken on their wires, lose their look of flying, then droop and begin to fall away, scattered by the blunt arrows of time into bits and pieces, leaving part of a breast or neck perhaps, a wing here, the cobwebby shadow of a once gallant plume. I went over to the cabinet, peered through the glass at the picture of the natives of Aru, and then at the coloured pictures, one by one, and finally the maps.

Cranston's fingers, through which you could still see daylight, tapped the glass. One finger pointed at the islands. "He's here. This one called Manoba." For a while I stared at the map, wondering how I could have missed seeing that in miniature it was really the same as the one on Cranston's wall, until I remembered how Dora's makan profile had just then taken my attention; and Cranston's map was on a larger, too-many-trees-for-the-wood scale, delineating a different world altogether from the simplified and long dead world preserved under glass, a world in which Manoba was no larger than a pinhead and only named because of the species of great bird of paradise that was said, years ago, to have lived on the higher reaches of its hills.

I thought: So it's Daintree after all; Daintree who could give my life purpose, or whose end will best illustrate the one I'll come to, for lack of it.

4

I HAVE often been tempted to set Melba free in defiance of Griffin's and Daintree's warnings that she would die in the forest, violently in all likelihood. Her increasingly difficult sulks if I leave her alone almost suggest she knows that time is running out and that she is becoming a practical problem for the man she sings to. Does she know I am going and expect to be deserted? As I said to Krishi in The Automobile Emporium: what does a man like myself do with a parrot? What problems of transportation lie ahead, what formalities have to be tackled to smooth her passage through customs and veterinary sheds? Perhaps none, perhaps too many. She watches me rip leaves from the calendar and sometimes I ask her whether she fancies Lew, or Lew's children who often stand like three naked little savages and watch her feed. When I say "Lew" she opens her beak and arches her wings which I'd take as a sign of her approval of him if it weren't for the fact that whenever he comes near her she sits dumb and resentful, watching him with an eye that looks as balefully red as a ruby. With Daintree it is different. She makes a great show of feathers for him.

But it's only to myself she sings. We are committed to each other. When she shrieks and rages and I lose my temper with her we are acting out the part of lovers; and so when I pick the cage up and swing off down the hill on the first stage of the long journey home I shan't feel embarrassed as I did on the morning I left Jundapur and found her presented to me by Krishi and Dora. Krishi had bought her for me but Dora handed her over because when Hari Janmal delivered the cage after breakfast she noticed that its circular handle could be passed over my hand to my wrist like a big bangle with a monstrous charm suspended from it. I had given her handkerchiefs. The cage, with Melba in it, was her rakhi, she said. Krishi said that he couldn't stand the thought of the parrot going through life shouting "William Conway!" unless she had William Conway close at hand to hear. Love's path never ran smoothly, he said, but there were limits to the obstacles that should be put in its way. And the parrot would be my personal bird of paradise. The present was given in affection, but also, I fancy, ironically, and I think that on the wholly social level it amused them to see the son of the Resident leaving Jundapur in this somewhat undignified way. In Muzzafirabad Cranston said, "What on earth have you got there?" which exactly expressed my own feelings, and Melba's too, possibly. From the moment the handle of her cage came onto my wrist until we were aboard the SIAT boat that brought us to Manoba we regarded each other with caution and suspicion and perhaps twinges of shame when people stared. Even the scarf of tigers and monkeys I bought for her artificial darkness failed to excite her. But when she smelled the open sea she eyed me with renewed interest and somewhere in the Malacca straits she began to sing. Perhaps her ancestors had straddled piratical shoulders.

She ignores Kandy, but I believe she only does so from an excess of sensibility for my feelings because the alterna-

tive would be to shriek at her. I suppose she associates
Kandy with the infidelity she prefers to desertion. When
Kandy has gone I promise Melba a home of her own, hot in
summer and warm in winter, with flora imported from
South America, and great spaces in which to spread her
wings. I also promise her that no woman shall be taken into
that house on a permanent basis unless she has passed through
the searing fire of Melba's scrutiny. Even if Melba understood
I'm sure she wouldn't believe me; but the tyranny of the
genes must be respected in our habits of love: like must
follow like in our affections, and will, unless the trap is
sprung by the unwary, sensuous foot.

When Cranston said, "What on earth have you got there?"
I told him it was a mock bird of paradise, the only kind
that could easily be obtained living, unless you visited islands like Manoba, which I intended to.

We were more our old selves. He was relaxed, just back
from a successful conference in Rangoon where he'd probably expanded his horizons, not yet involved with what the
banks of eyes saw on the rows of slides, but more with
what his own eyes saw: Conway with parrot and the flush of
gate-fever on his cheeks, the fever of Man'bah, Man'o-bah,
Manoba, an island which linked Conway's boyhood to a man
he knew but had never met, connected the *Paradisaeidae*
through Pig Eye to the present; not a violent flush but one
suitable to a rise in the temperature of his curiosity or of
his new obsession with the ends that people came to; a curiosity neither grave nor dignified; yet not haphazard, because
his passion for form and order had been met by a precision
of myth and symbol and this warmed him as he might have
been warmed by a personal achievement.

Were there any Foundation facilities I could make use
of in Manoba, I asked? A bungalow, say, with air conditioning
plant, refrigeration, an illuminated bar; casual but essential

amenities, necessary aids to a consumer's digestion? Cranston lifted a finger that in the old days would have flicked his nose but now rubbed it thoughtfully. He asked me how long I expected to be in Manoba. I said I didn't know, but I had to be back in London in ten months' time, which meant that I had about nine months to do what I liked with, providing I threw my itinerary away and honoured my sabbatical year. "Is that what you're on?" he said. "I thought it was business." There was a bungalow, not much more than a hut, one of two that belonged to the Foundation, but if I intended to use it for a week or so he would have to get in touch with The Straits, Islands and Archipelago Trading Company who had an interest in it too, and on whom I'd depend for more ordinary amenities like food and drink. He knew nothing about the birds of paradise. All in all he thought Manoba a poor bet for them. I should do better in New Guinea itself, shouldn't I?

I said, "The birds are an excuse. Is there anything I can do for Daintree?"

Some drink themselves senseless, others twist wedding rings, some row across water to shoot dummies, others open doors and brandish old men's spears; some sit like slowly ageing spiders in the middle of mindlessly efficient webs and incur risks to the reputations of the organizations they work for and to their own. For there is risk for Cranston who has made himself personally responsible that nothing untoward will come of Daintree's continued employment.

When I first saw Daintree I thought Cranston's reliance on him, faith in what he believed Daintree still fundamentally was and would be until he fell dead, dangerously misplaced. The flamingo-pink light that spread over the clearing where Daintree's bungalow stands reminded me of that other unearthly light, rosy-bronze, that spread around the clearing on the lake isle. His boy, a Malay with hospital orderly experience, stood guard on the veranda, tried to stop me entering. I pretended to misinterpret his gestures and not to understand the stilted English in which he said that Doctor Daintree was out and that he would deliver the letter I was waving in front of him and refusing to let go of. We grinned at each other. He couldn't bring himself to hold me off by force because of my white skin and my white suit. When he ran out of means to delay me he didn't follow me in but stayed out there on the veranda, ashamed for Daintree and ashamed of himself, but resigned otherwise to what I should see, a sitting room in a state of terrible disorder and, having passed through it, a bedroom even worse, stinking of stale alcohol, with Daintree lying unconscious on his back on the bed, with his shirt open exposing the ribcage. I went back to the veranda, gave the boy Cranston's letter of introduction and returned down the track, moved by what I had seen because the tale of the kennel was fresh in my mind.

Once when Daintree was talkative drunk (and since he found and read everything I had recorded up to my father's death and the use to which Anne and I put his money, Daintree has drunk no less but talked a bit more), he said, "Cran's a fool. Tell him that, next time you write him one of those letters." He would not say why in his opinion Cran was a fool. For him talkativeness when drunk consists in questions he doesn't seem to want the answers to, exclamatory and allusive statements which are mostly disconnected for the listener but no doubt progressively logical in his mind where they must be linked by thoughts that don't find their way into speech. I have stopped trying to fill in the gaps. "Why do you write down all that stuff? . . . They'll go to the bad those kids of Griffin's. . . . There was this man in Java, what was his name? He was a mess. I've not seen a worse mess. . . . Cran's a fool."

Perhaps he meant Cranston was a fool because of something he had once done that I don't know about but which

remained in Daintree's opinion as illustrative of him; or
he may have meant Cranston was a fool to employ him, to
buy his time, to have spent so much of his own time and
energy on finding job after job for Daintree, which I know
he did. Daintree never completely let him down, always
brought the jobs to an end himself, before things got to
the stage of their being ended for him, by saying, "I'm finished. Get rid of me." All over the East, wherever the Foundation was active, Cranston moved him. There were months
in which he never drank at all, months when Cranston
thought the tide had turned and Daintree could presently be
persuaded to retire, and do so honourably, tackle the text
book he had talked in the old days of writing, on the
psychology and treatment of tropical diseases. And then
the pattern would be repeated, drunkenness, irascibility
which made him impossible to work with; never a bad mistake, never a professional failure that could be pointed to
as proof that Daintree was actually finished, but the margins
were getting narrower in places where the work he did
was public and supposed to be important, and eventually
there was only Manoba left, an island the Foundation had
found neglected after the war and assumed responsibility
for, to the relief of the mainland medical authorities who
had their own work cut out. When Daintree came to Manoba
the island enjoyed western health and was ranked as a
place where one of its young field officers could cut his
teeth. A determined old drunk could do no harm. Cranston
said, "I suppose I always knew that Dane would end up
there, that when we sent him to Manoba that was the last
stop, the place he'd die in." Cranston tried twice to provide
him with an assistant. Daintree kicked the first one out, the
second left of his own accord after a week saying that Manoba
wasn't big enough for the two of them, that he couldn't
imagine a sphere of medical operations that would be big
enough. The Foundation tried to get Cranston to pension

Daintree off but Cranston wouldn't. He said, "He could drink himself to death in a couple of weeks if he decided to. He's got the will for it. He's also got the will to go on living." After the failure of the two assistants, Cranston spared time he could ill afford going twice to Manoba. On his last visit Daintree said, "Don't come again, Cran. Get rid of me if you want, I'll be dead before I make a mess of Manoba, but I don't want to see you again." Daintree sent his periodical reports as was required of him, acknowledged receipt of his supplies, toed the line it was necessary to toe to satisfy the authorities on the mainland but never answered the personal letters Cranston had now given up writing. When Daintree died on the job, as Cranston said he knew he must, the news would reach him from the medical officer on the mainland who, by then, would have taken over. Manoba no longer interested the Foundation. They would be as relieved to get rid of it as others had been relieved for them to assume responsibility in 1946.

It took Cranston a month to arrange my visit. I think he delayed to give me time to change my mind. I completed my Indian itinerary, left Melba with him as a hostage for my own intentions. Even on my return to Muzzafirabad the sailing date he gave me was a tentative one that needed to be confirmed. "Are you sure?" he asked. But he wanted me to go. If Daintree showed signs of failing in his promise not to make a mess of Manoba I might be able to get word to him before the mainland authorities found out. And he didn't want Daintree to die alone. The boat, a SIAT freighter, was slow and casual. It was August when I rode Griffin's lighter into the lagoon. Now, according to my Manobaon calendar, it is February. I have another tentative sailing date, from Griffin, I have not seen the birds and Daintree hasn't met the boy with pebble and sling. I shall ask Griffin to confirm my passage. I think there are no living birds on the island and that Daintree was hinting at what he knew for a fact when he said he expects they've all been killed off. It is curious how neither Griffin nor Daintree, nor anyone on the island, will quite admit the birds are gone. The distant wawk-wawk-wawk, wok-wok-wok˙ which the boys told me was their cry was probably made by another boy, for my benefit.

When there's no duty as such to go back to, going back becomes a duty in itself.

There are two Manobas: the island of china ducks in flight across a wooden wall, of jazz and rock and roll and crates of cargo, bottles of rum and whisky, Kandy's orange bundle and ship's cigarettes in circular air-sealed tins; brown-skinned men who fish from boats and work in the SIAT plantation in cast-off trousers got from SIAT sailors, brown-skinned women who cover their breasts, gut fish and laugh in doorways; of light and airy valleys in the interior where the people who get their living from the earth line up, put out their tongues, make wry faces and watch Daintree in detached dispassionate amusement; and there is this other Manoba, which perhaps I shall take with me, a dark, forgotten island whose warriors challenge your approach, make magic out of tins and mysteries out of birds: the island Daintree enters in drunken sleep, the island that enters him, that enters me, perhaps enters Griffin and all the people who inhabit it, enters us and darkens our eyes, broods in us at night before storms and throbs in us with the suddenly heavy pulse of the sun passing its zenith. It is this other Manoba Cranston pictures when thinking of Daintree, this other Manoba I pictured myself, that I came to to wait for Daintree to die in, to be there at hand should he want as he died some flicker of warmth from a fire other than the one he brought into the world himself: another fire, pale, damp and smoky, but one that might have told him his own had been worth bringing. That, in the end, was all I could offer. I have no work behind me that can be dismissed or forgotten by others as Daintree's work before the war has been forgotten. My protest finds no outlet such as Daintree's finds, breaking syringe needles on tough bark. Its only outlet has been in coming to Manoba, unless you count the way I clouted Anne back when she clouted me, and the time I was within an ace of emptying Stephen's bedroom of all those images which nothing particular in themselves together defined the image of a world that had never existed and never could exist but was the world his elders tricked him into believing in because they themselves had been tricked into believing in it and held it still in a kind of repute, like a myth or legend, against all their worldly judgment, using it as one of the few remaining means by which they could forget that if they suddenly closed their eyes and listened the only real sounds in the world would be those of chewing and swallowing and champing and regurgitation, the gasp of dying animals, the crash of tree trunks, the snap of stalks, the whirr of machinery turning things into other things, the ring of hammers, the screech of chisels, the crunch of bone on bone and of mind on mind.

Not that Anne would hear any of that, for she is a great consumer, wholly committed to it. I am hard on her, I know, but she is content with what she thinks she is, and is therefore nothing in my opinion. For her nothing has any meaning until she has got her teeth into it. Whatever she touches she ravages with her ignorance of its previous existence, her greed for it while she wants it, her destructive dismissal of it when she has finished with it. For her the world was born on the day that she was born and will die when she dies. And there will probably be at least a score of people to mourn her and put expensive flowers on her grave, for unlike Daintree, whom only Cranston and I and perhaps Griffin will mourn, she has never yet staggered drunken and dishevelled into the clubhouse and cried: The buggers are leprous, and probably never will, has never caused, in public, a moment's unease to anyone, but has only sucked and munched her way steadily through life in the company of other suckers and munchers, masking that cold and empty face with an expression of lively intelligence and a flawless English complexion.

Since Daintree found and read part of this record I have kept it under lock and key in an old, scratched black deed box Griffin gave me, that came from Adelaide and smells of rank metal and catches me high up in the nostrils when I open it. "Why do you write all that stuff down?" Daintree asked, but was not interested in the answer it would have been difficult to give him: For myself, for Anne and Stephen, for my father and Aunt Sarah, to sublimate what I suppose a world that finds it more convenient to reduce a man's life to two brand-words on a label than to examine the contents would call my Oedipus complex. And since Daintree found and read it, our more frequent conversations have only served to widen the gulf there was between us from the beginning. Even his show of taking me into the valleys which followed his reading of part of what I'd written was a blow struck publicly in the cause of his privacy. He wanted to show me that as a doctor he could still go through his monkey performance; just as I in going with him established my monkey interest in bright-feathered birds. But this performance and this interest only heightened the mystery of our deviation from the ape.

If I stand in a certain way, holding myself in my broader, heavier fashion in the attitude that was my father's, I can feel the flesh transformed into armour-casing and understand, so, how the light might fall on it and produce a radiance. But what would first cause him to put such armour on remains obscure. I no longer feel that it is important to know, or to know the answers to the questions I would have asked him in Gopalakand but didn't, not wanting him to be diminished by the futile answers he might have had to give.

And these days, because I've seen Daintree, and heard him, and understood both the cause and nature of his behaviour, when I imagine this room in Manoba as quite another room, with Dingy Row sitting where I am sitting, like myself, pen in hand, papers close, and my father coming in to make his denunciation, I no longer think of Father as old and foolish and out of touch, because the voice in which he makes his protest is no longer either querulous or coldly precise, but like Daintree's, hot and angry; and however misplaced his judgment was in terms of history and in the light of practical affairs, I see his denouncement then, and the frigid, desolate admission of failure that slipped out later from his exile in the Dhooni hills, as proof that within all his silence and coldness there burned the likeness of a noble aspiration; and then I see only what was honourable in the name they gave him, Old Very Light; and bitterly regret that not once in my life did I sit with him and let him feel that I understood how vulnerable is the illusion that a man has of his own importance, not of his importance to others, but of his importance to himself, and how to speak of what drives him to sustain the illusion, of the means he finds to drive himself, of the dark that falls on him when the illusion is gone, is virtually impossible.

EPIGRAPH

"Thus one of my objects in coming to the far East was accomplished. I had obtained a specimen of the King Bird of Paradise (*Paradisea regia*), which had been described by Linnaeus from skins preserved in a mutilated state by the natives. I knew how few Europeans had ever beheld the perfect little organism I now gazed upon, and how very imperfectly it was still known in Europe. The emotions excited in the mind(s) of a naturalist, who has long desired to see the actual thing which he has hitherto known only by description, drawing, or badly-preserved external covering—especially when that thing is of surpassing rarity and beauty, require the poetic faculty fully to express them. The remote island in which I found myself situated, in an almost unvisited sea, far from the tracks of merchant fleets and navies; the wild luxuriant tropical forest, which stretched far away on every side; the rude uncultured savages who gathered round me,—all had their influence in determining the emotions with which I gazed upon this 'thing of beauty.' I thought of the long ages of the past, during which the successive generations of this little creature had run their course—year by year being born, and living and dying amid these dark and gloomy woods, with no intelligent eye to gaze upon their loveliness; to all appearance such a wanton waste of beauty. Such ideas excite a feeling of melancholy. It seems sad, that on the one hand such exquisite creatures should live out their lives and exhibit their charms only in these wild inhospitable regions, doomed for ages yet to come to hopeless barbarism; while on the other hand, should civilised man ever reach these distant lands, and bring moral, intellectual, and physical light into the recesses of these virgin forests, we may be sure that he will so disturb the nicely-balanced relations of organic and inorganic nature as to cause the disappearance, and finally the extinction, of these very beings whose wonderful structure and beauty he alone is fitted to appreciate and enjoy. This consideration must surely tell us that all living things were *not* made for man."

(*The Malay Archipelago:* The land of the orang-utan, and the bird of paradise. A narrative of travel, with studies of Man and Nature. By ALFRED RUSSEL WALLACE: Vol. 2. Macmillan & Co., 1869)